A monster w̶i̶t̶h̶
A doom that has no end . . .

Gloved in scarlet blood, two colossal hands descended
into view, and with an impact that almost knocked Erim
from his feet, tore into the earth, clawing Qanar-Sharaj out
of the ground as though it were a toy.

There stood the Riddled Man, a titan now, red cascades
pouring from his wounds. A greater power loomed above
him, a towering assembly of interlocking dull-black wheels,
rotating slowly, ominously, bristling with spikes. What was
this sinister machine?

But presently he saw that it was not a machine at all—
the wheels were covered with thousands of darting, horribly
vigilant red eyes.

Tchernobog, he thought. *Emperor of Hell!*

"No!" Erim shrieked. "God save us!"

THE BLOOD OF THE LAMB
THE DEVOURING VOID

MARK E. ROGERS

ACE BOOKS, NEW YORK

This book is an Ace original edition,
and has never been previously published.

THE DEVOURING VOID

An Ace Book / published by arrangement with
the author

PRINTING HISTORY
Ace edition / November 1991

ISBN: 0-441-06827-8

Ace Books are published by The Berkley Publishing Group,
200 Madison Avenue, New York, New York 10016.
The name "ACE" and the "A" logo
are trademarks belonging to Charter Communications, Inc.

PRINTED IN THE UNITED STATES OF AMERICA

10 9 8 7 6 5 4 3 2 1

What Has Come Before

This is the second part of THE BLOOD OF THE LAMB.

The first part, *The Expected One*, told how the Kadjafi people had come under the domination of Batu, the Khan of the Mirkuts; at Batu's insistence, an order of Kadjafi wizards, the Sharajnaghim, have begun an investigation of Essaj Ben Yussef, a miracle worker and would-be Messiah who seems to pose a threat to the Khan's rule. Three inquisitors are dispatched—Erim Sawalha, an expert theologian; Nawhar Barak, a specialist in the detection of false miracles; and Sharif Ben Shaqar, reputed to be the mightiest sorcerer since the legendary Mancdaman Zorachus.

On their way to their encounter with Essaj, the three witness the near-rape of two sisters, Khalima and Zehowah, by a troop of Black Anarites. The Sharajnaghim intervene, but not before the sisters' father, Khaldun Al-Maari, is killed by the Anarites. Discovering that the inquisitors were journeying to find Essaj, the women join them, intending to ask Essaj to return with them and raise their father from the dead.

Meanwhile, Qanar-Sharaj, the home of the Sharajnaghi Order, has been wracked by a series of grisly murders; all the victims have been members of the Council of Masters, and have been killed by demon-sendings. Khaddam Al-Ramnal, the Order's second-in-command and Master of Sorcery, maintains that the murders are the work of the Black Anarites, although certain superficial evidence points to Samadhi Hijaz, the Order's Master of Intelligence, and Massoud Namtar, the Science Master, who thoroughly detest each other.

Khaddam is attacked by a sending and barely survives; Samadhi manages to have Massoud imprisoned on suspicion of murder. Ultimately, Khaddam receives a summons to visit the Khan, who informs him that a Black Anarite has penetrated the Order and risen to high rank.

While Khaddam is still with Batu, word comes that the Order's Grand Master, Ahwaz, has been murdered; on his way back to Qanar-Sharaj, Khaddam is attacked yet again, this time by the demon Morkulg the Mask. Khaddam survives, even though a Master who has accompanied him, Samra Ghazal, is killed.

In the meanwhile, Erim, Sharif, and Nawhar have reached Bishah, the city where Essaj has been preaching; there they attempt the exorcism of a demoniac who calls himself Horde, and are badly mauled. But Essaj appears and saves them, effortlessly casting out the demon and healing their wounds.

As it turns out, Essaj is perfectly happy to have the Sharajnaghim observe him; they spend some time in the household of his uncle, Terzif, meeting Essaj's disciples and his mother, Yasmin. Essaj makes no secret of his divinity; plainly his doctrine is heterodox, but his miracles cannot be dismissed as mere trickery. Nawhar is infuriated, but Erim finds himself being swayed by certain of Essaj's arguments; to further complicate matters, he falls in love with Khalima, while Sharif becomes enamored of Zehowah. To Nawhar's horror, his comrades marry.

Essaj announces his intention to preach in Thangura, and agrees to resurrect Khaldun; the Sharajnaghim join him as his company journeys south. Eventually they reach the inn where Khaldun was killed; true to his word, Essaj wrenches him gasping out of the grave. Erim's old faith is swept away by this stupendous miracle, but Nawhar's detestation for Essaj is only reinforced. The seeds of a terrible enmity between Erim and Nawhar have been planted.

And now—*The Devouring Void*.

Chapter 1

By the time Khaddam's party returned to Qanar-Sharaj, the conflict had been quelled; Akram had the situation well in hand. Many of Samadhi's and Massoud's men had been confined to quarters, as well as followers of other Masters—members of all factions had joined in the fighting, protecting friends, or simply choosing sides. Twenty men had been killed, more than a hundred wounded. Luckily, the combatants had confined themselves to simple physical strife. No sorcery had been brought into play—yet.

Khaddam received a full report from Akram; as the Martial-arts Master departed Khaddam's study, Samadhi arrived.

"What was Batu's message, Khaddam?" the Intelligence Chief asked, without any preliminaries.

Khaddam ignored the question. "You seem to have lost control of your followers again."

"And I'm horrified by their actions," Samadhi replied. "Still, they were reacting to—how should I put this?—extreme circumstances."

"You're horrified by their actions, yet you make excuses for them," Khaddam answered. "Twenty men dead, Samadhi."

"Too many of them mine," Samadhi answered hotly.

"I weep for them. But Akram told me that your faction started the fight. That they tried to snatch Massoud from his chamber."

Samadhi tapped his foot impatiently. "What was the Khan's message?"

"I don't think you'll care for it," Khaddam replied.

"Tell me."

"If you insist. Batu received an anonymous communication to the effect that a Black Anarite *has* penetrated our Order."

Samadhi looked as though someone had slapped him. It was a few moments before he recovered. "An anonymous communication?" he asked. "Why did Batu put any trust in that?"

"His brother had an agent at Khaur-Al-Jaffar. The man confirmed the message."

"This . . . spy that's supposedly among us . . ." Samadhi's voice trailed off.

Khaddam eyed him carefully. "Yes?"

"Did Khassar's man learn his name?"

"No. The only thing we know is that the spy entered the Order as a young man."

Samadhi loosed a little sigh.

"Do I detect a note of relief?" Khaddam asked.

"Wouldn't you be relieved if you were in my situation?"

"Why so?"

"Because my theory still holds up."

"Which part of it? That the killings weren't committed by a Black Anarite?"

"That Massoud is our man," Samadhi answered. "Nothing you've said excludes him."

"Even so," Khaddam said, "I intend to have him released."

"You have no authority," Samadhi protested. "He was imprisoned on the orders of the Grand Master. You can't rescind—"

"Not until *I'm* Grand Master, true," Khaddam replied.

"You might not find the Council so willing to oblige."

"You want the post yourself, is that it?"

"Perhaps. And perhaps Akram wants it as well."

"He has no desire to be Grand Master. How many times has he said so?"

"And you believe him?" Samadhi asked.

"You're grasping at straws, and you know it. He didn't even want to become a Master. Not everyone seethes with ambition the way we do. It will come down to the two of us. And as for the rest of the Council, *including* Akram—I think they'll support me. They generally do."

"They might change their minds when they learn you want to

free Massoud," Samadhi answered.

"I think not," Khaddam said. "I'm inclined to believe that they'll trust *your* arguments less than ever, now that we've heard from the Khan."

"As I said," Samadhi replied, "Massoud wasn't exonerated—"

"True enough. But you've expended far too much energy maintaining that the Anarites weren't involved. The most important issue *never* was finding the killer. It was whether or not we were actually at war. On that larger matter, *I* was right. And I'm right about Massoud as well."

Samadhi fumed for a few moments. "And if you become Grand Master, what will you do with me?"

"I'll consult the Council, of course. But I can't have you in charge of Intelligence any longer."

"You leave me no choice," Samadhi said. "I must oppose your elevation, whatever the cost."

"Do your worst," said Khaddam.

"So be it," said Samadhi, and stormed out.

Massoud reclined on a carpet, head on hand, looking across the chessboard at the men who had been assigned to guard him. They had withdrawn some distance from the low table, whispering about their next move. Massoud was unsure of their names; he had three different sets of keepers, and all were Khaddam's men.

At last his opponents returned. Their self-appointed leader picked up a rook, smirked triumphantly at Massoud, and captured one of his pawns.

"Hah!" he said.

"That's hah *Sibi*," Massoud reminded him. "I may be your prisoner, but I still outrank you." Sitting up, he swooped down on the rook with his queen.

"*What?*" the guards demanded in collective disbelief.

"Mate in three," Massoud announced.

They scrutinized the pieces. The leader struck himself in the forehead, groaning. One of the others struck him as well, snarling: "Shahib, you fool!"

"Do you concede?" Massoud asked.

They nodded in unison.

"But you want revenge, of course," he said.

They nodded again, faces grim with determination.

"Plenty of time for that," Massoud answered, and began replacing his pieces on the board. When he finished, he asked: "Isn't it about time you fellows took white?"

Shahib said: "*Sibi*, we're four against one—"

"My point exactly."

They whispered among themselves once more.

"Very well," Shahib said heavily. They changed places with Massoud.

But having the first move did little for them. Massoud quickly established control of the center of the board, and his endgame proceeded with characteristic efficiency. So intent was he on the board that he barely noticed when one of his antagonists placed himself directly at his shoulder.

"—ll me," the man gulped.

Massoud did not even spare him a glance. "What?" He laughed, advancing a pawn. "Mate in two."

"Kill me," the guard said.

Massoud looked at him at last.

The man was drawing his sword.

Too late, Massoud began to retract his hand from the pawn. A flashing fan, steel blurred before Massoud's eyes. There was a thump. Chesspieces and his dark-brown hand bounced into view.

The guard snatched the severed member out of the air, raising it high above his head. Two of the other men thrust their blades into his chest, but he slipped off the blades, blood rilling down the front of his tunic.

Massoud got to his feet, moving back from the table. Fighting the temptation to stare at the stump of his wrist, he kept his eyes fixed on the man who had wounded him.

The adept was retreating swiftly towards the wall on Massoud's left, still holding the Master's hand aloft, shrieking a spell in a high-pitched, childlike voice. Even as his back came up against the door, the severed hand vanished from his grip, his fingers twitching convulsively shut about the space it had occupied an instant before.

"Kill me!" he screamed, now in his own voice. "*Kill me!* KILL ME KILL ME KILL—"

The others closed in. Despite his pleas, he parried a lunge, wounding one. Then their swords slipped past his defense.

Massoud thought he was stabbed ten more times at least. As the guard slid down the wood, his companions stepped back, staring at him.

"Too late," came the child's voice once more.

Massoud snatched a cloth from a meal-tray, pressing it against his wrist. "Push him away from the door!" he shouted, his skin chilly with sweat. "We have to get out!"

"Do it, Yoseh!" Shahib cried, pushing one of his comrades towards the corpse.

Yoseh looked over at Massoud.

"Haste, man!" Massoud shrieked, the mere exertion of crying out causing his vision to swim.

Yoseh bent, reaching for the body—

There was a ferocious snap. Even as the Adept touched the corpse, its eyes flashed green; the whole center of its face, everything between the brow and mouth, buckled inward.

Yoseh jerked back, but a fine coil of green light leaped from the dead man's mouth and snared Yoseh's arm. The limb snapped straight out, jerking towards the corpse's maw, fingers uncurling. Yoseh screamed, straining against the coil, unable to escape.

With a crunch, the corpse's head collapsed, and was sucked down into the throat. The neck puckered, seizing the collar of the dead man's tunic; sleeves and trouser-legs crept upwards along their limbs, whose nether extremities were themselves retracting, as though the body were devouring itself. And even though no visible opening remained, the lightning-coil still crackled from the shrinking mass, holding Yoseh in thrall.

"Help me!" he wailed.

Shahib started towards him.

"No!" Massoud shouted. "Don't!"

But Shahib had already touched the snared Adept. Green energy crackled from Yoseh, capturing Shahib as well.

The third guard stood off, assuming a stance, flinging bolts into the mass that had been the corpse. They seemed to have no effect.

The thing was hovering above the floor now, collapsed into an almost spherical shape, sheathed in tightly stretched cloth. The dead man's feet and hands still protruded at crazy angles, but were rapidly disappearing, as if the limbs they terminated had been pulled, shoulder and hip first, into the sphere's interior.

Massoud watched in helpless horror. Magic was denied him; Samadhi had seen to that with his damned spells. And now Samadhi's sending was here to finish him.

The cloth stretched over the sphere went completely red, then split, vanishing through a tight crevice, which disappeared in turn. No skin showed on the mass now; there was only a surface of shining crushed flesh, ceaselessly churning, as though stirred from within.

Sweat rolled down Massoud's face. The floor seemed to be pitching beneath his feet. It was impossible to think. Sheer dizziness was sealing his doom. He had to stop the blood from his wrist.

Across the room, the sphere had stopped contracting. The lightning-coil that had snared Yoseh and Shahib was thickening, growing more powerful, drawing them forward. Yoseh's fingertips touched the red mass; his sleeve ripped into fragments, the grey rags snaking down along the coil as though they had lives of their own, slithering beneath the churning surface of the sphere.

Yoseh loosed a single screeching note before his voice cracked and deserted him. His skin was splitting, unravelling from fingers to shoulder, parting in a score of places to reveal twitching ruby muscle, individual patches worming their way down the coil.

Off to the side, the third Adept kept pummelling the sphere with bolts, still in vain.

Does he have any other tricks? Massoud wondered frantically, undoing his belt one-handed, wrapping it above his stump with fumbling fingers, pulling it taut with his teeth to choke off the blood.

Yoseh's arm was denuded of muscle by now. Ripping loose from his shoulder, it was pulled into the sphere. The coil vanished with it, and Yoseh rocked back, freed from the current; as the contact broke, Shahib tore himself away as well.

Then the lightning whipped back into view, seizing Yoseh's head. A moment later, the man's face was all grinning teeth and bone, naked but for beads of blood and strings of flesh that were even then crawling towards the energy-coil; his eyes spun hideously along the spiral as they were plucked from his sockets.

The other two Adepts staggered over to Massoud.

"What can we do, Master?" Shahib asked.

"Can you conjure?" Massoud demanded.

"Nothing to stop that thing," they answered.

"Something to *distract* it?" Massoud asked, exasperated by their stupidity.

Shahib's comrade entered a stance. Clad in a corselet of scales, a dwarvish creature with a doglike head appeared, holding a short bow.

"Is that the best you can do?" Massoud asked the man who had conjured it.

"I'm sorry," the Adept said. "The Influences . . ."

The creature looked at the sphere, which had now doubled in size; Yoseh was gone, utterly devoured. The archer sniffed disdainfully and plucked a shaft from its quiver.

"Most wicked poison," it told Massoud gruffly, indicating the arrowhead. "Can Master do better?"

In spite of everything, Massoud laughed, his legs wobbling. "Save us, good servant."

The creature whirled and put the arrow into the sphere. Fletching and all, the missile sank from sight.

"Out to my window," Massoud said, and together with the remaining guards, retreated through an adjoining room into his bedchamber. There the single casement had been set with thick iron bars.

"Have to rip them out," Massoud gasped, sinking to one knee. Vision greying, he asked Shahib's companion: "Can you summon anything else?"

"Exhausted," the man said.

"I might be able to," Shahib said, assuming a stance, letting force into the ceiling.

"Blast the bars, damn you!" Massoud cried. "Weaken them! Then summon something to pull them out!"

He turned. The dog-archer was retreating steadily across the adjoining room, pursued by the sphere, striking it with arrow after arrow. The lightning-spiral lashed out repeatedly, but the dwarf dodged and ducked, evading it each time. Were its shafts doing any damage?

The archer backed across the threshold. At last the whipping coil seized it, reeling it in towards the sphere.

Massoud flinched and swore, almost ordering Shahib's companion to banish the creature. But the Master knew he could not afford such generosity, even to so valiant and faithful a retainer.

As for Shahib, he was still forceletting, the bars ringing as his bolts struck them; would he ever be done?

The sphere paused on the threshold, stripping the armor from the archer, peeling the flesh from its arms. Somehow the dwarf managed to pry its head up from the surface of the sphere, straining to look back at the Sharajnaghim.

Massoud's will cracked.

"Banish it," he cried.

The Adept beside him sobbed with relief, spoke the words. The archer disappeared. The sphere drifted forward once more.

Behind Massoud, the strikes had stopped; Shahib was uttering a spell.

But the time was up. The emerald spiral lashed towards Massoud.

The man next to him sprang forward, the coil taking him instead.

Shahib had fallen silent; Massoud looked round. A large dark mass floated beyond the window; three black tentacles knotted round the bars.

Bones crackled. Massoud looked back at the sphere. The man who had sacrificed himself was hanging in midair above him, head and one arm already gone, his remaining hand lifting, pointing at Massoud, running with green fire.

The coil leaped the narrow distance, striking Massoud full in the face. His cheeks and brow seemed suddenly full of fishhooks; the coil hauled him up and forward, off the floor, reining him towards the corpse's fingers. The digits brushed Massoud's nose, sent an excruciating charge coursing through his skull—

Then he found himself plummeting, the hooks gone from his skin. He struck the floor with a grunt.

The lightning was withdrawing along the dead man's arm, withering, growing dim. Victim and sphere sank slowly towards the floor. Blood had begun to drip from the descending mass; strings and small chunks of dismembered meat fell away.

Most wicked poison, Massoud thought, blackness creeping in at the edges of his vision. Had the venom actually worked?

There was a loud grate behind him. Shahib's creature was dislodging the bars; but it seemed the escape-route might not be necessary after all.

The sphere settled to the floor, and instantly lost its shape, crushed meat splaying out in all directions. Blood drained from the flesh, forming a ruby tarn.

Massoud rose, pressing himself against the wall next to the casement. At last he had time to wonder why the demon hadn't simply possessed *him*; given the entity's effect on its host, that would have been the simplest way to dispatch him.

But he was wearing several protective talismans below his robes, graven with the three-letter name of God; perhaps they had shielded him from invasion.

"It's over," he told Shahib. "You can send your friend back."

The Adept banished the tentacled creature.

There came a pounding from the antechamber; someone was beating on the front door.

"Open it," he said. "Fetch me a surgeon, quickly."

Shahib didn't stir.

Massoud reached towards him. The man slowly took his sword out of his scabbard, offering it to Massoud hilt-first, trembling violently.

"Kill me," the Adept said.

It was a heartbeat before Massoud realized what was happening. Then he snatched weakly at the blade.

"Too late," came the child's voice.

The Adept flipped the sword out of Massoud's reach, caught the hilt, and thrust.

Massoud felt a bitter sliding coldness under his chin, then blossoming pain. But worst of all was the obstruction of his throat, the inability to breathe or swallow. Resigned to death, he hoped only that Shahib would pull the sword out again.

The Adept loosed the weapon. Massoud tried to remove the blade, but was unable with only one hand.

Reaching for his own throat, Shahib gloated down at him, pretending to choke.

✛

Chapter 2

With the news of Massoud's death, Akram and his men braced
for a new round of violence, but it never materialized. The
Numalian's innocence had been proven beyond a shadow of
a doubt; Samadhi's men were shamed into passivity, and with
Akram's troops stationed everywhere, Massoud's followers were
unwilling to goad them.

It was generally agreed that the elevation of a new Grand
Master could not wait. Khaddam obtained an emergency meeting of the Council, and to no one's surprise, the proceedings
went entirely his way—Samadhi's opposition counted for nothing.

The Spymaster had been completely discredited. It was not
only that he had been wrong about the Anarites; Massoud's
imprisonment and helplessness in the face of the sending counted
heavily against him as well. Allowed to remain on the Council, he
was nonetheless suspended from his post as Chief of Intelligence.
The state of war was acknowledged.

And Khaddam was elected Grand Master.

An abbreviated elevation ceremony was decided upon for the
following morning. Afterwards, a second meeting of the Council
would convene to consider replacements for the slain Masters,
and the prosecution of hostilities against the Anarites.

Khaddam's meal was long cold by the time he arrived at Sigrun's
chambers.

10

"Poor Chabela," Sigrun said. "She hasn't spoken a word since the news came."

"If only Ahwaz had listened to me," Khaddam said, shaking his head in disgust. "God help me, but I've come to hate Samadhi."

"Was it Morkulg again?" Sigrun asked.

"No. By dispatching him twice in such a short period—first against Ahwaz, then our party on the road—the Anarites must have exhausted their privilege for the time being. Massoud was attacked by a much less powerful demon." Khaddam indicated his dinner. "I don't have much appetite, I'm afraid."

Sigrun took the plate away. "When are you going to arrest Samadhi?"

Khaddam did not respond.

Returning, she declared: "He's the killer."

"Did I ask for your opinion?"

She settled across from him once more. "Everything points to him."

"Everything pointed to Massoud as well," Khaddam said.

"All right, then," Sigrun answered. "Who's first on *your* list?"

Khaddam took a sip of wine. "Samadhi," he acknowledged.

"I knew it," Sigrun said.

"There was a moment, just after I told him of the Khan's message—he seemed so relieved when he learned that Khassar hadn't discovered the Anarite's name. And now there's this business with Massoud. It's not just that Samadhi engineered his imprisonment . . ."

"He worked the spells that prevented Massoud from defending himself," Sigrun said.

"And the ones that were supposed to *protect* Massoud," Khaddam went on. "He could have annulled them. Or laid them defectively. Or chosen precisely the sort of entity that could penetrate them.

"Even so, there must be more to it than him. It's all so *obvious* . . ."

"Obvious?" Sigrun asked. "He's forestalled arrest long enough to murder five Masters."

"In which case I'm a fool not to have stopped him before now," Khaddam replied. "Another possibility that I'm not too anxious to admit."

"You saw through his arguments about the Anarites. You can still take credit for that—and for trying to shield Massoud."

"This may come as a surprise to you," Khaddam said, "but I'm not in the least bit interested in taking credit."

"Pardon me, My Lord," Sigrun said, regretting her choice of words. True, he was an ambitious man; no one knew that better than she. But she could also see that he was genuinely disturbed with himself.

"Not at this moment, at any rate," he went on. "The most important thing is *proving* Samadhi's guilt—if indeed he's responsible."

"What are you going to do?"

"As Grand Master, I can have him watched. And his quarters searched. Also, there's information in the Book of Masters, names of villages where he supposedly lived in his youth . . . Khassar said the spy joined us as a young man. *If* Samadhi's an Anarite, he would *have* to have spent several years at Khaur-Al-Jaffar; he might even have been raised there."

Sigrun raced ahead: "And if no one in those villages remembers him—"

"Then he's concealing something about his past," Khaddam said. "I've already dispatched riders. We should know in two days or so."

"Are you going to arrest him in the meanwhile?"

"I don't have any evidence."

"You're Grand Master. Do you need evidence?"

"If I wish to avoid problems with the Council. And also, I'm afraid, my conscience demands it. Suppose he's innocent? And suppose I consigned him to prison, and he met Massoud's fate?"

"I don't care," Sigrun said. "You should be more ruthless."

"Is that so?" he laughed. "Let me tell you, I'm quite ruthless enough."

Khaddam was ordained Grand Master the next morning; the Council met, although Samadhi did not appear. The first matter to attend to was the replacement of the slain Masters, and the reordering of the Seventh Level. Khaddam's elevation left a vacancy at Sorcery, which would normally have been filled by Samadhi; by general acknowledgement the most powerful wizard on the Council after Khaddam and Samadhi,

Mufkadi Umar, was taken from Science and given the Wizard's Chair.

For the post of Intelligence Chief, Khaddam proposed Sayid Al-Mashat, a member of the knot and Samadhi's second-in-command. Sayid was not yet a Master, but the Trials could be swiftly arranged.

As for Samadhi, it was decided that he would be made Master of Logic—technically, a promotion over his post as Spymaster, but in actuality a situation in which it was thought he could do little damage.

Murad Abu Kaukab, the Master who oversaw the Order's trading affairs, a lieutenant of Ghazal's, succeeded to the office Ghazal had held; a second member of the Knot, Ahmed Fawzi, was to be inducted into the Seventh Level to replace Murad at Trade.

Finally Khaddam advanced the names of two more of his "Serpents," Raschid Zekowi and Karaz Al-Kara. Khaddam's choice to succeed Shoua, Raschid had served primarily as a drill instructor, but was well versed in medicine, being constantly called upon to administer aid to students injured during practice. Karaz, on the other hand, was given Mufkadi Umar's chair at Science, where, as Samadhi's subordinate, he could act as a check on his nominal superior.

The Council then turned to Akram's plan for the attack on Khaur-Al-Jaffar. Akram unrolled two vellum maps on the table, holding the edges down with small stone weights. One map showed a section of the Andohar mountains and the land to the south; the second depicted in some detail the Anarite fortress and its immediate environs.

"According to our best estimates," Akram began, "there are at least fifteen hundred Anarites at Khaur-Al-Jaffar. It's my opinion that we would need a force at least half that strong to take the fortress—provided we achieved complete surprise."

"Seven hundred and fifty men," said Mufkadi Umar. "How could such a large force approach the castle undetected?"

"Through our various enterprises, we control a large fleet of river-boats," Akram said, and pointed to a blue line on the first map. "Sailing north on the Gura, we'd come within a week's march of the fortress. Our men could travel upriver concealed, and disembark at night—under the eaves of the Rohaz Forest, here." He indicated a green area on the map. "The region's thinly settled, and even if we're seen, the inhabitants have no love for the Anarites. Once we reach the mountains, we can put the gorges and ravines to excellent use. And there's a way—a perilous way—for an advance force to slip into the castle itself."

"Go on," Khaddam said.

Akram went to the second map. "Khaur-Al-Jaffar is situated on the rim of a dead volcano. A narrow road leads to the main gate; the slopes flanking the road are covered with iron spikes, driven into the stone. There are two smaller entrances to the east and west, opening on the rim of the crater; but the gates are very strong."

"And approach from behind?" Mufkadi asked.

"Barred by the lake that fills the crater."

"Are there any openings in the crater-wall, below the castle?"

Akram nodded. "A huge sewer-mouth."

"We could send swimmers," Mufkadi suggested.

"Under cover of darkness," Akram agreed. "But the Anarites know that the sewer's a potential liability. Some time ago, they populated the lake—*stocked* it, if you will—with all manner of ferocious creatures: dragonsharks, huge serpents and crocodiles, God knows what else. The beasts congregate at the opening, feeding on the remains of sacrificial victims. Any swimmer who approached would be devoured."

"Could we lure them away?" Khaddam asked. "With blood, perhaps?"

"I considered that," Akram answered, "years ago when I first tried to formulate a plan of attack. But I immediately saw what appeared to be an insuperable problem: it would take too long for the blood to diffuse through the water. The crater is, after all, half a mile wide."

"Couldn't we conjure some kind of winged being?" Khaddam asked. "It could carry a bag of blood across the crater, puncture it and fly back, dripping a trail into the lake."

"That occurred to me too," Akram said. "But such a creature would have to be very large, to carry enough blood. It might attract attention, even at night."

"Luckily, though, we don't have to resort to such measures. Recently in the library, I happened upon a description of the volcano by a Malochian naturalist who visited Khaur-Al-Jaffar with a diplomatic mission. According to this fellow, the crater's not quite dead. Heat rises from a submerged vent on the northern side, causing the water to circulate. Given that, we could indeed lure the creatures away from the sewer. Our men might be able to reach the opening unmolested."

"Swimming with the current, I presume?" Khaddam asked.

"No. The best place to descend into the crater is on the south side, near the fortress. But the current's fairly weak. It shouldn't be much of a hindrance."

"And once our men enter the sewer?"

"They open their waterproof packs, dress themselves as Anarites, and find their way up into the castle. We have plans of the interior—"

"Twenty years old," Sayid Al-Mashat pointed out.

"Even so, I doubt the inside has undergone any extensive changes," Akram answered. "Our men should be able to reach one of the exits that open on the rim, and overpower the guards. Our whole force could then slip inside."

"Why not send demons to do the same work?" Mufkadi asked.

"The entire surface of the fortress—and the crater wall beneath— are graven with counterspells," Akram explained. "Unlike Qanar-Sharaj, Khaur-Al-Jaffar is located in a geographical nexus that permits defensive magic on a vast scale."

"But we'll be able to use spells inside the walls?" Mufkadi asked.

"Yes," Akram answered.

"The plan would appear to allow very little margin for error," Khaddam observed.

"Unavoidable, given the objective," Akram replied. "Or so it seems to me. If you can think of a better scheme, I'll gladly defer to it."

"That won't be necessary," Khaddam said. "For what it's worth, I'd also given the matter some thought. The problem of diffusing the blood stymied me as well. I was none too comfortable with the idea of laying a trail by air, but—"

At that moment, a greyclad entered.

"What is it?" Khaddam asked.

"*Sibi* Samadhi, Grand Master," the Adept answered. "He's in the infirmary—"

Several Masters sprang to their feet.

"Was he attacked?" Khaddam and Mufkadi demanded.

The messenger shook his head. "He slashed his wrists."

"Is he conscious?" Khaddam asked.

"He was when I left," the Adept said. "He asked to see you, Grand Master."

Akram looked to Khaddam. "Adjourned?"

"Adjourned," Khaddam said heavily, and left with the messenger.

When Khaddam arrived in the infirmary, Samadhi was being borne on a litter from an operating table to one of the private rooms; the Grand Master waited outside until Samadhi was settled in his bed and the attendants had gone.

"Thank God you've come," Samadhi said weakly as Khaddam entered.

"Aren't they going to give you any blood?" Khaddam asked, closing the door. Samadhi's face was very pale.

"Doctor Mahad has to find someone with the right sort," Samadhi said. "It seems I need a rare variety. But he said I'll survive in the meantime. I didn't lose too much. He gave me something for the pain. . . ."

"Why did you do it?" Khaddam asked.

Samadhi closed his eyes. "Isn't it obvious?"

Khaddam sank into a chair. "Tell me."

"I learned you were delving into my past."

"And?"

"The third village I named in the Book of Masters . . ."

"You never lived there," Khaddam said.

Samadhi nodded, opening his eyes once more. "I was already at Khaur-Al-Jaffar."

Khaddam stared quietly at him.

"I *was* a Black Anarite," Samadhi said.

Khaddam shook his head slowly.

"It's true," Samadhi persisted. "Surely you suspected. Why else did you send the riders?"

"But I didn't want my suspicions *confirmed*," Khaddam said tonelessly. "Even about you."

"They still think I'm theirs," Samadhi said. "I've been giving them false information."

"The Anarites?"

"Yes. I came to Qanar-Sharaj as a spy. But—I fell in love. With God. With the Order . . . It was such a relief. You don't know what it's like among the Anarites. The fear, the mistrust. The hatred you feel for everyone, including yourself, the loathing of flesh—I never overcame it fully. Healing-spells are quite impossible for me, did you know that? That's why I had to come here, reveal what I'd done to myself . . ."

"A Black Anarite in the Council of Masters," Khaddam said. "Chief of Intelligence. No wonder you argued that they weren't behind the attacks."

"No," Samadhi replied. "You have it all wrong."

"Do I?" Khaddam asked, an edge rising his voice.

"They're *not* responsible. Who'd know better than I?"

"Why should I believe you?" Khaddam demanded.

"Why would I have confessed?"

"So you could cling to your position even after you were exposed."

"Do you think I'm stupid enough to hope for that? I knew I'd be arrested. And when you add the fact that I tried to kill myself . . ."

This line of argument stopped Khaddam cold. Suicide was considered the ultimate sin by the Sharajnaghim; Samadhi's attempt was sufficient all by itself to guarantee his expulsion from the Seventh Level.

"I was mad with despair," Samadhi said. "First the Khan's message, then Massoud's murder . . . I couldn't bear it. I've always been a proud man. Proud and sinful. But I thought the Order needed me. I imagined that I could sanctify my ambition. Wipe out the stain of my years with the Anarites. I was such a fool . . ."

"But if you were so full of remorse," Khaddam said, "why didn't you let yourself die?"

Samadhi lunged into a sitting position, trembling. "Because I *am* a Sharajnaghi! Because I *couldn't* break God's law." Blinking dizzily, he sagged back down again. "I'm part of the *Comahi Irakhoum*, even if it rejects me. God will know I didn't betray it. What else matters? I won't die in despair. I have much to answer for, but I won't send myself to Hell."

"I wish I could believe you—"

"You *must*," Samadhi begged. "If you blame all the killings on me, the murderer will *still* be at large. Worse yet, you'll embark on this pointless war . . ."

"Samadhi," Khaddam said, face pinched with weariness and disgust, "Ghazal and I were attacked by Anarites on our way back from Dhamar. Morkulg was conjured by them. He vanished the instant I loosed a sending on Mahayoun . . ."

"It might have been a coincidence," Samadhi answered. "Perhaps the attackers broke off simply because they exhausted their power."

Khaddam groaned. "I *might* be willing to entertain such a possibility—*if* all the other evidence were not so heavily against you."

Samadhi smiled bitterly. "I don't blame you. Nonetheless, I'm telling the truth."

"Oh, God, my skull hurts," Khaddam said, lowering his face, pressing his palms against his temples. But after a few moments, he heard Samadhi weeping and looked up.

"Stop it," he said.

"It's not for myself," Samadhi replied. "It's for the Order. The night is coming, and I'm powerless to help."

"I think, Samadhi," Khaddam said, "that we have had quite enough of your help."

Rising, he made for the door.

✛

Chapter 3

Khaddam placed Samadhi under heavy guard. Then he ordered Sayid Al-Mashat, the soon-to-be Intelligence Chief, to make a thorough search of Samadhi's apartment. Sayid and five assistants examined every book and dismantled every piece of furniture; ultimately Sayid discovered a small coffer hidden high atop a bookshelf. Inside was a mannikin covered with tiny blades. He sent for Khaddam.

"It's a model of the automaton that attacked me," the Grand Master said. "Was there anything else in the coffer?"

"The figure was wrapped in three rolls of parchment," Sayid replied, signalling. An adept handed the rolls to Khaddam.

"Chemical formulae?" Khaddam said, examining one.

"Some pyrotechnic substance, I'd say," Sayid answered.

"And I'd wager it's one of Massoud's explosives," Khaddam continued, looking at the other parchments. "Rituals for enlargement and animation . . . hmmm." He picked up the mannikin. "Perhaps this isn't a model after all."

"I wonder who it was intended for?" Sayid asked.

"It doesn't matter now," Khaddam replied. "We have all the proof we need to send Master Samadhi to the block."

"But, *Sibi*," said one of Sayid's men, plainly troubled. "What about a confession?"

"Are we going to bother, *Sibi*?" Sayid asked.

"Not if it means torture," Khaddam answered. "I'm certain we have our man."

19

"But the Rules of Evidence, *Sibi* . . ." Sayid's man objected.

"The Rules be damned," Khaddam said. "I'm not going to be legalistic about this. I'll see if I can't convince him to acknowledge his guilt. But I won't put him on the rack."

"You think he'll confess, My Lord?" Sayid asked.

"He's already admitted he was sent as a spy." Khaddam wagged the mannikin. "Let's see how he reacts when I produce this."

After instructing Sayid and his aides not to speak about what had been discovered, the Grand Master returned to Samadhi's chamber in the infirmary.

Samadhi had just received an infusion of blood; much of the color had returned to his face. Khaddam ordered the donor and Doctor Mahad from the room, then showed Samadhi the coffer and its contents.

"We found these in your study," he said.

"I've never seen them before," Samadhi asked. "What are they?"

Khaddam related his theory about the mannikin.

"That's all very well and good," Samadhi said. "But the damned thing isn't mine."

"*When* will you give up?" Khaddam asked.

"Someone planted the coffer."

"Make it easy on yourself."

"Make it easy?"

"Confess," Khaddam said.

"I'm as innocent as you are," Samadhi insisted. "We've both been used. Can't you see that? Massoud too, for that matter. God in Heaven, it's ingenious. The killer gave you two suspects—me and Massoud. But he intended *me* to be the scapegoat all along. He even knew about my past, alerted the Khan . . ."

"What are you talking about?" Khaddam demanded.

"He had to show that there was some *reason* for thinking I was a Black Anarite. But he had to do it indirectly. So he sent the Khan that anonymous message . . ."

"Please, Samadhi. You're only making me angry—"

"*Listen to me!*" Samadhi cried. "Can't you see that there's something very wrong with all this? Why would I have left the figure in my quarters? Why would I have kept it at all, once Massoud was dead? The whole *point* of it was to incriminate him . . ."

"Who knows why you did it?" Khaddam asked. "Maybe you intended to use it on me or Ghazal, but didn't count on us being summoned by the Khan. Maybe it slipped your mind afterwards. Perhaps you even wanted to be caught. It doesn't matter, Samadhi. Can't you see that? You're finished. And you're going to die. The only question now is whether or not you're tortured before we send you to the headsman."

"You won't do it," Samadhi said. "You wouldn't do it to Massoud . . ."

"We had no real evidence against him."

"That wasn't the reason," Samadhi answered. "And it's not the reason now. I know you, Khaddam."

"The Rules of Evidence—"

"It has nothing to do with them. You're just not cruel enough."

"I wouldn't count on that if I were you."

"I'd be confessing a lie in any case," Samadhi answered. "It would just strengthen your delusions. I won't have that on my conscience. The sooner you realize you're wrong, the better." He paused. "When are you going to move me to a cell?"

"As soon as the doctors say you're ready," Khaddam replied.

"And when will you try me?"

"Within the next few days. The sooner we turn you over to the Khan, the better."

"Expecting trouble?" Samadhi asked.

"That depends."

"On what?"

"Whether or not Sayid's men keep quiet."

But in spite of Khaddam's instructions, someone let the information slip; by noon the following day, the whole Order knew, and the halls were smoldering once more. All the hate and suspicion which had been stirred up in the previous weeks was now directed towards Samadhi. In denouncing him, Massoud's followers soon found they had avid competition from Samadhi's own men, who went far out of their way to disassociate themselves from their former master, one group even burning him in effigy. There was little enthusiasm for due process; the chief controversy was whether he should be executed immediately—without recourse to the Khan's headsman—or tortured at length. Pandemonium erupted twice outside the infirmary, with furious Adepts and brown-robes making determined efforts to press inside. But a company of Akram's best troops managed to disperse them both times.

Khaddam decided it was imperative to move Samadhi to more secure quarters as soon as possible; Akram elected to oversee the transfer himself. The doctors pronounced Samadhi fit enough, and he left the infirmary protected by fifty men who advanced along the corridors in a lockstep phalanx, quarterstaffs presented at the ready.

Even so, a turbulent crowd defied them at one junction.

"Disperse!" shouted Akram.

"Show him to us!" a greyclad, one of Massoud's lieutenants, replied.

"Silence!" Akram ordered, stepping into the first rank of the phalanx.

"Show us the traitor!" the Adept cried.

"What do you want?" Akram asked. "To murder him on the spot? Hasn't enough blood been spilled?"

"Not yet!" Massoud's man shrieked. "Give him to us, *Sibi!*"

"Consider yourself under arrest," Akram thundered.

The man's eyes flamed defiance. "Why not arrest us all?"

Akram stood silently for a few moments, pondering the situation. Resting his quarterstaff on his shoulder, he moved forward, beckoning the man as if to parley.

The greyclad came to meet him. "I knew you'd see reason, *Sibi,*" he said.

Akram swung his staff forward.

Collarbone smashed, the man collapsed with a howl.

In the crowd beyond, two Adepts entered stances. Akram was amazed, not only by such mutinous behavior, but because they were resorting to sorcery; even their comrades seemed startled.

But astonishment did not delay Akram's reaction. Cocking the staff back, he hurled it like a spear. With a loud *bock!* it took one man square on the point of the chin.

The second turned to look. Rushing forward, Akram seized the rebounding staff before it could strike the floor and swept the man's legs out from under him. As the fellow struggled to get back up, Akram drove a heel into his groin, then glared at the others, roaring:

"I said, disperse!"

They hesitated, muttering, shaking their heads.

"Do it!" Akram bellowed.

The mob melted sullenly away. Fairly certain there would be no more trouble, Akram detailed men to take the wounded to the infirmary.

The phalanx continued its advance. But as it passed through the junction, the mob swiftly reassembled behind it, raining clay bottles and other refuse on Akram's men. The Master sent a runner for reinforcements before going to confront the mob once more. The crowd commenced a rhythmic chant:

"Samadhi! COME OUT! Samadhi! COME OUT!"

"Silence!" Akram cried.

They ignored him, if they even heard; a bottle came hurtling, end over end. Whirling his staff, he smashed the vessel in midair, retreating into the phalanx.

More voices took up the chant. Turning, jumping to look over the troops ahead, he saw that a second mob was approaching from the front. Blowing three notes on a horn, he signalled the phalanx to halt, thrusting his way into the middle of the formation. Catching sight of Samadhi, he bellowed:

"Satisfied, traitor?"

Samadhi fixed him with a deathly, grieving stare. As close as they were now, with all the uproar Akram could hear only part of the reply:

"—not my doing."

To his horror, Akram was so moved by Samadhi's expression that he almost believed him. But the spy was undeniably a marvellous actor, if nothing else. Twenty years he had been in the Order, rising through the ranks, breaking bread, mouthing prayers—and serving the Black God all the while.

Almost as though he were reading Akram's thoughts, Samadhi shook his head.

The mobs grew steadily bolder, moving close to the presented quarterstaffs. Akram wondered: was help on the way? Had his runner even escaped?

There came the crack of a magic bolt. He saw one of his men go down. Quarterstaffs rose and fell. More bolts flew; some of Akram's men dropped their staffs and responded in kind. The mobs erupted, rushing at Akram's troops.

Magic ceased as the sides closed—in such constricted conditions, it was impossible to maintain stances.

Akram's men held firm for a few moments. Then the ones in front began to waver; blood was flying. Shouldering forward, he saw that their antagonists had drawn their shortswords. Men with staffs were no match for them in such a press.

Good God, Akram thought. He had never envisioned such madness. *Has it truly come to this?*

His troops were reaching for their own shortswords now, but a salient had already been thrust into the phalanx. Stabbing furiously, a young brown-robe lunged at Akram, his face a mask of mindless rage.

Akram drew and parried, stabbed him beneath the ribcage. As the fellow slid off the point, features slackening with approaching death, the Master recognized him; Akram had labored to correct his technique just the day before. Apparently the lesson had not taken—

Something struck Akram on the back of the head.

What? he thought. Had the other mob broken through as well?

He spun. The rear of the phalanx seemed to be holding. It occurred to him that he had heard a shattering noise. Had he been hit by a flying bottle?

His legs began to wobble. He could feel blood flowing down his neck. A dead greyclad dropped against his side; Akram's legs folded under him. There were a few black seconds. Then he thrust the dead Adept aside and got back to his feet.

All was chaos before him. His men were still fighting, but the phalanx had disintegrated; he had been unconscious longer than he had thought.

Samadhi staggered towards him. Blood was fountaining up the side of his face from a wound between shoulder and neck. Halting, he gave Akram that grieving look one last time, then toppled on all fours, a dagger buried hilt-deep in his back.

Akram lurched a step forward—and immediately sank to his knees.

Dressed all in black, a small figure pulled the knife out of Samadhi and wrenched him up by the hair. The red blade jabbed into his side, his temple, his throat. His wounds poured out such torrents that Akram could think only of a wineskin, punctured in many places.

Samadhi's assailant let him go. The spy crumpled, splashing in his own blood.

Straightening, his slayer loosed a ululant cry of triumph that ripped through the surrounding din; setting her foot on Samadhi's corpse, Massoud's widow Chabela lifted her dagger on high—an instant before one of Akram's men stabbed her in the lungs.

What have we become? Akram wondered, blinking.

Chapter 4

As night approached, Erim returned to the grave of Khaldun
Al-Maari, staring down into the pit, pondering what he had seen
earlier that afternoon.

Mind my works, Essaj had said. Erim could think of nothing
else, so full of astonishment and wonder that he felt his heart
would burst. Whatever the nature of Essaj's power, whether or not
he was benign, it was manifest to Erim that the man represented
something totally unprecedented. The possibility that the miracles
were mere trickery, or any kind of sorcery, Erim could no longer
entertain even for a moment. He was no expert in such matters;
but he *had* buried Khaldun. And now Khaldun was alive again.

Nawhar appeared on the other side of the pit. Somehow the
sight of him made it seem a yawning gulf.

"Essaj is possessed," he said. "There's no other answer."

Erim nodded at the grave. "In short, you can't explain this."

"Possession *is* my explanation," Nawhar said. "And I'm quite
comfortable with it."

"Are you?" Erim asked. "What then should I make of those
scratches on your cheeks? You looked as though you were going
to rip your face off this afternoon. You were just as astonished
as I was."

"I don't deny it," Nawhar said. "I'd never heard of a demon that
could restore a corpse to *actual* life. Obviously, my knowledge
was limited."

"Obviously?"

26

"It's much easier for me to believe that," Nawhar said, "than to believe that Essaj's power is innate. That it stems from some sort of divinity. There are many kinds of demon—almost certainly more kinds than we have experience of. On the other hand, our experience of human beings demonstrates an unbridgeable gulf between us and God. We are fallible. He is not. He is self-existent. We are contingent. He is immortal. We die. He is goodness itself. All our righteousness is as filthy rags. He is omniscient, omnipresent, omnipotent. We are little scurrying animals who are lucky if we manage to feed ourselves every day. And Essaj is merely one of us."

"Merely the one who raises the dead," Erim answered.

"A display of tremendous power, certainly," Nawhar said. "Also a finite display. Even if we grant that Essaj's power *is* innate, that still wouldn't justify a claim to divinity."

"But such a test would cast doubt on *any* miracle," Erim protested. "When God parted the Inland Sea, it didn't require *all* His might—only enough to perform the miracle. Nonetheless, anyone who witnessed such an event would be mad not to see His hand in it. There is a point at which skepticism becomes a kind of insanity, Nawhar."

"And what point is that?" Nawhar demanded.

"When we see a man torn alive from his own grave," Erim shot back.

Nawhar smiled; Erim had never seen him show so many teeth. They gleamed wickedly in the twilight.

"You believe in Essaj, don't you?" Nawhar said.

"I believe that the universe is stranger than we suppose—stranger than we *can* suppose. That we are confronting a very great mystery here, and that we should approach it humbly."

"Humbly? What does that mean?"

"That perhaps we shouldn't rush to send Essaj to the block, simply because he defies our understanding."

"He overturns our doctrines as well," Nawhar countered.

"There may be more to our doctrines than we realize," Erim said. "I have faith in them. I believe that they're consonant with reality. But if Essaj is not an evildoer—or a madman—or possessed, then they must also . . ."

"Be consonant with *him*?" Nawhar cried. "Are you aware of what you're saying?"

Erim shrugged. "Interesting question," he said. "Maybe I'm not thinking straight. I'm extremely troubled. But it's more than the miracles—more than what I've seen. Remember what Ahwaz told us? About his dream?"

Nawhar looked annoyed. "Something about turtles? What does that have to do with—"

"He said he was visited by the Grand Master Ghaznavi," Erim said. "And that Ghaznavi had a message for me."

"Which was?"

"That his three-horned reptile was *not* found near Bishah."

"So? It was just a dream. Senseless, as dreams always are."

"No, Nawhar. Think: what did Essaj give me for a wedding-present?"

"A carving of . . ." Nawhar's voice trailed off.

"Ghaznavi's reptile," Erim said.

"Coincidence," Nawhar answered.

"If so, a wondrous one indeed."

"Perhaps Essaj saw a skeleton," Nawhar suggested. "The mountains are full of bones . . ."

"Exactly what occurred to me. But Ghaznavi's beast was found far to the south. Which is what Ghaznavi wanted me to remember."

"Perhaps it also lived in the north."

"The stone in these mountains is too ancient. Far older than the layer that the reptile was discovered in."

"Perhaps Essaj simply read your mind," Nawhar answered. "You're willing to credit him with every other power imaginable—"

"He told me he *invented* the animal," Erim said.

"It follows from his other claims, I suppose," Nawhar replied acidly. "Even so . . ."

"Ghaznavi wanted me to know that Essaj was telling the truth," Erim continued.

"I'm not going to listen to any more of this," Nawhar announced, and started back towards the inn, scratching.

Erim stood alone by the grave for a few moments, then followed at a distance.

In the common-room, Sharif sat at a table not far from Khaldun and his daughters, admiring the way his father-in-law was ignoring the rude behavior of the help. They were all staring at him, and whenever he summoned them, they responded with some trepidation, as though they suspected he was a ghost. One had even gone so far as to prod him with a broom-handle.

As yet, Khaldun had not been informed of the marriages; he distrusted Sharajnaghim, and the sisters had insisted on telling him in their own good time. He was a cedar-wood merchant, and Zehowah had told Sharif that the man who procured wood for Qanar-Sharaj had sharped her father several times.

In spite of that, Sharif thought she and Khalima were being overly cautious. He was relatively certain that he and Khaldun would get on fine, although he was not sure why. He also guessed that Khaldun and Erim would find each other relatively agreeable. After all, Sharif liked Erim.

Nawhar came into the common-room, making directly for the stairs. As he stalked wordlessly past, Sharif felt a fleeting chill, and wondered what was bothering him now. Nawhar *had* been very put out by Khaldun's resurrection.

Erim appeared, joining Sharif. "Have they told him yet?" he asked, nodding towards Khaldun.

"No," Sharif whispered.

Their father-in-law swallowed a huge mouthful of mutton, his latest plate clear at last. He had already emptied three others.

"Told me what?" he asked.

Sharif looked down at the table, suddenly sure that Khaldun was going to despise him. Erim coughed.

"Come now," Khaldun said. "I have very sharp ears."

"You do indeed, sir," Sharif managed at last.

"And I know you saved my daughters from the Anarites, for which you have my eternal gratitude. But what happened after that?"

"Excuse me, father," said Khalima. "How exactly *did* you know?"

"I saw it," Khaldun said.

"Saw it?" Zehowah asked. "You were already . . ."

"Dead?" Khaldun paused. "Yes," he said slowly. "I suppose I was . . ." He snorted. "But that's neither here nor there. What happened after they saved you?"

"Well, sir," Sharif said, "we got to know your daughters . . ."

Khaldun gave him a bird-of-prey stare. "*Know* them?"

Sharif spluttered. "*Just* know them. Not *know* them, if you see what I mean . . ."

"But, Sharif . . ." Zehowah interrupted.

"*But?*" Khaldun demanded.

"We're married, father," Khalima broke in quickly. "Erim there is my husband, and Sharif—"

"*Married?*" Khaldun said. "To a pair of *Sharajnaghim?*"

"They've been very good to us," Zehowah said.

"Do you care nothing for my blessing?" Khaldun answered.

"You were dead, father," Khalima pointed out.

"You could have waited," Khaldun snapped.

"With all due respect, sir," Erim said, "I think you're being a bit . . . er, unreasonable."

Khaldun grumbled something.

"We had no one, father," Zehowah said. "We were completely on our own."

"And think," Khalima added. "The times have been so hard lately. You've said a dozen times you couldn't afford decent dowries for us. Now you needn't worry about it."

"Where will you live?" Khaldun asked.

"At Qanar-Sharaj," Sharif said.

"Aren't you fellows supposed to be celibate?"

"Not anymore. That is, there's a rule, but it's not enforced. There's a whole quarter reserved for women. Erim and I can put your daughters up quite comfortably."

Khaldun mulled the situation over. "No dowries?" he asked.

"You owe us nothing," Sharif assured him.

Khaldun looked at them sharply. "Do you two have anything to do with Shafaz Birsavi?"

"Who?" the Sharajnaghim asked.

"He buys lumber for your Order."

"Never heard of him," Erim said.

Sharif rubbed his chin. "Shafaz, Shafaz—I think I drubbed him in a practice duel."

"A wizard's duel?"

"Smashed his chest in."

Khaldun's face brightened. "Did you, now?"

"As I recall."

Khaldun snapped his fingers. "About three years ago?"

"Yes."

"So *you're* the one who broke his ribs!" Khaldun asked.

"It's a small world, isn't it?" Sharif replied.

"I really shouldn't be so delighted, but—God is just."

"He is indeed, sir."

Khaldun laughed. "Come over here, the two of you. Sit down, sit down." He signalled a porter. "Wine for my sons-in-law."

The man brought goblets and a fresh bottle. Sharif found the vintage faintly reminiscent of Essaj's wine; it was nowhere near so strong or good, but it still transported him, for the briefest instant, back to the garden in Bishah. He smiled at Zehowah.

"Excuse me, sir," Erim said to Khaldun after a time. "Might I ask you a question?"

"Ask away, young man," Khaldun replied.

"What was it like?"

"What was what like?"

"Being dead."

Khaldun lowered his goblet. His expression grew thoughtful, as though he were searching for the proper words.

"The pain went away," he began. "That was the first thing. I began to feel . . . well, *separate* from my body, as though I were just drifting out of it, rising into the air.

"Suddenly I realized that I was looking down at myself. I saw the whole battle in the courtyard, lingered just long enough to see the Anarites surrender. Then I was drawn into a kind of tunnel."

"A tunnel?" Erim asked.

"In the sky. There was a light at the end of it." Tears welled up in Khaldun's eyes. "My wives were in the light. That part of it was wonderful, simply wonderful. There were others too, but I don't remember who they were . . . We were all waiting, you see."

"For what?"

"Our bodies."

"You knew Essaj was going to raise you?"

"No. We were waiting for the Resurrection of the Dead. *All* the dead."

Sharif felt a crawling at the nape of his neck. "But where were you?" he asked. "Heaven?"

"No," Khaldun said. "That's what's so strange. I think it was Hell. Someone kept saying that it had to be harrowed—that the

Lamb had to be slain before we could see God."

"Hell doesn't sound so bad," Sharif observed.

"It wasn't," Khaldun said. "There just wasn't anything to eat." He sipped his wine, staring. "I still can't quite believe it. It all seems like some kind of dream. Was I truly dead?"

"I can assure you, sir," Sharif said, "*dead* is hardly the word."

✠

Chapter 5

Nawhar lay on his bed, chewing strip after strip of his pain-deadening bark, obtaining no relief. His joints were aflame; his skin crawled and twitched, full of needles. He was losing Erim— in all likelihood, had already lost him. And he was beginning to wonder if his own sanity were not slipping away from him as well. No matter what he had told Erim, he was not at all comfortable with his explanation of Khaldun's resurrection. As far as he knew, in all of human history, the barrier between the living and the dead had never truly been breached. It was reasonable enough to postulate the existence of demons with such power; even so, that was begging the question.

There is a point at which skepticism becomes a kind of insanity, Erim had told him. But Erim had it exactly wrong. It was the possibility of nascent belief that terrified Nawhar now—the very specter of Essaj himself. What was he doing in Nawhar's world? If, as Nawhar thought, the physical universe was a manifestation of his own sinful insanity, what did Essaj's coming portend? Was he the thin end of the wedge, the initial intrusion of a yet more radical madness? Nawhar was seized by a suspicion that he was falling somehow, that material perception was corroding his mind, producing hallucinations of healing and resurrection. . . . Would he too come to believe in the charlatan from Amran?

Never, Nawhar told himself. How could he accept the man's doctrine? Even if true, it only rendered Essaj that much more loathsome. If God became matter, would matter somehow be sanctified? To Nawhar, the suggestion seemed, if anything, more

33

absurd than the idea of Infinite Being squeezing itself into a finite receptacle. The Almighty would merely have demonstrated His willingness to turn Himself into meat and blood and shit. If the source of everything was so hopelessly corruptible, what reason was there for worship? For preferring existence to nonexistence at all?

Nawhar sat up on the edge of his bed, joints protesting. Normally, he was only this sore early in the morning—was the deterioration of his bones accelerating? Perhaps it was merely because he was in such a disturbed state—he had noticed that his various complaints worsened whenever he was upset, sometimes horrifically. The night of the wedding, he had been driven to scratch a large area on one shoulder blade virtually to shreds.

He rose to try some of his stretching exercises. They proved acutely painful at first, but he kept at them stubbornly. The anger in his joints slowly subsided. He began to relax.

The room was very hot; the kitchen was beneath it, he knew. It was well past midnight, but he guessed the embers in the oven must still be smoldering, the heat rising through the ceiling . . . between that, and the exertion from his exercises, he was awash in sweat. As uncomfortable as he was, he did not take his tunic off, distressed by the thought of his own nakedness; scrubbing himself through the cloth with both hands, restraining himself only with some effort from raking the great itching scab on his shoulder blade, he went out onto the balcony, which extended the full length of the building.

"Who's there?" came a voice.

Nawhar looked round. He could make out the shadowy form of a man, but could not see his face.

"Who is it?" the man pressed.

This time Nawhar recognized the voice: it was Jalloud's.

"Nawhar," he said.

"Have you come out to admire the stars, Sharajnaghi?" Jalloud asked.

"I couldn't sleep."

"Perhaps your conscience is bothering you," Jalloud said.

"While yours is quite clear, I take it," Nawhar replied.

"As a matter of fact, yes."

"I don't doubt it," Nawhar said. "Given how freely you criticize your master . . ."

"What are you talking about?"

"Your boldness in pointing out Essaj's inconsistencies. You must be a man of very high moral character."

"You flatter me," Jalloud said.

"I tell the truth as I see it," the Sharajnaghi said. "You think he doesn't go far enough sometimes, isn't that right? That he doesn't act in accordance with his own teachings?"

Jalloud laughed. "Are you trying to pry me away from him?"

"I notice you haven't denied anything I've said."

"I question Essaj precisely *because* I respect him so much," Jalloud replied.

"And when he veers off the path a bit, you set him right."

"I wouldn't put it quite that way, but—"

"You're his conscience, aren't you?" Nawhar broke in.

"Let's just say I think very deeply about his teachings," Jalloud answered, after a time.

"But what of his teachings about himself? Who do you think he is, Jalloud?"

"I think he's made himself clear enough on that point—"

"I didn't ask you about *his* opinion. I asked you for yours."

"He is My Lord."

"Your Lord?"

"The Son of God."

"As well as God Himself?"

"Yes."

"Then tell me, Jalloud," Nawhar prodded. "Why does God Himself need you for a conscience?"

"That was your word, not mine," Jalloud answered.

"Why does God Himself allow His uncle to keep a spacious house, in violation of His teachings?"

"God can do whatever He pleases."

"Certainly," Nawhar agreed. *Except become flesh*, he thought. "But surely He's constrained by His own goodness. And a good God would not make one law for some men, and another for the rest."

"You *are* trying to trip me up," Jalloud insisted.

"You mistake my intentions," Nawhar answered. "You're such an upright fellow—I would hate to see you expend your virtue on such a ruinous course of action."

"And what course is that?"

"Following this imposter. This blasphemer."

"You have no idea what I've seen," Jalloud answered. "The comfort he's given to the poor . . ."

"But if he's truly God, and he truly cares about the poor," Nawhar objected, "why hasn't he simply abolished poverty altogether, with a sweep of his hand?"

Even as Jalloud considered this question, one answer occurred to Nawhar—obviously, God had *always* declined to abolish poverty. But Nawhar was not about to show this lout the way out of his difficulties.

"Essaj *comforts* the poor," the Sharajnaghi continued, "because he can't redeem them from their plight."

"He raises the dead—"

"But you care about the *living*, don't you? The perfection of *this* world. You want results here and now. The mighty laid low. The humble exalted." Nawhar was guessing here, but he had encountered men like Jalloud before—lunatics who thought the physical universe could be rendered quite cozy if only property and class were eliminated. Nawhar regarded such men with a contempt that bordered on the perfect; but he was quite content to use the man's errors to destroy his belief in Essaj.

"The Master won't fail me," Jalloud said. "He'll overturn the whole world."

"Perhaps he will," Nawhar said. "Perhaps he'll drive the Mirkuts from the land, and make himself king, and conquer all Thorgon Karrelssa. Maybe he'll raise a dead man every day of every year. But would all that make his partiality towards his uncle any less hypocritical? Would it make up for all the times he's favored Anwar at your expense?"

Once again Nawhar was guessing. But it seemed reasonable to surmise that Jalloud was nursing any number of hidden resentments. It was generally so among power-seekers; and Jalloud plainly hungered to wield vast powers—all for the sake of the poor, of course—as the Expected One's right hand.

"What do you know about that?" Jalloud demanded.

"I only know what I've observed," Nawhar answered, pleased by the reaction he had fetched. "I wouldn't presume to tell you about your relations with Anwar and Essaj. Certainly you're the best judge of whether or not you've been slighted."

"It's none of your business," Jalloud said.

"Whatever you say," Nawhar answered. "But I only mentioned it to reinforce my main point—that Essaj isn't God. Do you actually believe that God would treat a man of your character the way Essaj treats you?" He paused. "Anwar *is* the favorite, isn't he? I'm not mistaken about that, am I? I would hate to think that I've misjudged your master—"

The only sound from Jalloud was an angry, hissing exhalation.

"God Himself—perfect justice—has chosen Anwar over you," Nawhar said. "Over *you!*"

"Stop it," Jalloud snapped. "He hasn't chosen at all."

"How do you enjoy being weighed in the balance—"

"I told you—"

"—and found wanting?"

"Shut your mouth!"

"Please don't be angry with me," Nawhar said. "If you can't bear the thought of your inferiority, console yourself. With the obvious truth—that you're *not* wanting. That Essaj isn't God."

"Not one more word out of you, Sharajnaghi."

Nawhar thought he had already done enough. Going back into his room, he fell asleep without the slightest difficulty.

Jalloud, on the other hand, spent a restless night, fretting over Nawhar's arguments. His weary mind was still chafing itself as the company departed the following morning. Some of the other disciples joked about his dark-rimmed eyes, but he made little attempt to respond, consumed as he was by his inner debate with Nawhar.

The company stopped near midday in a grove at the bottom of a hill. Jalloud wanted to catch some sleep, but was still too agitated. He ate some bread in a futile attempt to settle his stomach, then went some distance from the others, coming to a stream.

There he found Anwar. Knee-deep in the water, the latter was bent well over, peering at the bottom.

"Thought I'd try and catch myself some lunch," he said, and leaned a bit closer to the water. "I *see* you—" His hands darted downwards. There was a commotion beneath the surface. He splashed a step forward, breathing out loudly through his nostrils in frustration.

"Ahh," he said sourly, then looked up at Jalloud. "What's the matter with you? You've hardly said a word all morning."

"It's nothing," Jalloud replied.

"Perhaps you should speak to the Master," Anwar said, returning his attention to the water.

"I don't know," Jalloud said.

"It always helps me."

Jalloud found the assurance in Anwar's voice horribly irritating. "Does it now?" he asked pointedly.

"Come, come," Anwar said. "Why are you acting this way?"

"I spoke with that Nawhar fellow last night."

"And?" Anwar thrust his hands into the water again. This time they reemerged with a large trout. He tossed the fish onto the riverbank. "He seems harmless enough to me," he said.

"Harmless?" Jalloud asked. Noticing the fish flopping towards the stream, he flipped it back with his foot.

"Malicious, but rather pathetic," Anwar replied. "Small. Not someone I could ever take seriously—" He broke off. "Hoo now. Just *look* at that big beauty!" He lunged again, catching a second trout. Tossing it over with the first, he marched to the bank, wiping his hands on his tunic, looking very pleased with himself.

"Have you ever had any doubts?" Jalloud asked.

"About what?"

"The Master."

Anwar laughed. "Why should I want to admit such a thing? To you, of all people?"

"You have, then."

"I'm human." Anwar looked closely at Jalloud. "And I suppose you are too, eh?"

Jalloud sat on a fallen log. "I'm so tired. But my brain's on fire. That damned Sharajnaghi—"

Anwar sat next to him. "What are his arguments beside the Master's miracles? What authority does he have, that little unhappy twisted man? He doesn't even have the sense to ask the Master to heal him—Khalima told me all about it. He's a complete fool. Simply because we have to suffer him gladly doesn't mean we have to *listen* to him."

"He's not as stupid as you think," Jalloud replied.

"Are you saying that he *must* be intelligent if he managed to worry you? I can't accept that. The world's full of learned idiots.

The Sharajnaghim don't know anything, in my opinion. Not anymore. They used to do a lot of good, but they're too much part of the world now. Money-grubbers, corrupt and power-hungry. And when the Master comes into his kingdom, and everything's put right, there won't be any place for them at all."

"*If* the Master comes into his kingdom," Jalloud said.

"And what could stop him?"

"What if he's not who we think?" Jalloud asked.

"And who *do* you think I am?" came a voice from behind.

They rose, turning.

There stood Essaj.

"Tell me, Jalloud," he said.

Jalloud could not bear to look him in the eye. "You . . . are the greatest teacher . . . the greatest man . . . I've ever met."

"And you, Anwar," said Essaj. "Who do you say I am?"

"The Expected One," Anwar said, without the slightest hesitation. "The Son of the Living God."

Essaj nodded. "Good for you, Anwar son of Habid. You are steadfast, a rock." He laid his hand on Anwar's shoulder. "And upon this rock I will build my church, and the gates of Hell will not prevail against it. Whatever you declare loosed on earth will be loosed in heaven, and whatever you declare bound shall be held bound."

Jalloud was stunned. All he could think of were Nawhar's sneering words:

God Himself—perfect justice—has chosen Anwar over you. Over you!

"No," Jalloud breathed.

"What did you expect?" Essaj asked. "You don't believe."

Jalloud hurled himself to his knees. "Then help my unbelief."

"Be patient," Essaj answered.

"Be patient," Jalloud answered. "That's all you ever tell me."

"Because you haven't listened. But don't despair, or do anything you might regret. Nothing has changed between you and me."

"Nothing?" Jalloud asked, leaping back to his feet in a fury. "Are you saying that I *never* believed?"

"I still count you my friend," Essaj answered. "Content yourself with that, for now. If you're not against me, you're for me."

"Please," Jalloud said. "It's not enough—"

"You're not against me, are you?"

Jalloud shook his head, quivering. *Not yet, My Lord*, he thought.

The party pressed on into the lowlands; after several days, Erim made out a sprawl of ruins, surrounded by palm trees.

Al-Asriyeh, he thought, and went to warn Essaj.

"Master," he said, "my friends and I passed that village on our way north. The Mirkuts massacred the people for harboring rebels. The bodies were left unburied as a warning—some were nailed to those trees with arrows. I thought perhaps you might want to avoid—"

"No," said Essaj.

"There will be some risk of disease . . ."

"I think not," Essaj answered.

"I don't understand, Master," Erim said. "*Why* do you want to go through?"

"I'd like to see for myself what the Mirkuts did," Essaj replied. "I've led rather a sheltered life. Amran suffered very little during the invasion."

"But, Master," Erim said, anxious to dissuade him, "why do you need to *look* at all? Given who you claim to be . . ."

"I can't see everything at once," Essaj replied. "I can do nothing a man can't do."

"You raise the dead."

"Still, I am a man."

"Men can raise the dead?"

"One can."

"But they can't be all-knowing?"

"This world is too small for that. It is one thing to have a power, another to use it. If I am to remain bound by this world, I must walk softly."

"I'm not sure I follow you."

"Think of it this way," Essaj replied. "A man wrote a story, and put himself in it. Now. Was the man in that story him?"

Erim knit his brow. "In one sense, yes . . ."

"But?"

"In another sense, the character wasn't him at all."

"No? You must try to imagine a *real* storyteller, then."

"But the character *isn't* the author," Erim insisted. "He's just an abstraction."

"Just an abstraction," Essaj laughed. "Have you never heard that God thinks Himself?"

"I'm familiar with the notion."

"It is a good one," Essaj declared. "As for me, I am thinking of myself as a Son of Man. I have descended into your story. But if I were to spread my wings, I would tear this little world apart. And if I were to open my eyes, what would withstand my glance?"

That brought Erim up short. All along, Essaj had spoken with such offhandedness that Erim, although completely attentive, had not appreciated at all the transcendent strangeness of the man's words; here Essaj was, explaining the nature of his divinity in some detail, and he might as well have been discussing the weather! It was thoroughly disconcerting. Erim would have expected far more drama, whether from heretic, demon—or God.

"You know," he said after a time, "I've often thought of this world as a kind of story. Did you read my mind, Master?"

"No," said Essaj. "You read mine." He shaded his eyes. The village was not far now. "So. Let us see what our brethren have wrought."

Erim steeled himself as the palms loomed close, waiting to be deluged by a flood of horrible memories from his childhood. Stripped clean by insects and carrion birds, the transfixed corpses were little more than skeletons. They might have been there for years. Erim was relieved; it was hard to see his slaughtered father and brother in those fleshless relics.

The party moved through the trees and in among the ruins. Remains were scattered everywhere; wild dogs had torn them apart. It was apparent from the size of the bones that most had belonged to women and children. The Mirkuts always followed the same pattern—the men had been forced to watch their wives and young ones slaughtered before being led away for target practice . . .

At last Erim felt the old hatred boil up in him, and turned to Essaj. Essaj's expression was sorrowful beyond words.

"Well, Master," Erim said, voice clenched with rage. "Now you've seen. You say you're the Expected One. When will you sweep the foreign vermin from this land?"

"Never," Essaj answered.

"What?" Erim cried.

"The Mirkuts are not so great a matter as you imagine."

"You can look at this butcher's yard and still say that?" Erim demanded.

"Yes," Essaj said, nodding. "Still."

Amid the sorrow, Erim perceived a hint of satisfaction; had Essaj been testing himself?

"But, Master—" Erim began.

Essaj raised his hand. "Let us be off."

✢

Chapter 6

The company made camp shortly afterwards. Pushing on at daybreak, they came before noon to the road that led to Qanar-Sharaj, and halted at the junction. Five miles across the fields, the great white dome gleamed in the morning sun.

Khalima and Zehowah received blessings from Essaj, and went to say farewell to their father. Essaj turned to Erim and Sharif. Nawhar stood at a distance with his horse.

"So," Essaj said. "Here we part company."

Before the Sharajnaghim could speak, Anwar thrust himself between Essaj and them. "And what are you going to tell your Masters about My Lord?" he asked.

"The truth, I hope," Erim replied.

"You *hope*?" Anwar demanded.

But Essaj said: "It is enough."

"Good-bye, Master," Erim said.

"Thank you for your hospitality," Sharif added, bowing. "You've been very gracious."

"It was nothing," Essaj answered.

The two joined their wives. Khaldun was brushing away a tear as they came up.

"You take good care of my girls, now," the merchant admonished.

"You can count on it, sir," said Sharif.

Erim seconded him with a nod.

"Will you be all right, father?" Khalima asked.

"Don't worry," Khaldun replied. "If the house hasn't burned down, I'll manage. Come, daughters. Give me a kiss."

They gave him several apiece. At last he pushed them gently away.

"Now," he said. "Off with you."

Tearfully, they obeyed. Essaj's party continued towards Thangura, Khaldun bringing up the rear, looking over his shoulder now and again, waving. The Sharajnaghim and their wives remained some time at the junction.

"Must we wait here in the hot sun?" Nawhar asked. "How many times do you need to wave goodbye?"

They ignored him. Climbing onto his horse, he started forward by himself; the others followed presently, after mounting up as well.

As they neared Qanar-Sharaj, Khalima grew steadily more astonished. The structure seemed virtually a city in itself, with tall whitewashed walls. Towers stood at each corner, and flanked the massive gate; dozens of cupolas surrounded the gigantic dome in the center of the roof.

"Is it all one building?" Khalima asked.

"The largest in the world, or so I'm told," Erim said. "There are vast granaries, smithies, stables, armories. We have splendid doctors and spotless infirmaries, running water, wonderful baths, a library second to none—think of a book, and chances are we have it. We send men all over the continent, just looking for scrolls and texts."

"About anything?"

"Absolutely. Some of our more interesting finds have been laundry-lists and inventories."

"Laundry-lists?" Zehowah asked. "What's interesting about them?"

"Everything—if they're two thousand years old," Erim replied. "They're baked clay tablets, written by our ancestors in a tongue very different from ours. Languages change over the years, you see. So does writing—the words on the tablets were set down in the form of little wedges, dug into the clay with reed styluses."

"And you study these matters?" Khalima said.

"I don't," Erim replied. "But some of my friends are fascinated by the ancients, and they've told me about them. Myself, I'm a specialist in philosophy. Sharif's field is sorcery, as you must have guessed. A Sharajnaghi must study God, magic, and the martial arts. But few of us are truly gifted in all three pursuits, and the Order takes account of this. We're encouraged to take up any branch of knowledge that suits us, provided we fulfill our basic duties."

Zehowah laughed. "What about cooking?"

"Oh," said Sharif, "we have very good cooks. The science is well developed among us."

"You should see the old recipe-books in the library," Erim put in. "Our cooks can draw on two thousand years of experience. And believe me, some of the oldest are amazingly good. Sometimes, on feast days, we're served nothing but classics."

"Are there gardens?" Khalima wondered.

"In abundance," Erim replied. "The largest is inside the Women's Quarters, as a matter of fact. You'll both have private plots—small ones, but big enough for vegetables. If you want them."

"Of course we do," Zehowah said.

"We *love* gardening," Khalima added.

"You *love* it?" Erim asked.

Khalima nodded gravely, trying her best to communicate the high seriousness with which she regarded this subject.

They approached the gate. Nawhar had dismounted beneath the arch; he was talking agitatedly to the guards.

"What happened to Samadhi?" Sharif heard him ask.

"Massoud's wife," a guard replied. "She stabbed him to death . . ."

Erim shot Sharif a glance as if to say: *Surely we couldn't have heard that.* But as they came up, Nawhar told them:

"Five Masters were killed while we were gone," Nawhar told them.

They jumped down from their horses.

"Samadhi was behind it all, apparently," he said. "He confessed to being a Black Anarite . . . Chabela struck him down."

"Why?" Erim asked.

"He murdered Massoud," Nawhar answered.

"And who else?"

"Shoua, Ghazal—and the Grand Master."

"Ahwaz?" Sharif cried.

"A stroke carried him off," a second guard said. "But it was brought on by the sending."

"There was some fighting," Nawhar continued. "Between Samadhi's followers and Massoud's. Apparently Master Akram was wounded. Fratricide, in Qanar-Sharaj . . ." His voice trailed away.

Sharif was so sick with grief and rage that he thought he might vomit. "And what are we going to do about the Anarites?" he demanded.

"I'll tell you what we *should* do," the first guard said. "Slaughter every one of the bastards."

"The Council's been meeting every day," the second said. "We don't know what they're planning yet, but there's something big afoot."

"Who's Grand Master now?" Erim asked.

"Khaddam," a third guard answered.

"Have the other Masters been replaced?"

"Some. *Sibi* Murad took Ghazal's chair; Mufkadi Umar was at Science, but now he's in charge of Sorcery. The other posts won't be filled until Khaddam's men are elevated to the Seventh Level, but the trials have been arranged for the next two days."

"So," said Erim. "How many members of the Knot will be on the Council?"

"Five—provided they pass their trials."

Erim observed: "Khaddam can certainly take comfort in that."

Sharif thought this sounded like a veiled accusation; evidently the first guard thought so too, and said hotly:

"He's also gone through Hell. He was attacked *three times*. The first sending exploded, filled him with metal fragments and blew one of his eyes from its socket."

Erim winced.

"Who are those women, by the way?" the first guard asked.

"Our wives," Sharif said.

"Very well, then. Come on through."

Brown-robes took the horses. Leaving the sisters in a waiting-hall, Erim and Sharif went to arrange accommodations for them. Returning, they reported that apartments in the Women's Quarters would not be available for a day or two.

"A wing's under repair," Erim explained.

"Where will we sleep, then?" Khalima asked.

"Guest rooms, of course," Erim answered, holding up two keys.

After seeing their wives to their lodgings, Erim and Sharif set off for their own chambers. Upon entering Qanar-Sharaj, Sharif had noticed a queer, bristling quality in the air; he felt it very keenly now. There was a good deal of shouting in the distance; passing a group of Adepts and brown-robes, he overheard part of a fierce conversation about the morality of killing prisoners of war. The proponents of the traditional Sharajnaghi teaching— that prisoners should be spared—seemed to be very much in the minority. "Times change!" their opponents shouted repeatedly.

Sharif found himself siding with the majority. Five Masters murdered by sendings—he began to find the tense atmosphere a kind of tonic. He was in no mood to pacify himself.

Better rage than grief, he thought. *Let it build. Save it all for the Anarites* . . .

Reaching their rooms, he and Erim deposited their bags, then asked a neighbor who had replaced Massoud at Doctrine. Learning it was Arghun Khan, they went to make their report.

"I wonder where Nawhar is?" Erim asked.

"He's probably with Arghun already," Sharif answered. "Or the new Spymaster."

They soon discovered that Arghun had been given Iyad's apartment; going there, they found him overseeing the movement of Iyad's great desk by four grunting brown-robes.

"Arghun?" Sharif called through the open door.

Arghun ignored him until the desk was settled in its new place.

"What do you want?" he demanded.

"We're here to report on Essaj."

"Come in," Arghun answered, then sent one of the acolytes to get Sayid Al-Mashat.

"Sayid?" Sharif asked.

"He's in charge at Intelligence now," Arghun answered.

"So," Sharif said. "I suppose we should congratulate you on your promotion."

"Thank you," Arghun said. "But considering my new status, I think you'd best address me as *Sibi* now."

"But you haven't been elevated yet . . ."

"Then you might as well begin practicing," Arghun answered.

Sharif was stung by his tone. Unlike the rest of Khaddam's Serpents, who were fairly personable, Arghun was known for his haughtiness—he came of an Urguz noble line, or so he claimed—but this was unpleasant even for him. His slanted eastern eyes narrowed still farther.

"Do we understand each other?" he asked.

"Yes, *Sibi*," Sharif said.

"In the meantime, until Sayid arrives, you and Erim can help my men."

"Help, *Sibi*?"

"With my furniture," Arghun answered, and pointed to a chair. "Put that—" He looked about the room. "Over there."

After a time, Sayid appeared—with Nawhar.

Dismissing the acolytes, Arghun settled behind the desk. Sayid pulled up a seat, stationing himself nearby.

The two made for quite a contrast. Small and dark, Arghun favored his steppe ancestors; Sayid was a great bear of a man, his red hair clearly reflecting Malochian blood.

"I have matters to attend," he said. "Let's keep this brief."

Nodding, Arghun addressed Erim and Nawhar: "Did you find Essaj Ben Yussef?"

"We did, *Sibi*," Nawhar answered.

"In your opinion, is there sufficient evidence against him to bring his case before the Full Council?"

"Manifestly, *Sibi*," said Nawhar.

"You uncovered evidence of fraud?" Arghun Khan asked.

"No, *Sibi*," Nawhar answered. "Heresy."

"Erim?" Arghun asked.

"He made statements which would certainly, under most circumstances, be considered incriminating . . ."

"But you have reservations?" Sayid asked.

"The miracles, *Sibi*," Erim replied.

"Miracles?"

"Nawhar could discover no trace of fraud."

"If Essaj is a heretic, that's entirely irrelevant," Arghun said.

"He raised a man from the dead, Master," Erim answered.

"What?" Sayid and Arghun asked.

"He has powers, *Sibim*, indisputably," Nawhar broke in. "But in my opinion, he's demonically possessed."

"These incriminating statements," Arghun said. "What were they, Erim?"

Seeming not to hear him, Erim resumed: "He also exorcised a demon, a Great Demon, without recourse to ritual—"

"Answer the question!" Arghun snapped.

"Very well, *Sibi,*" Erim answered. Quickly he recounted Essaj's most outrageous claims.

"Astonishing," Arghun said.

"Is he insane, do you think?" Sayid asked.

"If he is, *Sibi,* he gives no obvious sign of it," Erim replied. "That is, apart from the basic nature of his claims."

"Sharif," Sayid said.

"Master?" Sharif asked.

"Were you present during any of this?"

"Yes, *Sibi,*" Sharif answered. "In particular, I heard Essaj claim the power to forgive sins."

"I think this merits the Council's attention," Arghun pronounced.

"I agree," Sayid said. "Nawhar, you're dismissed."

Nawhar left immediately.

Sharif said: "What about Erim and m—"

Sayid cut him off. "Nawhar informed me that you two have taken wives. Followers of Essaj."

"Yes, *Sibi,*" Sharif acknowledged.

"And you intend to keep them here?" Arghun asked incredulously.

Erim and Sharif nodded.

"That would create an intolerable situation," Sayid declared.

"You *will* put them aside," Arghun said. "You've had your pleasure . . ."

Completely dismayed, Sharif could only manage a sputter. But Erim kept his wits:

"With all due respect, *Sibi,* you can't force us to do that. Even the Grand Master has no authority—"

"We shall see, Erim," said Arghun.

"Times change," said Sayid.

Times change, Sharif thought. Hadn't he found himself assenting to that very argument quite recently, in connection with something else? But before he could fully retrieve the memory, Sayid dismissed him and Erim, and Sharif forgot all about it.

✛

Chapter 7

Despite the recommendations of Sayid and Arghun, the Council put the matter of Essaj off for several days. Given the fact that some sort of offensive against the Anarites was clearly being contemplated, Erim was not at all surprised. Even so, the delay was torture for him. He suspected that the hearing was going to prove a supremely ugly confrontation between him and Nawhar— and he wanted to put it behind him as soon as possible.

That his friendship with Nawhar was already finished, he had no doubt—unless he turned against Essaj. But he could not imagine what might cause such a change of heart. Essaj was not the Expected One that Erim had been yearning for, a man of war who would crush the invaders and drive them from the land; but upon reflection, even though his conclusion frustrated him horribly, Erim had decided that his notion of redemption was too primitive, however much it fired his blood. Indeed, the very fact that Essaj thought the Mirkuts no great matter made him, after a fashion, even more persuasive. There was nothing *significant* about him that Erim wanted to believe. The nature of the redemption promised by Essaj remained a mystery, but Erim found himself strangely certain that he would submit to it, whatever it might be. That certainty terrified him; it was a leap in the dark, plainly irrational, its consequences unforseeable. Nonetheless, somewhere between Al-Asriyeh and Qanarea Sharaj, he had come to believe.

He had no idea of how long he could remain a Sharajnaghi, but he did not intend to leave the Order until he was expelled. He loved the *Comahi Irakhoum* dearly, and could not bear to think that he had betrayed it. That left him only one course of action— to try and convert his colleagues. It was his deepest wish that there would be no rupture between the Old Dispensation and the New; if Essaj *was* God, it was not inconceivable that duty to him and the Order might be the same thing.

I call you traitors because that is what you are, Horde had said.

But Erim was determined to prove the demon wrong, at least in his own case.

Two days after their return, he and Sharif encountered Kourah Kislali, Samadhi's one-time aide; he was now assisting Sayid. The conversation turned quickly to the murders.

"You know, it's interesting," Kourah said. "But Samadhi never confessed."

"He admitted to being a Black Anarite," Sharif said.

"He admitted that he was *once* a Black Anarite," Kourah replied. "He claimed to have had a conversion. And maintained steadfastly that he wasn't behind the killings."

"Was he threatened with torture?" Erim asked.

"Khaddam decided against it—indeed, the evidence was already very strong. And then Samadhi was killed."

"Are you saying that his guilt remains an open question?"

"I wouldn't go that far," Kourah answered. "Still, it *is* interesting, though, isn't it?"

The discussion ended there; but Erim, unsettled, sought Kourah out again later that evening.

"I fear I might have overstated my case earlier," Kourah said.

"Regarding Samadhi?" Erim asked.

"Yes."

"Exactly how much do you know about the investigation?"

"As much as anyone at this point, I suppose. I worked with Samadhi *and* Sayid, after all."

"Well," Erim said, "I've already heard several different accounts—of the killings, that is. You wouldn't be willing to start at the beginning with me, would you?"

"You're very curious about this," Kourah observed.

"Indulge me. I was away for some time, and I'm *desperate* to hear the unvarnished truth."

"Unvarnished?"

"The official story. Isn't that the same thing?"

Kourah laughed. "Very well, then. The *official* story."

Embarking on a detailed recount, Kourah held Erim in rapt fascination for two hours.

"Good Lord," Erim cried at last. "I have to get back to my wife. Can I speak to you again tomorrow night?"

"Certainly."

"And might I take some of this down? I'm thinking of writing an account."

"So am I," Kourah answered. "Perhaps we could collaborate."

"Done," said Erim.

Kourah finished his tale the following evening, lending Erim some of his notes. Erim took them to the Women's Quarters, where Khalima and Zehowah had moved into adjoining apartments. Sharif and his wife were visiting Khalima when Erim arrived.

"Khalima tells us that you've opened your own investigation," Sharif said.

"She's exaggerating," Erim replied. "Let's just say I'm trying to distract myself."

"From what?"

"Thinking about the hearing tomorrow."

"Shouldn't you be planning your line of attack?" Sharif asked. "You *are* going to argue against Nawhar, aren't you?"

"Does that bother you?"

"Why should it?" Sharif said, shrugging. "I have no opinion, so how can I grudge you yours? Now, if Essaj is brought to trial, and the Council finds against him, that's a different mat—"

Zehowah clapped a hand over his mouth, as though to keep him from making an objectionable joke. Gently Sharif thrust her arm down, not looking at her. Plainly to forestall an argument, Khalima asked Erim hurriedly:

"What did you learn from Kourah tonight?"

Erim gave a summary.

"And so," he said at last, "I keep coming back to the same question. Who's benefitted from all of this?"

"Khaddam," Sharif answered. "He's Grand Master, and controls half the votes on the Council."

"But Khaddam was away from Qanar-Sharaj when Ahwaz was killed, and was attacked at virtually the same time. Not to mention twice before that."

"Could he have arranged the attacks?" Khalima asked. "To draw suspicion from himself?"

"It would've been quite a trick," Erim answered. "Particularly with the first sending. If he'd suffered minor injuries, perhaps a case could be made. But by Kourah's account, he was ripped half to tatters. *Mortally* wounded. If it weren't for the healing-spell, he certainly would have died. It's a bit much to imagine that he could have counted on surviving."

"But who's benefitted *besides* Khaddam?" Khalima asked.

"The Serpents," Erim said. "Five of them elevated, all as a result of the killings."

"But that doesn't make sense," Khalima answered. "You said that they all owe their positions to Khaddam."

"Yes," said Erim.

"Then why would they have tried to kill him? If they'd succeeded, he'd never have become Grand Master. And they wouldn't have become Masters themselves."

"Not necessarily," Erim replied, irritated by this challenge from his wife. "They were still ideally placed."

"Oh, this is nonsense," Sharif answered. "They'd never have gotten into the Seventh Level."

"Mufkadi Umar was chosen before Khaddam was attacked," Erim countered. "Perhaps they thought he'd plead their case."

"All by himself?" Khalima asked. "That's lame."

Erim glared at her. "Well, maybe it isn't *all* of them," he said angrily. "Perhaps the object was simply to penetrate the Council, find out our secrets, and kill as many Masters as possible. One of the Serpents *might* have been certain he'd be selected, even without Khaddam's help. Or the killer might have been the first Serpent selected—Mufkadi."

"That's all very well," Sharif said. "But why would this lone Serpent—or all of them together—want to do any of this?"

"Suppose the Anarites realized that Samadhi had been turned?" Erim asked. "Wouldn't they have sent someone else?"

Khalima sighed. "Honestly, do you know what I think?"

"No," Erim said sourly.

"I think you really can't explain the attack on Khaddam."

"Your argument *does* get rather tortured after that," Sharif added.

Erim growled.

"Oh, let's not get nasty about this," Zehowah said.

Erim decided there was some wisdom in her words.

That night, in his dreams, Erim saw Qanar-Sharaj standing white against a wall of shadow, as though a huge storm were rolling up from the south. There was a rumbling in the air, and at first he thought it was thunder. But he saw no lightning, and the more he listened, the more the rumbling sounded like the working of a machine, a grinding of huge wheels or gears.

Gloved in scarlet blood, two colossal hands descended into view, and with an impact that almost knocked Erim from his feet, tore into the earth, clawing Qanar-Sharaj out of the ground, lifting it on high trailing an avalanche of soil. Erim craned his head backwards, gaping.

There stood the Riddled Man, a titan now, red cascades pouring from his wounds. Pressing the building between his palms, he raised it before his hooded face as though it were a toy.

Yet mighty as he was, a greater power loomed above him, a towering assembly of interlocking dull-black wheels, rotating slowly, ominously, bristling with spikes. There was an intensely sickening quality about their remorseless motion; merely to look at them was to imagine being crushed. So vast was the mountain they comprised that Erim wondered how the heavens could over-arch it. What was this sinister machine?

But presently he saw that it was not a machine at all—the wheels were covered with thousands of darting, horribly vigilant red eyes.

Wheels and eyes, Yasmin had said, describing the angel that had announced Essaj's birth. Yet this thing was no angel, Erim knew.

At least, not anymore.

Tchernobog, he thought. *Emperor of Hell* . . .

The Riddled Man's hands began to crush inward. Fissures snaked through the walls of Qanar-Sharaj.

"No!" Erim shrieked, rushing forward. He was puny, impotent, a mere ant watching the destruction of its nest, but he had to do *something* . . .

The Riddled Man continued to press. Huge sections of masonry fell away. Qanar-Sharaj was crumbling before Erim's agonized eyes. The gears behind the Riddled Man spun faster and faster, their rumble becoming a rib-shaking roar.

"God!" Erim screamed. "God save us!"

As if in mocking answer, Qanar-Sharaj shattered into powder. Erim wailed, staggered and dropped. But the worst was yet to come.

Black fluid gushed from between the Riddled Man's hands. Thick and viscous, without sheen or glint, it poured to the ground without splashing, forming a black ocean that stretched from horizon to horizon within seconds, racing towards Erim like the shadow of some unimaginably immense bird.

"BEHOLD!" thundered the Riddled Man, as the black tide rose about his feet. "THE BLOOD OF THE LAMB!"

Erim turned to run, but the darkness caught him before he had taken two steps. For an instant he felt as though he was being swept up in a wave—then there was only pressure piled upon pressure, the universe turned to lead, constricting, squeezing, tightening around his throat, flattening his skull and ribcage, pinching his blood veins shut, pursuing *Him* through the collapsing shell of his body no matter where he fled, biting off bits of his soul, eradicating the very boundaries of his self . . .

"Wake up!" came a dim voice.

Erim knew he couldn't possibly be hearing it—there was too little left of him. Still, it persisted:

"Erim! Wake up!"

He tried to open his eyes, but it was useless. They had already been crushed, obliterated . . .

"Wake up, damn you!"

He was being shaken now. A stinging blow landed on his cheek. He was sure it would do no good, but he opened his eyes anyway.

Panting violently, Khalima was leaning over him, staring at him desperately. His chest ached; he gulped air.

"Thank God," Khalima moaned.

"I had a nightmare," he said. "I've never had one so terrible . . ."

"You cried out," Khalima answered. "You began making this horrible wheezing noise, then stopped breathing altogether . . ."

"I was being crushed," he said. "Crushed out of existence by a black wave. I saw Qanar-Sharaj destroyed by a giant—he was riddled with arrows—and this black liquid gushed out and covered the whole world . . ."

Khalima laughed.

He sat up. "You think it sounds absurd, do you? You have no idea of how terrible it was. Worse than Hell. Do you hear me? *Worse than Hell!*"

She laughed again, but he could tell it was fear this time.

"How . . . how could you know, Erim?"

It *was* impossible to explain; yet that did not diminish his dreadful certainty.

There came a knock from the adjoining door. "Are you two all right in there?" Sharif called.

"Yes," Khalima said. "Everything's fine."

Erim stared at her, shaking his head. "Something monstrous is going to happen," he whispered.

✠

Chapter 8

While Erim and Sharif were at the Council, Khalima and Zehowah decided upon a serious inspection of the Women's Quarters; it was a disturbing experience, at first. None of the other residents would speak to them, although speaking *about* them was another matter. Wherever the sisters went, they seemed to be the topic of furtive conversations, and from what they could glean, their belief in Essaj had everything to do with it. Apparently the conviction was already widespread that he was a heretic.

"I don't think I'm going to like it here," Zehowah said.

"Well, we should try our best to fit in," Khalima answered. "We must be good witnesses for the Lord."

Putting on a brave smile, she addressed a tall blonde woman who had just emerged from a doorway:

"Excuse me. We're looking for the garden."

"Garden?" the other asked.

"The vegetable garden," Khalima replied. "We're new here, and we were told that we'll have private plots . . ."

"I know who you are," the woman said. "The ones Erim and Sharif brought back."

"Why, yes. My name is Khalima."

"And that must be Zehowah."

Two older women scurried by as though there was a danger of plague.

"Don't speak to them," one whispered to the blonde.

"I'll speak to whomever I please," she answered. "After all, I am the Grand Master's . . ." She paused.

"Wife?" Zehowah asked.

The blonde gave her a bittersweet smile. "My name's Sigrun," she answered. "Come, I'll take you anywhere you wish."

"You're the first person who's been willing to talk with us," Khalima said as they walked along.

"You're newcomers," Sigrun answered.

"Oh, I don't think that's why," Khalima said.

"What then?"

"We're followers of Essaj Ben Yussef."

"Well, that probably has something to do with it," Sigrun admitted.

"But you don't mind?" Zehowah asked.

"I don't know much about the man," Sigrun answered. "Perhaps you could tell me."

"What if it makes *you* angry?" Khalima asked.

"I doubt it will," Sigrun said. "I'm not quite so sure about things as some of the people around here. I come from up North, you see."

"You're a pagan?"

"I'm not certain."

"And they tolerate you?"

"They have to. I'm the Grand Master's . . . wife. As for my faith, I'm *inclined* to think there's only one God, though I pray to some of the others sometimes, just to make sure. My mother believed in the One. You may never have heard this, but there are a goodly number of His people in the Northlands. A Sharajnaghi Master named Raschid Kestrel went there long ago, back in the time of Zorachus."

"Zorachus?"

"He was a Sharajnaghi too, but betrayed the Order. He became the ruler of a city called Khymir—a very wicked place. Some say he was the most evil man who ever lived. You should ask Erim about it. It's a fascinating story. Ah, here we are . . ."

They stepped through a doorway into a huge sunlit enclosure divided into many small green plots. The air was full of a rich mixture of green and flowery smells. Insects buzzed from blossom to blossom.

"Where would our plots be?" Khalima asked.

"I don't know. But we could ask."

They went over to a fat, middle-aged woman who was setting up bean-poles.

"New arrivals, Almasta," Sigrun told her.

The woman eyed Khalima and Zehowah, grunted, and led them to the far side of the enclosure along a stone walk.

"You can have these," she announced.

"They'll do," Khalima said.

"They'll have to," Almasta replied, and went back the way she had come.

"Pleasant sort," Zehowah said.

"Now," Sigrun said. "About this Essaj of yours—"

"Yes?" the sisters asked.

"Your husbands have started some amazing rumors."

"What do you want to know?" Khalima answered.

"Does he really have the most perfect teeth in the world?"

Nawhar arrived early for the Council; only Akram had preceded him. The Master looked up briefly from the book he was studying and instructed Nawhar to sit.

Three chairs had been placed between the wings of the Masters' semicircular table. Nawhar settled in the one on the left, feeling uncommonly free of his usual discomforts. He was not at all anxious; indeed, he was looking forward to the hearing. After all, the outcome was hardly in doubt—the case against Essaj was devastating. The only question was how far Erim was willing to go in defending the blasphemer. Nawhar's guess was that he would stop just short of immolating himself; that way he could remain in the ranks, secretly undermining the *Comahi Irakhoum* with lies, scheming to rise as high as possible, the better to spread the contagion of Essaj's doctrine. That Erim had come to believe in Essaj, Nawhar was certain; and Nawhar saw it as a sacred duty to expose that fact. If all went as he intended, the hearing would lead not only to Essaj's downfall, but Erim's as well. Nawhar had come to feel nothing but loathing for his onetime friend. Even summoning a *memory* of his former affection was all but impossible.

Suddenly Nawhar realized that Essaj's conviction might lead to the execution of Erim; if Essaj was a heretic, surely an unrepentant follower . . . Nawhar smiled, imagining a headsman's axe being thrust into his hands, the weapon surprisingly light and wieldy; Erim was kneeling with his neck stretched over a block, and Nawhar, filled with righteous anger, seeing the traitor so perfectly positioned to take the stroke, lifted the axe to strike . . .

No, Nawhar told himself. He could not allow himself to fondle such thoughts. Vengeance was not his goal. All that mattered was the purification of the Order. He reminded himself that Erim's repentance would be the best outcome. Not perhaps a very likely one, and surely nowhere near as satisfying to contemplate as the thought of the traitor's head dropping from his neck. But Nawhar knew he must keep his emotions in check.

Other Masters joined Akram. Erim and Sharif arrived, taking their seats. Sharif planted himself diplomatically between Nawhar and Erim.

How feeble, Nawhar thought. *As if to keep us from arguing, when the whole point of this meeting is for us to fly at each others' throats. Only Sharif would come up with an idea like that.*

Khaddam entered at last, along with the members of the Knot. The Serpents had already passed their Trials; rumor had it that some had demonstrated a level of accomplishment that had taken the judges quite by surprise.

Khaddam led the Council in prayer, then nodded to Arghun Khan, who, as Master of Doctrine, would conduct the hearing. Off in a corner, a grey-robed scribe dipped his quill in ink.

Arghun rose. "This session of the Council has been convened for one purpose: to determine if there is sufficient evidence to indict Essaj Ben Yussef on the grave charge of heresy. We will begin with the accounts of our three investigators; they will be allowed to challenge and correct each other. Any member of the Council may question them at any time. Erim?"

"*Sibi?*" Erim asked.

"Tell us about your first meeting with Essaj."

Nawhar thought Erim spent far too much time on the battle with Horde—clearly he was trying to inflate the the threat posed by the demon, the better to magnify Essaj's triumph. But Nawhar detected no untruths, try as he might.

Arghun interrupted the testimony at Erim's lapse into unconsciousness on the tomb steps, just after the exorcism.

"Nawhar?" he asked.

"*Sibi?*"

"Did you observe this so-called exorcism?"

"Yes."

"Erim said he saw no trace of magic. What about you?"

"I didn't witness the event under the best of circumstances," Nawhar answered. "But as far as I could tell, there was no magic."

"And what about mere trickery?"

"There was no sign of that either."

"Are you convinced that the man was truly possessed?"

"He manifested all the signs," Nawhar answered.

"And the spirit in question was a Great Demon, just as Erim said?"

"It was I who first made that determination," Nawhar said.

Arghun turned to Sharif. "Do you have anything to add?"

"Well, *Sibi*," Sharif said, "regarding the head wound that Erim mentioned—"

"Yes?"

Sharif pointed to his brow. "As you can see, there's not even a scar. Essaj healed it with a touch, just a touch, as soon as he dealt with the demon. There was also the Mirkut whose face had been scraped away. Essaj restored it—"

"He healed my arm as well," Erim put in. "And then there's the matter of the demoniac's eyes—"

"Enough," Arghun said. "We're getting ahead of ourselves. Nawhar: did you witness these healings?"

"I didn't actually see Erim's wound close," Nawhar answered. "But when I rolled up his sleeve, it was gone. Once again, there was no detectable magic or trickery.

"Essaj then went to Sharif. The head-wound simply sealed under his fingers. I saw it very clearly.

"It was the demoniac's turn after that. As Erim said, his eyes had burst. But when Essaj passed his hand over the man's face, the eyes were restored."

"*Restored*?" asked Arghun and Khaddam.

"God's truth, Masters," Sharif said. "I saw it too."

"And while this was happening," Nawhar continued, "the Mirkuts retrieved their comrade from the tomb. The man's face was destroyed. Meat and bone, nothing more. But Essaj merely spat on his palms, and placed them onto that muck. When he lifted them, I thought he hadn't succeeded—the man's skull was still covered with bloody scraps. Then Essaj wiped them away, and there was the man's face, underneath."

Arghun and the rest of the Council were silent for a few moments.

"Might Essaj have had something secreted in his mouth?" Akram asked. "A drug, perhaps?"

"If so," Nawhar replied, "it must have been a formula unknown to us. It would represent a healing-magic completely beyond our capabilities. And when one considers that our healing-spells derive from the Angel Shuriel Himself . . ."

"Was the man's face *actually* removed?" Arghun asked. "You said there was a bloody mass that Essaj wiped away . . ."

"False wounds *can* be made from animal blood and flesh," Nawhar said. "But if we assume the various wounds were false to begin with, we must address the matter of accomplices. And ultimately we would have to explain why Sharif and Erim were co-operating with a charlatan they had never met.

"There's also the question of the demoniac's eyes. I could see a good *inch* into his skull. In my opinion, it would be impossible to counterfeit such an effect."

"And Essaj healed another Mirkut as well," Sharif said. "One whose ear had been torn off."

Khaddam laughed. "Did Essaj give him a new one, or simply put the old one back on?"

"The latter," Nawhar answered. "But he suggested that they wash it first."

"This is preposterous," Khaddam said.

"Nawhar," Arghun said uncomfortably, "are you suggesting that the miracles are genuine?"

"Nothing of the sort," Nawhar replied. "But my doubts stem from Essaj's doctrines, not his works."

"Very well, then," Arghun said. "What happened after you left the cemetery?"

The hearing proceeded thus at some length. Erim was questioned in great detail about his interrogation of Essaj, and rather to Nawhar's surprise, made no effort to minimize Essaj's blasphemies. Nawhar could only second his account.

The Masters did not evince much interest in the matter of the woman taken in adultery; they seemed to find Essaj's actions uncontroversial. Nawhar was irritated by this, but was in no position to vent his displeasure.

At last Erim came to the raising of Khaldun.

"The man must not have been dead," said Sayid Al-Mashat.

"Sharif and I washed the body," Erim said. "It already stank. The eyes had sunken. The blood had settled. . . ."

"Nawhar," said Sayid, "did *you* help them wash it?"

"No," Nawhar replied. "But I saw a sword driven through the man. He had several other wounds as well, any of which would have been mortal. I don't doubt that he was dead."

"Was it the same man that Essaj raised?" asked Murad Abu Kaukab.

"Unless he has a twin," Nawhar said. "Moreover, he was buried under three feet of earth, wrapped only in a blanket. Even if there had been a double, and some sort of conspiracy worked out in advance to fool us, there would have had to be some means of sustaining the double beneath the ground, supplying him with air. But when I examined the grave, I found no trace whatsoever of any sort of apparatus."

"He might have been drugged," said Karaz Al-Kara.

"Even a man in a catatonic state must breathe," Nawhar answered.

"So," said Akram. He had not spoken for some time. "Even though you believe the miracles are false, you're convinced there's a supernatural explanation, aren't you?"

"Yes," Nawhar replied. "Demonic possession."

Up till that point, he and Erim had not clashed at all. But now, to Nawhar's delight, his onetime friend finally chose to engage him.

"There's no evidence whatsoever for that," Erim said.

"Oh?" asked Arghun. "And when did you become our authority on false miracles?"

"I humbly bow to Nawhar's judgement—so long as he confines himself to his own field. And he's stated plainly that he was unable to detect any magic or fraud. As for possession, I know as much about it as he does. And I have never heard of a demon capable of restoring a body to *actual* life."

"So, then," Arghun asked, "how do you explain these wonders?"

"I wouldn't dare to," Erim replied.

"Please, Master," Nawhar said. "Ask him what he means by that."

"I'm not sure I see the necessity," Arghun answered.

"Did you not notice a certain wariness of expression, *Sibi*? On one level he speaks the truth—indeed he does not know how to explain these things. On another level, he lies, because he has an explanation—which is that Essaj *is* who he claims to be."

"Do you believe in Essaj, Erim?" Arghun asked.

"Let us grant for the sake of argument that I do," Erim answered. "How would that strengthen Nawhar's theory? He hasn't contested my account of the facts. He admits that a supernatural force is responsible, then insists it has to be demonic simply because he detests Essaj's doctrines. Now, if it comes to that, I detest Essaj's doctrines also. I am horrified by them, you must believe me. Nawhar has said they are a spear pointed at the heart of our religion; how could anyone argue otherwise?

"*But*. To say that one must then insist on Essaj's possession is simply too great a leap. Indict him for heresy if you must. But don't try to explain him."

Nawhar gave a dry laugh. "What a performance!" he said. "I trust, Masters, that you listened very carefully to those marvellous turns of phrase. He grants for the sake of argument that he believes in Essaj—thus neatly implying that he does not, while assenting to the opposite. He says he's horrified by Essaj's doctrines. But one might very easily be horrified by the truth—or what one *perceives* to be the truth—if it means total separation from one's Order and one's God. He gives my estimate of the threat that Essaj poses; he says he cannot imagine how I could be refuted. Well, who would know better than he? But he does *not* admit that I am right."

"Am I the subject of this hearing?" Erim asked. "Are my beliefs relevant at all, provided I'm telling the truth? If so, shouldn't Nawhar's be relevant as well? Consider what this man believes—that the physical universe was not created by God, that matter is the principle of evil, that procreation is sin. Do you think for one instant, Masters, that these beliefs do not condition his view of Essaj? It is indeed hard to accept the idea of God made flesh. But Nawhar's attack on it has nothing to do with Sharajnaghi orthodoxy. It stems from his own heresy, a deranged view of reality that comes perilously close to that held by the Black Orders—"

"How *dare* you?" Nawhar spat, rising from his seat. But before he could say anything else, his whole body erupted in a murderous itch; he gasped, digging at himself with his nails, sitting once more.

"See how he reacts," said Erim. "The thrust has gone home, has it not?"

Nawhar battled to reassert himself over his squirming poisonous flesh. "He imputes heresy to me simply to mask his own—"

"*Neither* of you are under investigation," Akram said.

"Has Erim tried to hide anything about Essaj?" Arghun asked Nawhar.

"No," Nawhar answered.

"Then we can continue," said Arghun.

The hearing moved rapidly to Erim's most damaging testimony: an account of his conversation with Essaj just before they reached Al-Asriyeh.

"He seems to have abandoned all attempts to conceal his doctrines," Khaddam said. "He let his guard down completely."

"I think he knew how thoroughly perplexed I was by that point," Erim answered. "Perhaps he no longer saw me as a threat. Or hoped to convert me through sheer frankness."

"I have a question," said Akram. "It's somewhat beside the point, but I'm afraid I must ask. Where was Essaj born?"

"Before he began to preach, he lived in Amran, *Sibi*," Erim replied. "But I don't know if he was born there."

"He wasn't," said Sharif. "Zehowah told me. He was born in Nabatiyeh."

Akram's eyebrows lifted. "Nabatiyeh?" he demanded. "Are you *sure*?"

"That's what she said, Master," Sharif answered.

Khaddam regarded Akram. "Why do you ask?"

"And how old is Essaj?" Akram asked, ignoring him.

"Thirty-two," Erim replied. "No—thirty-three."

Akram laughed softly, shaking his head.

"Don't keep us in suspense," Sayid said.

"Thirty-three years ago, *I* was in Nabatiyeh," Akram replied. "I was still in the old Khan's army. There was a story going round that the town had just been visited by three White Anarite Masters. The last three, I expect—the ones who dissolved the Order."

"What were they doing in Nabatiyeh?" Khaddam asked.

"Supposedly, they had discovered something strange in the heavens—the White Anarites *did* set great store by astrology— and this sign led them to Nabatiyeh. No one in the town had noticed anything unusual, but the Masters had sworn there was a star."

"And what did this sign portend?"

"The birth of the Expected One," said Akram.

The chamber grew very quiet.

"They had come to bring him gifts," Akram continued after a few moments. "But they refused to reveal who he was."

"Why?" Khaddam asked.

"I don't know. But the Old Khan wouldn't have welcomed the Expected One any more than Batu. Indeed, he dealt with false messiahs rather more harshly, if I recall."

"Why then would the Anarites have revealed *any* of their story?"

"Impossible to say. Perhaps one was simply incautious. Perhaps a servant was drunk. Perhaps the whole story is untrue."

"But you don't think it is, do you?" asked Murad Abu Kaukab.

"No," said Akram. "Here we have Essaj, this mighty miracle-worker. If he's a fraud, he's defeated the best efforts of our foremost expert to unmask him. He claims to be the Expected One. He's thirty-three years old, and was born in Nabatiyeh. I don't believe it's all a coincidence."

"Coincidence or not, it makes no difference," said Khaddam. "The man appears to be a rank heretic."

"He also appears to wield powers unparalleled in human history," Akram answered.

"Are you saying we couldn't arrest him?" Khaddam asked.

"I'm saying that perhaps we *shouldn't*. Not yet. In my opinion, the matter requires more study."

"The case against him is perfectly clear," Khaddam replied.

"Not if his miracles are genuine."

"They can't be genuine if he's a heretic."

"He can't be a heretic if they're genuine."

"You're not serious—"

"Listen to what I'm saying. I am *not* arguing that he's the Expected One. I find the reports of his heretical statements deeply disturbing. But I find the inexplicability of his miracles equally so. And I would feel more secure if we demonstrated their falsity before we indicted him."

"We have Rules of Evidence . . ."

"Which we can alter if we see fit. You yourself decided that no confession was needed from Samadhi. You're always lecturing us on the dangers of 'legalism.' Surely we need not rush to try Essaj. If indeed he's demonically possessed, as Nawhar says, we can determine that. Among other things, we could exorcise him. . . ."

"Not if the demon is too strong."

"We could at least make the attempt," Akram said. "We'll have to delay his arrest in any case. We can't hope to conduct a trial before—" He paused.

Before the attack on the Anarites? Nawhar thought.

"That's true," Khaddam admitted. "Erim, how long does Essaj intend to stay in Thangura?"

"A month at least," Erim replied.

"I see," said Khaddam. "Still, I can think of no reason to delay the indictment itself." He looked at the other Masters. "How say you?"

"Wait!" cried Akram. "Consider the testimony we've heard today! What if Essaj truly *is* the Expected One, and we set ourselves against him?"

"That's a chance I'm willing to take," Khaddam answered. "What about the rest of you? Murad?"

"I don't know," Murad replied.

Khaddam shook his head derisively, but continued:

"Sayid?"

"Indict him."

"Karaz?"

"Indict him."

The vote proceeded round the table. The other Serpents voted with Sayid and Karaz, joined ultimately by Khaddam.

Yet when it was done, the Council was evenly split.

Khaddam sat back in his chair, twisting a horn of his moustache, eyeing Akram hotly.

"You heard a story in Nabatiyeh," he sneered.

"Prove him a fraud," Akram answered. "It's not much to ask. Simply unmask him, and I'll hand him over to the Khan myself."

Khaddam motioned to the witnesses. "You're dismissed."

Chapter 9

Pleased that Erim had acquitted himself so well, Sharif rose and made for the exit with him. Nawhar marched out in front of them.

"How very impressive," Erim whispered to Sharif. "He's going to reach the hall first."

But all at once Nawhar stopped, staring at the door; they came up on either side of him.

Made of thick, polished Numalian hardwood, the door had been fashioned in one piece from a massive trunk. An infrequent visitor to the Council-chamber, Sharif had never given the object much attention.

Even so, he felt sure he would have recalled the relief that had been carved into it. Larger than life-size, it was of a voluptuous dancing-girl, all but nude, eyes closed, hands cupping her breasts.

"And where did that come from?" Erim wondered aloud. "Not exactly the sort of thing one associates with the Council."

"It's easy on the eyes, though," Sharif said, and nudged Nawhar. "Don't imagine you approve, eh?"

Nawhar stood silently, squinting at the carving. "Masters?" he called.

Hearing them deep in the midst of a heated argument, Sharif glanced over his shoulder. None were paying any attention. He looked back at the carving.

Small red beads had appeared on the hands. The beads became rivulets, revealing protruding black points, as though the palms covering the breasts had been transfixed with nails.

"It's a sending!" Nawhar cried.

The dancer's lips peeled back, revealing wooden gums lined with long dark spikes; her jaws opened, and Sharif saw that her whole mouth was full of thorns. Tiny points appeared between her eyelids, levering them open. Thorns bristled in the sockets.

With an undulant motion and a crackle of splitting wood, the sending pried herself away from the surface of the door; her hands fell from her bosom, which was shiny with blood. The palms had indeed been impaled—two-inch-long thorns jutted from the center of each breast.

The Masters were shouting to each other now. Sharif and his companions retreated.

"Get down!" came Khaddam's voice.

Sharif hurled himself to the floor with his companions. A tremendous salvo of strikes, bolts of every type, flew overhead, crashing into the Thornwitch in a multihued explosion; surely every man on the Council had unleashed a strike. The Thornwitch rocked back into the door, flattening against it.

"Don't stop!" Khaddam bellowed.

Blast upon blast struck the demon. Behind her, the door buckled down the center, finally parting, one half flying into the corridor, the other swinging back on its hinges. But the Thornwitch remained upright, taloned fingers hooked into the doorframe, head whipping left and right as she emitted a continuous whistling shriek.

Looking past her, out into the corridor, Sharif saw two men slumping against the far wall; apparently they had been struck by the hurtling door-fragment.

He was all but deafened by the crackle of the bolts and the demon's cries; dimly he heard Khaddam shouting for the other Masters to halt their strikes.

As the barrage ended, the Thornwitch started forward once more. It seemed to Sharif that she was making straight for him, but undoubtedly he was merely between her and the Masters.

Leaping to his feet, he withdrew a few paces, then stood his ground, assuming a Griffin Stance. The Influences were with him; he could conjure without forceletting. Behind him, Khaddam seemed to be conjuring as well.

The demon turned her palms towards Sharif. Their wounds bulged and squirmed, the wooden flesh creaking. Creepers streamed forth, lined with wicked backward-pointing spines.

But before Sharif could finish his spell, a saurian shape appeared at his side, enveloped in flame. His concentration snapped, but he realized the salamander was no threat.

Khaddam summoned it, he thought.

The creature charged headlong at the Thornwitch.

One of the barbed whips sprouting from her palms lashed at Sharif, catching him round the shoulders.

As the salamander closed in, rearing up on its hind legs, the demon interposed Sharif between her and it, clutching him to her spiked breast. His whole upper torso ripped and bleeding, Sharif barely felt the spines enter his pectoral muscles; but the salamander's heat on his back was so fierce that he thought he must have been set ablaze.

Khaddam roared, banishing the salamander. Abruptly, the heat was gone.

Helpless, arms pinned at his sides, Sharif looked up at the Thornwitch's face. The spiny eyes bristled like sea-urchins. The thorn-filled mouth moved towards his lips, the naillike teeth lengthening. Turning from the kiss, he felt the bitter-sharp fangs lance his cheek.

Someone approached on the edge of sight; it was Erim, thrusting with his sword. The flat of the blade slid across Sharif's brow. There was a loud crunch, and a shudder went through the Thornwitch. Sharif looked back at her face. Fully a third of Erim's blade had entered her left eye, nested amid the spines.

Shrilling a cry, the sending retracted the creepers, reaching for the swordhilt. Gasping as the thorns ripped free of his flesh, Sharif staggered back, Erim with him.

Khaddam and several others were conjuring now, but they broke off as the Thornwitch toppled suddenly forward, onto the floor—one of the door-wards had recovered and knocked her over. Throwing himself astride her back, he began to hack at her neck.

He seemed not to notice the creepers that snaked from each rent he opened.

Even as he raised his sword for a fourth blow, one of the spined whips flayed the skin from the back of his hand. The blade dropped from his fingers.

A second creeper seized the sword, while the third pulled his head back, jerking his mouth open. The blade screeched over his upper teeth as it drove down his throat. The Thornwitch rose to her feet, the door-ward's corpse sliding off her back.

Khaddam's salamander reappeared; evidently conjured by other Masters, a harpy and a huge lynx materialized on either side of the blazing shape. But instantly they shied away from it, apparently terrified by the flames.

The salamander leaped at the Thornwitch, trailing a sheet of fire. She bounded straight up, and it passed beneath her—just as several grey-robes, bodyguards who had been dismissed for the duration of the Council, burst through the door, drawn by the tumult. The salamander hurtled into them; robes kindled. Shrieking, the adepts hacked and stabbed at the creature.

Khaddam swore and banished it. The Adepts rolled to put out their burning garments. The Thornwitch wrenched the sword from her eyesocket.

With a yowl the great lynx sprang. The Thornwitch sliced its head off.

The harpy leaped aloft. With a sweep of her arm, the Thornwitch extruded a whip from her free palm, catching a wing and ripping it in half at the joint. The harpy dropped screeching.

Sharif re-entered his stance. He could hear the Masters conjuring frenziedly.

The Thornwitch came on once more, hacking at herself methodically with Erim's shortsword, tendrils bursting forth all over her.

The harpy bounded at her from behind. Creepers dangling from the back of the Thornwitch's neck licked out. The harpy sank down, all three hooked in her face; struggling hideously, she dragged along for an instant behind the demon, then vanished.

Sharif finished his spell. Smoldering red, a host of Ember-worms appeared, swarming over the Thornwitch's body. Strangely, there were many more than he anticipated—had one of the Masters duplicated the spell?

Smoke curled in innumerable wisps. The Thornwitch flicked some of the worms away—then seemed to decide that the rest did not pose enough of a threat. Sharif had expected the creatures to bore rapidly in, but they remained on the surface of her body, apparently unable to penetrate the hardwood.

Karaz Al-Kara and Murad Abu Kaukab bolted from either wing of the table, trying to get behind the demon.

Creepers shot towards them. Throat spewing blood, Karaz spun, smashing into the wall and sliding down in a scarlet smear. Ducking, Murad managed to save himself, but only for a second stroke of the whip. As he straightened, the side of his head became one vast ruby splash, a large chunk of something flying free as he crumpled.

Conjured beasts assailed the Thornwitch from all sides, some visible only for an instant before the thorns ripped home and they disappeared.

But Sharif saw several Emberworms slipping from view at last, crawling into the rents the Thornwitch herself had made. Smoke rose from the thorns in her eyes and mouth.

The demon resumed her advance, moving more swiftly now, as though she realized the end was near. Sharif turned and vaulted the Master's table. Erim had already taken shelter behind it.

As Sharif glanced back at the Thornwitch, creepers seized the chairs he and his companions had occupied, hurling them over the table. He dropped to one knee. To his left, Arghun Khan was struck in the shoulder, the impact twisting him to one side, the seat continuing past; to Sharif's right, Akram crouched, a chair-leg tearing a red groove in his scalp. With a single tremendous CRACK! the chairs shattered against the wall, raining fragments over Sharif and the two Masters.

"Bolts!" Khaddam was screaming now. "Drive her back!"

Sharif looked over the rim of the table. Beams hammered into the demon, and she began to reel; Sharif assumed the force was spinning her about.

Then he realized she was whirling on her own, moving like a smoking top between the wings of the table, creepers rising, whipping straight out, keening through the air. And she was hacking frenziedly at herself once more; with every blow a new creeper appeared.

The Masters dropped stance and hurled themselves down behind the table. The thorn-cyclone spread out over the table-top, spines rasping along the surface, the clawed tendril-tips rattling savagely against the chairs. Splinters and dust sprayed through the air. Lying on his back now, Sharif gaped up at a ceiling of whirling creepers. He turned his head, peering out from under the table.

Small glowing coals were showering the floor about the Thornwitch's feet, and the air had grown misty with smoke. She was surely burning now, being eaten away from the inside.

But would she be consumed in time? The table and chairs provided some protection from the cyclone of thorns, but were swiftly being worn away. Chips tumbled like snow from the swirling ceiling.

He looked back up at the thorn-cyclone. Suddenly a blazing streak shot out of it, striking the wall. It was a creeper, burned through, still flaming at one end.

More and more of them flew loose. The cyclone slowed. Sharif whooped for joy.

The creepers sagged over the splintered tops of the chairs, plucking and questing. Sharif scrambled away from the table. A tendril snagged his arm; he grabbed at it, hand recoiling as the thorns pierced him. He thrust himself towards the wall, felt the creeper part. The far end flew overhead, sputtering flame.

Rising, he put his back to the wall, pulling out his sword and using it to pry the vine loose from his arm. All around the table, the Masters were getting back to their feet, hacking at the weakening tendrils.

Out between the wings, the Thornwitch had stopped spinning, her torso running with fire, creepers dropping away on all sides. Her mouth was an inferno; flames spurted from her eyes. Her hands lifted, and like a sleepwalker, she moved slowly towards Sharif and Akram.

Khaddam entered a stance, flinging bolts once more. Charred fragments exploding from her body, she staggered but refused to fall. Burning tendrils snaked towards Akram and Sharif, then dropped and fell.

Other Masters followed Khaddam's example; Sharif joined in as well, hurling cataract-strikes into the blazing somnambulist.

The fingers jumped from her hands. One arm snapped off at the elbow, the other at the shoulder. Her brow shivered to bits in a blossom of smoke and flames; another salvo, and everything above her jaw was gone. A knee disintegrated; trailing a grey pall, the torso toppled sideways like a burning tree—

And vanished before it struck.

The burned-off creepers disappeared with it; even the smoke dissolved. Emberworms bounced on the floor.

Sharif uttered the banishing-command. Half the worms remained, though briefly—Khaddam dismissed the rest.

"It seems we think alike," he told Sharif, smiling faintly in approval.

"Yes, *Sibi*," Sharif replied.

Now that the battle was over, he remembered his wounds. His shoulders and chest were already stiffening. He looked down at his tunic. The fabric was completely black with blood.

Erim ran up to him. "Are you all right?"

"Do I look all right?" Sharif replied, feeling faint.

"Get him to the infirmary," Akram said.

Erim took Sharif by the arm and hand, walking him round the table, passing Nawhar. Staring murderously at Erim, Nawhar said nothing.

A crowd of Adepts and brown-robes had entered. The bodyguards who had been burned were even then being helped from the chamber.

Sharif looked for Murad. Raschid Zekowi was kneeling at the Master's side, signalling several of the Adepts. Murad seemed to be breathing, although his head was a welter of gore. Sharif guessed he had merely seen a piece of scalp flying from his skull.

Sharif turned his gaze towards Karaz. Shoulder against the wall, Karaz had crumpled in a sitting position, staring down into the largest pool of blood Sharif had ever seen.

"Come on," Erim said, easing Sharif towards the door. "There's no need to look."

The infirmary was not far. Sharif lowered himself onto a cot.

"Thank you," he said.

"For what?" Erim asked.

"Holding my hand," Sharif replied.

Erim gave it a squeeze. "Go on now. Into your trance."

When Sharif awoke, Erim, Khalima, and Zehowah were seated beside him. The windows were dark; he had no idea how long he had been unconscious. Zehowah gave a little gasp when she noticed his eyes were open.

"He's awake!" she cried.

"Feeling better?" Erim asked.

Sharif nodded.

"I was so worried . . ." Zehowah began.

"I wasn't in any danger," Sharif answered.

"That's what I kept telling her," Erim said. "But . . ."

"How is Murad?" Sharif asked.

"Fully recovered," Erim replied. "He came out of the Masters' Ward a short while ago. Arghun Khan's still in there."

"Broken shoulder?"

"And something worse, apparently. He barely managed to enter his trance. Raschid Zekowi thought his brain must have been rattled rather severely."

"Raschid would know," Sharif said.

"Now," Erim continued, "are you ready for the *real* news?"

"I suppose."

"Twenty or so Black Anarites were seen a few miles from here, engaged in a ritual."

"During the attack?"

"So I've heard," Erim answered. "Khaddam had Sayid do some tests—the sending was conjured where the Anarites were sighted."

"So," Sharif said. "That would certainly seem to demolish your suspicions about the Serpents. At least the ones on the Council."

"Perhaps," Erim conceded, then said quickly, as though to change the subject: "There was one other bit of information."

"Yes?"

"We're going to attack Khaur-Al-Jaffar."

Sharif beamed, relishing the prospect.

"Khaddam announced it," Erim went on.

"No secrecy?"

"There's no point. A full third of the Order's going."

"Well, it's about time," Sharif said. He laughed fiercely. "Khaur-Al-Jaffar."

"The preparations are already well underway."

"Splendid. What a lesson we will give! Are you in the mood to teach, Erim?"

"I think so," Erim replied.

✠

Chapter 10

Awash in blood, the Riddled Man proferred Nawhar the mirror-bright blade. Nawhar did not know if he should take it.

"Of course you should," said the Riddled Man from the shadow of his hood. "You're one of us; our deeds are yours. You share responsibility for everything we do, but also the glory. You might as well wield the blade."

It made perfect sense; Nawhar took the knife. The long blade was surprisingly light, the hilt pure comfort in his hand, perfectly fitted to his grip.

"Now come," said the Riddled Man, leading the way past the other robed figures, to the stone altar on which a large muscular man lay naked, transfixed by iron spikes driven into the stone through his elbows and knees. The battered face turned slowly towards Nawhar, swollen and bruised; he could not recognize it.

Even so, the sight kindled a murderous rage within him, a fury so sudden and violent that he did not even realize whom it was directed against. At first he thought its object must be the torturers. Lifting the knife, he almost flung himself upon the nearest.

But then he realized it was the victim himself that had aroused his rage, that the man's face was the perfect picture of everything he detested about flesh; it was helplessness, pain, dissolution, bottomless horror. The ravages it had suffered had only revealed its true nature—What was a face after all, but a mask over a skull?

"Strike," said the Riddled Man, now at his side. "Finish him. Finish it *all*."

Nawhar nodded, stepping forward. The victim's bleared eyes stared up at him, pleading—but for what? Succor from death—or life?

It did not matter to Nawhar. The confusion only made him hate the man more. Shrieking, he brought the blade straight down, sending the point deep into the wretch's throat. Nawhar tried to pluck the blade free, but the flesh sucked at the steel like soft clay; screaming once more, he wrenched it loose and stabbed again and again . . .

A black spot appeared on the man's forehead. Nawhar paused, staring, reminded of a scorch mark spreading through parchment. The discoloration rapidly took on a hollow look; the edges of the hole seemed to be curling downwards into nothingness.

Other chancres appeared, on the victim's arms and chest. Nawhar looked round. The spots were everywhere now, on the Riddled Man and his followers, on the walls, hanging in the very air. Nawhar's vision seemed to ripple and waver; then he realized that existence itself was sagging before his eyes, shot through with rents like a piece of rotten cloth, the gaps yawning ravenously, joining other gaps, forming huge devouring mouths.

Nawhar looked down at himself. He too was disintegrating, the fabric of his being falling to tatters.

All over his body, he was swept with a sensation like intense, gnawing hunger; his body seemed to be devouring itself. He could feel the muscles shrinking beneath his skin, the tongue vanishing in his mouth, his jaws clacking together as his teeth vanished from between them; in moments there seemed to be a vast opening in the center of his face. Vision vanished. The hunger grew ever more fierce.

But why was it indistinguishable from pleasure? The pangs were exquisite; surely even union with God was a poor substitute for the sweet, sweet gnawing. He was lost in ecstasy, hurtling towards ultimate consummation in the void . . .

He heard a loud bang; a cold breeze swept him. Maddeningly, he could feel his flesh returning, the rents in his being knitting back together. The void was spurning him, rejecting his love. Snarling with frustration, he opened his eyes, horrified to discover that he had merely been asleep.

Horrified, but not surprised. Undoubtedly such bliss was possible only in dreams.

He looked at the window. The shutter banged once more against the sill. He got up to close it, his flesh inflamed from scalp to toe despite the chill. Once the window was shut, he stood awhile in the darkness, scratching beneath his robes until his nails were blunted with clinging skin.

With the death of Karaz-Al-Kara, Ezzedin Moukarbal, who had been one of Massoud's closest lieutenants, was placed in charge at Science; one of his most vital tasks was to prepare several hundred crossbow-bolts incorporating his former Master's percussion-detonated explosive. Upon learning of this, Erim approached Ezzedin with an idea of his own: short lengths of explosive-packed lead pipe, sealed at both ends with mortar and spell-primed like the quarrels.

"Hand-thrown," Erim explained. "For use at close quarters. I expect they'd come in handy at Khaur-Al-Jaffar."

Receiving Ezzedin's approval, Erim made five prototypes. Given the size of the charge that they contained, it was considered unwise to test them in Massoud's indoor range; the Numalian had always conducted his most dangerous experiments at the shore, which lay a half-mile or so from Qanar-Sharaj's western gate. Taking his noontime meal with Khalima, Erim mentioned where he was going.

"I haven't seen the ocean in awhile," Khalima said. "Might I come with you?"

"I don't know . . ."

"It would look irregular, is that it? Is anyone else going to be there?"

"No. I'm off-duty this afternoon, remember? I can keep any company I like. It's just that I don't want to endanger you."

"Is there any chance they'll go off by accident?" Khalima asked.

"No."

"Just tell me how far away I should stand." She paused. "What are you going to call them?"

"I don't know," Erim answered. "I've given the matter some thought, but I want to see if the things work. I'd hate to attach some terrifying name to them, then find out that all they do is go *phhht*."

Once the noonday heat had subsided, they set out for the beach, passing through the west gate. Following a road paved with crushed shells, they entered a band of palms; beyond the trees rose tall red dunes dotted with green brush. Overwhelmed in places, stone walls had been erected to shield the road from the shifting sands.

At last Erim and Khalima emerged onto a broad flat beach. There was virtually no wind; the ocean was glassy.

Erim pointed. "Do you see those ruins over there?"

She nodded.

"I'm going to see if I can't blow them up. Stay here."

Eager to test his handiwork, he found himself halfway to the rubble before he even realized he was running. A tremendous storm had uncovered the tumbled brickwork a few years before; it was all that remained of a fishing village buried when the dunes first crept northwards. The ruins had been an ideal proving-ground for Massoud, his explosives adding immeasurably to the damage the ancient walls had already sustained.

Going into the shell of a small hut that stood apart from the other structures, Erim removed his pack and took out one of his bombs, then looked to see if Khalima was keeping a safe distance. She was at least a hundred yards away, still looking out to sea.

Off to the left, motion caught his eye—horsemen appeared from behind a dune, six in all. Two were clad in white; as the group drew nearer, he recognized Arghun Khan and Akram. Ezzedin was with them.

"Masters?" Erim asked, bowing.

"Ezzedin told us about your invention," Arghun said.

"This way you won't have to repeat your tests for us," Akram added. "If these things work, we must begin producing them as soon as possible."

"Very good, Masters," Erim said. "I'd suggest the animals be kept well back, however."

Akram and Arghun dismounted, along with Ezzedin; the bodyguards led their horses away.

"May I?" Akram asked, taking the sealed pipe from Erim and examining it. "You intend to use these inside the gatehouse?"

"They'd be the quickest way to kill the men in the towers, *Sibi*," Erim replied. Because of his prowess with knives, he was one of ten chosen to enter Khaur-Al-Jaffar in advance of the main force.

"If they work," said Arghun Khan, sneering slightly.

"Well, that's what we're here to find out," said Akram, handing the bomb back to Erim. "*Is* it going to work, Erim?"

Erim wanted to say *I think so,* but Akram's expression was so encouraging that he found himself saying: "Without a doubt, Master."

Akram nodded. "Good man. Go to it."

Erim led them over to a chest-high wall.

"What's the target?" Arghun asked.

"That wall directly across from us, *Sibi*," Erim said. "We should be safe from the blast. But we'd better take cover just in case. When you hear me say 'prime' in old Malochian, get down—the word will melt a capsule inside the pipe, arming the device."

"Just like the quarrels," Akram said.

"Exactly," Erim said. "Now here goes."

Pronouncing the trigger-word, he hurled the pipe straight-armed; ducking, he found himself face to face with Akram as the seconds passed.

"Don't worry," Akram said, just before the blast smote Erim's ears. Red sand rained from chinks above him. Unable to contain a whoop, he leaped back to his feet.

A gap four feet wide had been torn through the other wall; chunks of brick were still flying. One narrowly missed Arghun, who glared at Erim. But Akram cried joyfully:

"Give me one of those things!" Apostle of restraint he might have been, when it came to actual war; but few things delighted him more than advances in the art of killing.

Erim reached into the pack. As he handed the pipe to Akram, he could not resist a smirk at Arghun.

"So, then," Akram said, hefting the bomb, "I concentrate on this when I trigger the spell?"

"Yes, *Sibi*," Erim said.

Akram grinned. "Watch out!" he cried, throwing his arm back and uttering the trigger.

Erim started to crouch, but noticed Akram remaining upright; Erim straightened, watching the pipe sail through the air. It struck the other wall near the base, ripping a smoking mouth in the barrier. A fragile arch remained athwart the gap for a few moments, then collapsed.

"Now *that's* sweet," Akram laughed, casually dodging a bit of debris. "Give me another."

Erim obliged. Akram blasted a third hole in the wall, then two more.

"That was the last one, *Sibi*," Erim said, holding his pack wide open so Akram could see inside.

"Pity," Akram said. "Fine work, though. Damn fine work. What are you going to call 'em?"

"Well, seeing how destructive they are," Erim began, "I was thinking I might name them *Benshaqars*. After Sharif."

"Very well, then," Akram said. "*Benshaqars* it is. Would it be possible to prime several at once?"

"I expect, *Sibi*."

"Is it necessary to see them?"

"To be honest, I don't know."

Ezzedin said: "It shouldn't be—so long as you have a clear idea of where they are."

Akram asked: "How many do you think you can make in the next two days?"

"Fifty, if I had enough men," Ezzedin replied.

"You'll have them," Akram assured him.

Erim turned, looking for Khalima; she was standing with the bodyguards now.

"Who is that?" Arghun Khan asked.

"My wife, *Sibi*," Erim said, beckoning to her.

"Have you given any more thought to my advice?"

"What advice?" Akram inquired.

"As you know, she's a follower of Essaj," Arghun answered. "So?"

"We can hardly tolerate such influences on our men," Arghun explained. "I told Erim he should divorce her, of course."

"Of course?" Akram asked. "Essaj hasn't even been *indicted*. And even if he is—*and* found guilty—we can't make a man put his wife aside. Even if she *is* a heretic."

"We can at least force her out of Qanar-Sharaj," Arghun answered.

"For what?" Akram asked. "Poisoning the Women's Quarters with heterodox thoughts? The women can think whatever they want. What difference does it make? Ask your master, Khaddam. Sigrun's no believer. She's practically a pagan. God in heaven, at least we have something in common with heretics."

"Which makes them all the more deadly," Arghun replied. "Lies deceive more powerfully the more truth they contain."

"Indeed," said Akram. "A truth you might do well to contemplate. There are many kinds of heretic. Ones who offend against the sanctity of marriage, for example."

"I don't have to listen to this," Arghun answered, and marched off in the direction of the other men.

Akram looked at Ezzedin. "I wish to speak to Erim," he said. "Tell my guard not to wait."

Once Ezzedin had gone, Akram asked Erim: "Your wife introduced you to Essaj, didn't she?"

"Yes," Erim answered.

"I'd like to ask her a few questions."

"Of course, My Lord."

✠
Chapter 11

Akram's queries made Khalima uncomfortable at first, but once it became evident that he was not at all hostile, she warmed quickly to the task of witnessing to him. He was particularly interested in what she knew about Essaj's birth.

"Yes, there were three men," she said. "At least, that's what Yasmin told me. White Anarites. I didn't even know there were such things. But I believed her. It's very hard to disbelieve her, you know . . ."

"The order was disbanded about thirty years ago," Akram said. "Thirty-*three* years ago, to be exact. The last Masters argued that the days of lawful magic were ending, that wizardry would soon become so difficult that it would be possible only through the supplication of devils. And that warfare against devils would, of necessity, involve some other kind of combat."

"Did they ever describe this other way, *Sibi*?" Erim asked.

"No. They taught that the Expected One would reveal it." Akram addressed Khalima once more: "What else did Yasmin tell you about these men?"

Khalima thought for a few moments. "She said they were very polite," she replied. "She also asked them to point out the star they had followed. But they said it would take a great deal of training, and she supposed they must know what they were talking about. After all, they found Essaj, didn't they?"

"Hadn't the White Anarites maintained all along that the

Expected One would be born in Nabatiyeh?" Erim asked.

"Yes," Akram answered. "No one else took their prophecies seriously, but they did indeed say that."

"You know it's all true," Khalima said. "I can see it on your face."

"The only thing I know is that I'm mystified," Akram replied.

"So was I, Master," Erim said. "I suppose I still am . . ."

"So Nawhar was right," Akram observed. "You *do* believe in Essaj."

"Did I ever say otherwise, *Sibi?*"

"No," Akram said. "I thought Nawhar's analysis of your 'denials' was *witheringly* accurate. You're simply fortunate that your beliefs had nothing to do with the matter at hand."

"Fortunate?" Erim said. "No, Master. I *counted* on it."

Akram studied him.

"It's true, sir," Khalima said. "Erim discussed it with me beforehand."

"Is that so?" Akram asked.

"You can rely on it, sir."

"That's good to know," Akram answered.

Khalima sensed he was patronizing her, but did not mind. *He's a Sharajnaghi Master, after all,* she thought.

"Well, then," he said, "we'd better get back to Qanar-Sharaj. I've a long night ahead of me. There's still so much to do. Perhaps I should have gone with the others, but . . . Frankly, I find Arghun's company quite wearing. Furthermore, I suspect that Essaj may prove considerably more important than the raid."

"You've never said a truer word, sir," said Khalima.

"Oh?" Akram laughed. "And how long have you known me?"

"It has nothing to do with that," Khalima answered. "Essaj *is* who he claims to be. And if that's true, he's the most important thing that's ever happened." She paused for a few seconds. "Besides. True is true. You might have said things *as* true. But nothing *truer*."

"That's very well put," Akram said. "Not necessarily correct, but succinct. She has a good brain, Erim."

"But why should that matter, *Sibi?*" Erim prodded. "After what you told Arghun about the women . . ."

"I was simply trying to shut him up. My wife was one of the wisest people I ever knew. That's why I joined the Order after she died. It was one of the few places I could have an intelligent conversation."

They set off for the road.

"But what *will* you do if the Council finds against Essaj?" Akram asked Erim as they trudged along beside the dunes. "At the very least, you'll never rise above the Fifth Level. More likely, you'll be expelled from the Order."

"Well, *Sibi*," Erim answered, "If I'm expelled, I'll live with it somehow. As to remaining Fifth Level, I accustomed myself to that idea a long time ago. I'll never be a great sorcerer."

"That hasn't stopped some men," Akram replied. "Allowances have been made. Consider Raschid Kestrel."

"Who was he, sir?" Khalima asked.

"A Grand Master," Akram said. "A very great warrior, but no magician, and just barely a theologian. His whole reputation as a thinker rests on a single proof for the existence of God— a so-called 'ontological' argument."

"Ontological?"

"The argument runs like this. If something is perfect, it must be thought to exist. And so, if God *is*, by definition, perfect, He *must* be thought to exist."

"Oh," said Khalima. "I don't know. Sounds too simple to me."

"Well, it may be *wrong*, but it's nowhere near as simple as it seems," Akram said. "I might also add that Raschid's formulation of it is more complicated than the version I just gave you. It involves substituting the definition 'that than which nothing greater can be thought,' for 'perfect,' among other things. A lot of great minds have agreed that the proof is wrong. The problem is, none of them can agree on *why*.

"Actually, Raschid claimed that he didn't even invent the argument himself. He said a Kragehul barbarian first gave him the rudiments! But who could believe that?"

"How long ago did Raschid live?" Khalima asked.

"About three hundred years," Erim replied. "In his younger days, he was a good friend of Mancdaman Zorachus, if you can believe it."

"Zorachus?" Khalima said. "Sigrun told me I should ask about him."

"It's one of the darkest chapters in the Order's history," Akram said. "He was a Sharajnaghi Master, the mightiest sorcerer who ever lived."

"Greater than Sharif?"

"In terms of native power, probably *far* greater," Akram continued. "Sharif simply has access to techniques that weren't invented in Zorachus's time. Zorachus was actually capable of defeating two Masters at once; some say he even defeated three at once, one of them Ghorchalanchor Kletus, the High Priest of Tchernobog. In Khymir."

"Khymir?"

"A very wicked city that lay far to the north. It was dominated by the Black Priesthood, the most powerful of the Black Orders. Zorachus was Khymirian by birth, even though he was raised in the *Comahi Irakhoum*; his father had been a High Priest of the Black God. When the man who killed his father was himself overthrown, Zorachus was sent north to foment a civil war in Khymir, ultimately with the goal of destroying the Priesthood.

"But it was all a trap. Tchernobog wanted *Zorachus* as High Priest; and Zorachus's experiences with the Khymirians infected him with such a bitter hatred of everything human that he enlisted, ultimately, in the Black Lord's cause. His goal became the eradication of all human life; to that end, he attempted to become the Black God's incarnation.

"But Tchernobog's scheme was part of a larger plan; Tchernobog and Zorachus themselves were mere pawns—albeit with free will. God Himself had been planning Khymir's downfall all along. Raschid Kestrel managed to raise a Kragehul army, which stormed Khymir; the barbarians reached Zorachus before Tchernobog could enter him, and Zorachus was hacked to pieces. But he killed well over a hundred men before he died."

Erim told Khalima: "He created a whole *system* of evil, compulsion at every level of society. Not even the lowliest aspect of Khymirian life was free of it. As vicious as the city was before he came to power, it was a paradise in comparison."

"Was he worse than the Mirkuts?" Khalima asked.

Erim was silent, as though he did not want to admit this. But Akram answered:

"Once you bend the knee to the Mirkuts, and pay them their tribute, they leave you alone. They don't care about religion, or philosophy, or how people raise food or make money. They don't want to make life impossible—life has to continue in order for them to get what they want. Zorachus wasn't like that. He didn't commit his crimes to gain lesser goods such as power or wealth. What he wanted was negation, pure and simple. He regarded existence as a kind of plague, something that had to be cured."

"And he began as a Sharajnaghi?" Khalima asked.

"If he hadn't been sent to Khymir, he might well have become the Order's greatest son," Akram said. "Who knows what he might have achieved?"

"A horrible story," Khalima said, shivering.

"You asked," Erim said. "Didn't you find it interesting at all?"

"Horrible *and* interesting," Khalima acknowledged. "But why is it that terrible things should be so fascinating?"

"Well," said Akram, "not all of them are. The food in the Old Khan's army, for instance."

"You're not going to tell me about that, are you, sir?" Khalima said.

"Not if you don't ask," Akram replied.

Sigrun saw very little of Khaddam in the days following the attack on the council; deeply involved in the preparations for the raid, he worked dawn to midnight, sleeping in his own apartment. But at last the eve of his departure arrived, and he sent word that he would be spending the night.

Sigrun prepared a splendid meal, fully expecting that it would be long cold before he made his appearance. But, wonder of wonders, he was on time, and went well out of his way to show his appreciation of her efforts.

"You're so good to me," he said, finishing his second dish of lamb. "I should reward you."

"Indeed you should," Sigrun replied. "But how?"

"You've been my concubine long enough," he answered.

She was stunned. After six years, could it be that he actually intended to marry her?

"It's not seemly that the Grand Master of the Order should have a slave for a consort," he went on.

Her heart began to race. "Of course not."

"And so, I intend—"

"Yes?" she breathed.

"To free you."

Her shoulders slumped.

"Wouldn't you like to be free of me?" he asked.

"No, My Lord," she said, turning her face from him.

"Then I suppose I'll have to marry you, won't I?" he asked.

She looked sharply at him. "What did you say?"

"Really, Sigrun, you should listen more closely," he laughed.

She grabbed a handful of rice.

"You're not going to throw that at me, are you?" he asked.

She caught him full in the cheek with it.

"When?" she demanded.

He laughed once more, swiping the rice away. "When *what*?"

"Are you going to marry me?" she snarled.

He leaned back on his cushion, picking grains out of his beard. "As soon as I return."

"No you won't!" she cried. "You're going to be killed. I *know* it."

"No you don't. Because I'm going to be fine. I couldn't be more confident. But just in case, you'd better give me a magnificent farewell tonight. At least as good as that meal."

She came over to him on all fours. "You won't have any complaints."

"Patience," he said. "Not on such a full stomach."

She sat back on her heels, hands in her lap.

"Did I get it all out of my beard?" he asked.

Shaking her head, she leaned forward, twitching out a grain—and several grizzled hairs.

"Oww!" he cried.

"Serves you right," she answered.

Several hours later, as they lay in bed, Khaddam said:

"I understand you've become friends with Sharif's wife."

"Hmmm?"

"And Erim's?"

"Maybe someday," Sigrun said. "I don't use the word 'friend' lightly."

"But you like them?" Khaddam asked.

"Yes. Does it concern you?"

"You know they're followers of Essaj, don't you?"

"Of course. They're always telling me about him. Anyone who'll listen, in fact."

"And how convincing do you find them?" Khaddam asked.

"Well, Khalima—that's Erim's wife—does most of the arguing. She's very clever, in an unlettered sort of way, and she's getting better at answering me. Every day you can see the improvement. I suppose that's Erim's work . . ."

"But once again," Khaddam said. "How convincing is she?"

"Not very. Not yet. Of course, so much of it hinges on the miracles, doesn't it? And I haven't seen any of those."

"And if you did?"

"Who can say?" Sigrun answered. "I haven't even decided if the One God exists, so I really shouldn't be worrying about whether Essaj is His Son." She stroked Khaddam's scar-furrowed shoulder. "Would you still love me?"

"Love you?"

"If I came to believe in Essaj?"

He pushed her hand aside, turning to stare directly into her eyes.

"Don't," he said.

"One more time," Zehowah whispered. "*Please*."

"It must be well past midnight," Sharif said. "I *have* to get some sleep."

"And what am I going to do when you're gone?" she demanded.

"What did you do before you met me?" he asked.

"I . . . got along. But since you're still here, I shouldn't have to . . ."

"Get along?"

She rose up on both arms, squeezing her breasts between them. "Look at them," she said. "They're *perfect*. And they're for you."

He groaned.

"I won't always be this beautiful," she said.

"And I won't always be this tired," he replied.

She pulled the covers off him. "No," she said, straddling him with a swift, sure movement. "You won't."

She began to rub herself slowly against him.

"*Mmmm*," she said, taking one of her nipples between two long fingernails.

"That's not fair," he answered. Horribly, he could feel his enthusiasm starting to mount.

Reaching down with her free hand, she began to pinch one of *his* nipples. A few seconds of that, and the matter was settled. She rode him ferociously, squeezing him with exquisite skill. Again and again the question came back to him: how was it possible that he was her first man?

"That . . . that thing," he gasped when they were done.

"What thing?" she asked, curling up beside him.

"What you do with those muscles," he said. "Am I really to believe that your mother taught you *that*?"

"She said it was very important," Zehowah answered. "Actually, it comes naturally to dancers. One has to be very practiced with one's stomach . . . You've never seen me dance, have you?"

"Please, no," he said. "Not tonight."

"Silly," she said. "How can I dance without musicians?"

"Good point," he answered.

A few moments passed in silence. He gathered the covers back over him and was just about to drop off when Zehowah asked:

"Is Nawhar going with you?"

"No," he muttered. "With all his afflictions, he's no fighter. Why do you ask?"

"Because I'd hate to have you and Erim depending on him, that's all," Zehowah answered. "Especially Erim. Nawhar hates him now, doesn't he?"

"Something close to that, I suppose. But really, Zehowah, I must get some sleep—"

"He also hates Khalima and me, doesn't he?"

"I wouldn't be surprised."

"He'll turn on you too," Zehowah said.

"Why should he?" Sharif demanded, irritated. "I don't believe in Essaj."

"Not yet," Zehowah replied.

"Not *ever*," he answered. "Not if the Council condemns him."

"What do they know?"

"It doesn't matter what they know. I'm not wise enough to question them. But I've given myself to the Order. It means more to me than anything."

"More than me?" she asked in a wounded tone.

"Please, I'm so tired," Sharif answered. "Will you just let me sleep?"

Her voice weakened: "More than me?"

Sharif did not answer. But as he drifted away, he thought he heard her whisper:

One will stand back as his love is slaughtered—

A huge silhouette towered at the foot of the bed. Sharif could not see the man's face, but it appeared to be ringed with a black halo, a spiked wheel, turning slowly on the wall behind him . . .

"She's so beautiful," said Horde, nodding towards Zehowah. "What a pity to open her up. How *could* you let them do such a thing?"

Sharif's eyes snapped open.

But wasn't he already awake?

The towering shadow was gone. His whole body slimy with cold sweat, Sharif lifted himself violently on one elbow, turning towards Zehowah. She was sound asleep, undoubtedly had been for hours.

Sharif sagged back down, panting, Horde's voice still echoing dimly in his head:

How could you let them do such a thing?

✝

Chapter 12

Sharif and Erim had been assigned to Khaddam's company, which was to depart soon after sunrise. To confound hostile observers, there were a dozen such detachments, several of which had already embarked under cover of darkness in several different directions; the rest would leave at intervals through the day and into the following night. Proceeding to various Sharajnaghi enterprises along the Gura, they would sail upriver, debarking at the appointed place beneath the eaves of the Rohaz Forest.

But Akram had conceived of a way to hamper Anarite intelligence still further. It was known that the black-robes owned a small slave-trading concern in Thangura, and that their spies reported regularly to the compound. Hence, even as the first contingents set off from Qanar-Sharaj, thirty picked troops were already threading their way through the nighted back alleys of the great city, under the command of Ahmed Fawzi, the Order's Treasurer and Master of Trade. He had been in Thangura for several days, ostensibly to oversee matters at several Sharajnaghi-owned grainaries; the least obtrusive of Khaddam's Serpents, he was a soft-spoken fellow of middling height. His legs were bandy, and he had something of a paunch; but he was also possessed of an iron constitution, and the men behind him, some considerably younger, had difficulty keeping up as he trotted through the gloomy, rat-infested lanes.

The blackness was virtually absolute, impenetrable to the unaided eye; but the Sharajnaghim had partaken of a drug, invented by Dr. Shoua, that revealed otherwise invisible emanations. To

93

Ahmed and his men, the alleys were full of a dim, silvery light, with some objects, notably anything that was or had once been alive, standing out much more brightly than others. Rats were scuttling blots of luminosity, cats slinking pale ghosts. Trash-heaps smoldered colorlessly; wooden lattice-screens resembled heated metal grids.

The raiders were clad in linen tunics and trews, which had been dyed black to blend in with the shadows; but to eyes conditioned by the drug, the garments glowed like dim streaming flames. Hands and faces stood out clearly, greased though they were with dark paint, the pigment itself a source of emanations.

A number of dogs were tied in the alleys; with two sleepy exceptions, they began to bark as the Sharajnaghim approached, and were silenced by quarrels before they could make too much of a nuisance of themselves.

At length Ahmed halted the company. Directly across from the alley-mouth stood the Anarites' compound, the main building rearing up above the outer wall. Dark shutters, probably iron, battened the windows, but light leaked through crevices. Ahmed could hear screams, from the second storey by the sound of it, and a noise that might have been the cracking of a whip. Emitting a silvery glare that made Ahmed's eyes water, a torch blazed beside the gate. The portcullis was down. Three men squatted behind the bars, apparently playing dice.

Ahmed gave some thought to the torch. But it hung between the guards and the street; almost certainly its light would do more to conceal his men than reveal them.

Signalling two of his strongest mages, he stepped from the alley. Together they entered stances and whispered a binding-spell.

Across the street, the portcullis began to rise.

So intent were the guards on their game that it was a few seconds before they noticed what was happening. Even then, they did little more than leap to their feet and swear. One gawked at the cleat where the rope was tied, pushing back his helmet-brim, scratching his forehead in puzzlement.

Three of Ahmed's crossbowmen stepped forward.

"Now," Ahmed said.

The man looking at the stanchion was just turning. The bolt that struck him had been aimed just beneath his ear, but took him in the mouth instead. He sagged to one knee, making a strange mewling sound. The other two men collapsed with quarrels through the helmets, killed instantly.

"Come on," Ahmed said, running across the street, drawing his shortsword.

The guard with the bolt in his mouth looked up at him, the mewling becoming a high-pitched whine, his helmet still pushed back. Hardly glancing at him, Ahmed thrust his sword into the man's forehead, feeling the corpse dragging along behind him for a yard or two before the body pulled free of its own weight.

Dogs bayed, off to the left. A door opened in the main building, spewing hueless light down the steps.

"What's happening?" a man cried, framed in the arch.

Ahmed heard the *thap!* of a crossbow-string. The man staggered and screamed, a second bolt finishing him. He started to roll down the stairs, but jerked to a halt after a few steps, descent checked by the protruding missiles.

More crossbows snapped, and the dogs fell silent.

Ahmed pointed to the left, where a second stairway descended beneath the building, leading to the slave cells. A third of his men veered away. Even as he reached the main entrance, pausing on the threshold, he heard them summoning the entity they would use to break the cellar door.

Before going in, he allowed several crossbowmen to take the lead; the remainder of his troops swept along behind him, kicking down doors, rushing into rooms two by two.

"Who's there?" a voice called up ahead, beyond the arbalesters.

Two bowstrings answered.

A door banged open on Ahmed's left. Belly hanging, a nude man blinked stupidly at him. Ahmed stabbed him in the center of the chest. Sour with sleep, the fellow's last breath belched into the Sharajnaghi's face.

At the end of the corridor, Ahmed followed the crossbowmen to the second floor, smirking inwardly at the stupidity of its occupants. The fools were far too engrossed in their diversions— the screams and whipcracks had continued without respite.

At the top, the Sharajnaghim found a small votive chamber, its walls splashed with blood; to Ahmed's eyes, the stains were a luminous grey-purple against a field of velvet-black. There was

no one living to be seen, but a dead boy lay naked on the altar,
neck all but severed, the glow of his body several shades darker
than that of living flesh.

Dark lacquered surfaces reflecting the corpse's effulgence, three
idols loomed behind the altar. In the center was a wheel of pinioned
wings, all radiating from a cluster of staring eyes. To the right stood
a female fertility image from the lands south of Numalia, a spike
driven through its left eye, its groin and one breast all but chiselled
away. To the left was a figure like a newborn baby, its head covered
with meticulously represented spiders of several sizes and types.

A door opened slowly on the right; bare feet shuffled. Ahmed
saw a nude woman with a collar about her neck, her luminous body crisscrossed with white streaks that might have been
whip-weals.

Ahmed put a finger to his lips. Given the chains and her injuries, it was reasonable to assume she was a natural ally. But she
responded with a shriek, running back inside.

"After her!" Ahmed cried.

The crossbowmen poured through the door. Ahmed heard cries
of horror, then the discharge of several bows; the interior of the
room flashed bright orange, the first real color he had seen since
taking the drug.

Force-bolt, he thought.

The archway flared several more times. One of his men toppled
out, landing heavily on his back. Sheathing his sword, Ahmed
dashed past the prostrate form, assuming a stance as he crossed
the threshold.

Only one of his troops was still on his feet, tossing his arbalest
down even as Ahmed entered; the rest, several still holding their
bows, lay stunned on the floor.

Across the room, a still-writhing man had been pinned to the
wall with quarrels, his nude muscular body running with blood,
the fluid incandescent against the duller glow of his skin. Standing
atop a huge bed was another Anarite, clad in a robe, orange fire
bursting from his hands.

Ahmed's last man crumpled in the blast before he could raise
his shields; Ahmed's own bucklers materialized an instant before
the Anarite turned his bolts on him.

The shields held. The Anarite raised defenses of his own and
began shrieking a spell. Ahmed could not respond in kind; he had

not drained off enough power. Hoping to break the Anarite's concentration, he dropped a shield and laid on with cataract-bolts.

The Anarite completed his spell nonetheless. A tall, thin figure
appeared before Ahmed, its whole meager shape outlined with
serrations like teeth on a saw, its eyes and fanged mouth apertures
through which he clearly glimpsed the Anarite behind. Ahmed's
bolts began to fly wild, anywhere but at the demon. Switching
to another kind of strike, he fetched the same result.

The thing started towards him, body twisting side to side. It
appeared no thicker than a strip of tall marsh-grass. But like
marsh-grass, the demon could deal out terrible punishment—the
serrated arms crossed over its chest, then whipped sideways, one
limb slicing Ahmed's pectoral muscles clear to the ribs, the other
hissing through the bridge of his nose.

Shrieking, Ahmed drew his sword, slashing at the arms. They
parted with a sound like sheared parchment, fluttering to the floor;
the head fell away next. In the instant before it blinked from view,
the reed-demon curled backwards, crackling.

Ahmed flung his sword at the Anarite, crouching beside one of
his fallen crossbowmen. The Anarite dodged the hurtling blade
and began another spell.

Ahmed's arbalester had a bolt clutched in one hand, his cross-
bow in the other. Ahmed snatched the weapon, cocked it effortlessly with its "sorceror's wheel," then slid the dart into the
groove.

A second reed-demon appeared. But in repeating himself, the
Anarite had made a fatal error. Taking careful aim, Ahmed sent
a bolt though the demon's gaping mouth and into the Anarite's
stomach.

The demon vanished. Clutching at the bolt, the Anarite crumpled onto the bed, groaning.

Picking up his sword once more, Ahmed glanced at the man
who had been nailed to the wall. That Anarite was quite motionless now.

Ahmed looked slowly about the room. In the fury of combat,
many details had escaped him; now he understood the horrified
cries his men had uttered upon entering.

Two shredded shapes lay on the bed with the wounded Anarite,
covers beneath them one huge glowing bloodstain. It was impossible to tell their sex. A third corpse, still recognizably female,

hung from a rack off to the side. The woman who had rushed back into the room was crouching in a corner, staring, running her hands through her tangled hair.

Ahmed went to a window and opened the shutter. The surrounding houses were dark, the streets silent. To all appearances, the assault had not drawn the slightest attention. But that came as no surprise; Sayid's spies had reported that the Anarites frequently entertained themselves with their chattel well into the dark hours of the morning, and Ahmed guessed that their neighbors—many of them slave-traders themselves—had grown accustomed to the screams. He wondered how many Anarite spies would blunder into the trap in the next few days.

Feet slapped towards him. He turned to see the woman rushing at him with a knife. He parried coolly and ran her through, easing her off the point with an open palm against her face.

He looked back at the Anarite on the bed. Still on his back, the man was floundering over one of the flayed corpses. Ahmed rounded the bed and stared down at him.

"Why?" the Anarite gasped. "Why have you done this?"

"We couldn't let you warn your comrades at Khaur-Al-Jaffar," Ahmed answered.

"Khaur-Al-Jaffar?"

"We thought one of your spies might see our men departing," Ahmed replied. "We're going to destroy your Order, once and for all."

"But why?" the Anarite groaned. "We're the only reason you exist, the last Black Order . . ."

Ahmed smiled. "Last Black Order?" he asked, raising his sword. "What makes you think that?"

The blade swooped, cleaving the Anarite's brow.

In the morning, Nawhar went to the great dome to pray. Khaddam's company had assembled there, kneeling before the altar; the Grand Master stood upon the dais, invoking the Lord's blessing on his soldiers. Nawhar scanned the crowd, swiftly picking out Sharif and Erim.

He knelt, but could not compose himself. Just the sight of Erim was enough to make him tremble with rage. Nawhar seethed to think of the humiliation that he had suffered at the hearing.

What good is it, being orthodox? What difference does it make, if an arch-heretic can accuse you of heresy before the Council itself?

Nor had Erim been content to leave it at that. He had equated Nawhar with the priests of Tchernobog and the Black Anarites. It was tantamount to a charge of treason—such poisonous slander! Nawhar was the last Sharajnaghi. How could he betray the Order?

He could, perhaps, imagine it betraying *him*; but he represented everything that was good in it, the true center, the core of authentic spirituality. True, sometimes even he could not live up to his own ideals. But his vision—that was utterly clear.

He found himself staring at the plants covering the interior of the dome. The disease plaguing them had spread quickly in the last few weeks; there were very few green patches remaining, and great swaths of white stone showed through in places. Nawhar was reminded of the Order itself. Plainly, between the evil feelings that had been stirred up by the murders, and Erim's manipulation of the Council, it was badly infected. Nawhar could only hope that some good would come of the situation, that the contagion would destroy that which was corruptible, revealing the clean, sterile stone that was the Order's essence.

Khaddam led the troops in one last prayer, then came down from the altar. His men rose, Nawhar as well. Sharif and Erim drew near.

"Here to see us off?" Sharif asked.

Nawhar stared at them silently.

"We'd be thankful for your prayers," Sharif said. "We're going to need them."

"I'll pray for you, Sharif, certainly," Nawhar said, then looked freezingly at Erim. "And I'll ask the Lord to restore *your* senses."

"Well," Erim answered, "if that's the best you can do, I suppose I should be grateful."

"Why don't you pray to Essaj?" Nawhar continued. "Surely he can do more for you than I can."

"Don't be absurd, Nawhar," Sharif said.

"*Have* you ever prayed to him, Erim?" Nawhar prodded.

Erim shook his head.

"Why not? Surely, given what you believe . . ."

"Nawhar," Sharif said heavily, "we're leaving very soon. Must you ruin our last moments . . . ?"

"*Must* you keep company with this traitor?" Nawhar answered.

"Traitor?" Sharif asked. "Don't you think that's a bit strong?"

"Not at all," Nawhar replied. "Remember what Horde said: 'One will fight on my side when the final battle is joined?' "

"Yes, but which one of us will it be?" Erim asked. "Let us suppose Essaj is from God. *Then* whose side will *you* be on?"

"Erim," Sharif broke in, with a pained expression, "you're just rising to the bait. What good does it do to say things like that?"

"He has to discredit me," Nawhar said. "To keep you from thinking about his treason. Listen to your conscience, Sharif. You've always prided yourself on your loyalty to the Order. Your *perfect* loyalty. Mark my words. One day, it will be the Order or Erim. Be sure you make the right choice. For the sake of your immortal soul, be sure."

He searched Sharif's eyes. He had shaken the blockhead, he was sure of it. It was so simple to lead fools around by the nose; this was Jalloud all over again, except easier.

Only one thing puzzled Nawhar. Why hadn't he been able to turn the Council on Erim?

"We must go," the heretic told Sharif. Plainly he had also noticed the look on Sharif's face; and just as plainly, he was unsettled by what he had read there.

"Farewell, Sharif," Nawhar called after them. "God go with you."

Chapter 13

From Qanar-Sharaj, Khaddam's troop proceeded northwest to Ismailia, a small city on the banks of the Gura. Well after sundown, they boarded the cargo-vessels that had been requisitioned for their use. A brisk wind filled the lateen sails; after a scant three days, the flotilla reached the Rohaz Forest, a belt of scrub pines that grew in bitter, sandy soil where even grass could barely take root.

Khaddam ordered his men ashore. Concealed in the trees, a third of the raiding-company awaited them inland. Other detachments arrived in due time; the boats returned downriver.

Three Masters beside Khaddam and Akram had come on the expedition—Sayid Al-Mashat, the Intelligence chief; Raschid Zekowi, whose skill as a healer would certainly be tested severely in the fighting to come; and Arghun Khan. Meeting in Khaddam's tent, they conferred on various details of the campaign. One of the last unresolved issues concerned the distribution of Erim's bombs.

"It's too late to change my plans," Akram insisted.

"Nonsense," Sayid said. "You could certainly spare a modest number of these—what do you call them—'benshaqars.' "

"My men have been instructed in their use," Akram answered. "Yours haven't."

"It's simple enough to learn," Arghun said. "You said so yourself."

"It's not just that," Akram said testily. "If Sharif's party can't open the gate for us, we'll have to blast it down ourselves—

101

we can't use magic, and the explosive quarrels aren't powerful enough. The benshaqars *must* be reserved."

"But if Sharif succeeds?" asked Raschid Zekowi, a handsome man with very pale skin; the question was accompanied by an elegant hand-gesture that bordered on the effeminate. His masculinity was never questioned, however; he was the only Master with two wives, and had fathered numerous children.

"They must *still* be reserved for my men," Akram answered. "We're going first into the breach. If we meet shieldwalls, the benshaqars will be invaluable."

"And if *we* meet demons?" Raschid asked.

"If we're to keep our momentum, penetrate as deeply into the fortress as possible, we won't have time to stop and assume stances. In short, we won't *want* to answer demons with demons. Once again, the benshaqars—and the bolts—would seem the best solution."

Exasperated, Raschid and his fellow Serpents looked to Khaddam. But their patron only shook his head.

"Really," Khaddam said, "He's absolutely right."

"But, *Sibi* . . . " Arghun began.

"Enough," Khaddam replied.

Later that evening, as the Serpents took their leave, Khaddam invited Akram to stay and share some wine with him. They sat near the opening of the tent; the air was very still, heavy with the scent of the pines. Outside, the camp was dark and silent; fires had not been permitted, and the men had taken early to their bedrolls—Khaddam had informed them that he intended to cover thirty miles tomorrow.

"This is excellent wine," Akram said, and directed another squirt into his mouth from the skin bag the Grand Master had given him.

"I have a whole cask," Khaddam said. "Sent one of my men into Thangura to buy the best vintage he could find. Cost a fair piece."

"Isn't that rather an indulgence?" Akram asked.

"I have more money than I know what to do with," Khaddam said. "I've been investing some of my stipend. I should have been a speculator . . . anyway, life on the march is so ghastly. I thought I'd lighten our burden a bit."

"Which one of your men did you send? Raschid, perhaps? He's very knowledgeable about wines, isn't he?"

Khaddam laughed. "I *should* have sent one of the Serpents. The whole lot, in fact. Take them down a peg. They're very full of themselves lately."

"As if they think they're Masters," Akram agreed, and handed the wine back to him.

"You've put your finger on it," Khaddam said. "And I take full responsibility, as befits a Grand Master of the *Comahi Irakhoum*." He took a squirt from the bag. "You don't care for my apprentices very much, do you?"

"I like Mufkadi well enough," Akram answered.

"And the rest?"

"I can't say I have anything against them."

"That is, you don't like them, but you don't know why, exactly."

Akram swatted a mosquito. "Something like that. Actually, I suspect that they simply don't like *me*."

"There's probably something to that," Khaddam allowed. "I think they see you as my chief rival."

"That's absurd," Akram answered.

"Isn't it? God knows I've tried to enlighten them. I've told them how you had to be dragged kicking and screaming into the Seventh Level—that you're simply not a very ambitious man."

"Should I take that as a compliment?"

"The finest I can offer," Khaddam said. "I envy you enormously, believe me. The very idea of going through life without that little nattering voice in your head . . ."

"Voice?"

"The one I hear. Always stoking my anger, whispering about how I'm being taken advantage of, how I don't have enough control . . . It can't be satisfied. And fighting it is very wearying, believe me. I'm nowhere near as bad as I used to be, but I have far to go."

"Well, if you're so dissatisfied with yourself," Akram said, "pray for strength."

"I do. Constantly. But it's not so simple as that. The voice tells me to pray too, you know."

"Oh?"

"I prayed to become Grand Master, believe me."

"That strikes me as plausible."

"Not that I wished any harm on Ahwaz, mind you."

"Of course not."

"Undoubtedly God wants me to be more humble—but then, He puts the Order in my hands. Sometimes I think He's trying to confuse me."

"Why would He want to do that?"

"Maybe He doesn't trust me," Khaddam replied. "Certainly, He never trusts us with the whole truth—about anything."

"We couldn't understand it."

"He never trusts us with the ability to understand it."

"I think anyone who lusted for that would die a very frustrated man."

"Indeed," said Khaddam, then asked after a few moments: "Does it ever bother you, just being a pawn?"

"Why should it? I *am* a pawn. And I try to be a good one."

"It doesn't anger you, somewhere deep in your soul? The fact that you're trapped in a war between God and Tchernobog, a war you can't comprehend? You don't bear the least bit of responsibility, but you suffer anyway. And in the end . . ."

"I die and go to heaven," Akram answered. "No, I've never troubled myself about it. How else should the world be? What's the alternative? There are those who say they can imagine one, but we both know that's all bosh."

"Very true," Khaddam said. "It's one thing to say you can postulate a universe without evil. But to *actually* design it, and bring it to life—you're right. The only alternative is nothingness."

"Which is no alternative at all, to my mind."

Khaddam laughed. "Do you think so?"

"God is a necessarily existent being. If *something* exists necessarily, then *nothing* is out of the question."

"Oh, there are other schools of thought on that proposition," Khaddam said.

"That you take seriously?"

"No. Their arguments are bizarre, to say the least. Still, I find the fact that anyone could even entertain such notions curiously disturbing. Worse still, I've been troubled lately by a recurring dream . . ."

"Do you want to tell me about it?"

"Perhaps you've had it too. Raschid says he's talked to a dozen of the men. They've been losing sleep . . . Usually it begins with a man, nailed to an altar. He's been tortured horribly. And when he's killed, the void appears . . ."

"The void?"

"It devours everything. Sometimes it's like a black wave, sometimes like smoke, or holes appearing out of nowhere, like gaps in a cobweb."

"It sounds very horrible," Akram said.

Khaddam took a swallow of wine. "Beyond description. You've never had anything like it?"

"No. At least, not that I recall. The only ones I ever remember are about my wife. They're quite pleasant—until I wake up. . . . When did these nightmares of yours start?"

"Soon after Iyad died."

"Well, they probably don't mean anything."

"And it's just a coincidence that those other men have had them too?"

"Who knows? Don't worry about it."

"That's easy for you to say."

"Yes," Akram said. "It is. Hand me that skin, would you? One more taste, and I'm off. It's going to be a hard day tomorrow."

Khaddam gave him the wine.

"Ahh," Akram said, after his final swallow. "Once again, splendid stuff." He paused. "I take it you must have forgiven me for opposing you at the hearing."

"Over Essaj?" Khaddam said. "We've disagreed about so much, Akram. I've come to expect it, really."

"It is rather a tonic, isn't it?" Akram said, standing up. "Good night, Khaddam."

Preceded by a small scouting column under Sharif's command, the Sharajnaghim rose early and set out, pressing northwards through the pines, oftimes at a jog, their pack animals trotting beside them. Towards noon, the ground began to rise gently, and by the end of the afternoon, the mountains were visible from atop the swells.

The Masters drove their men at the same gruelling pace for the next two days, following a carefully chosen route through the least settled regions of the forest. As luck would have it, they encountered not a single soul.

But on the fourth day they approached the Great Slave Road, which wound its way out of the mountains to the east, skirting the fringe of the rocky uplands; merchants who had purchased human chattel at Khaur-Al-Jaffar followed it west to the Bishah Road, and thence to Thangura. Concealed in the pines, near enough to hear the clink of the chains, the Sharajnaghim watched several long caravans of misery plod by before dashing across.

Pressing into the foothills, Sharif's column maintained a distance of several miles from the main body. Erim was in the detachment; he had been observing Sharif closely ever since their departure from Qanar-Sharaj, wondering if Nawhar's words beneath the great dome had affected his friend. At the time, Sharif had clearly been troubled by the exchange, and he had, at intervals, been quite distant during the last few days. When Erim asked him about it, Sharif had explained that he merely missed Zehowah. Undoubtedly he did—Erim was terrified that he would never see Khalima again—but Erim knew there was more to it than that.

Two days north of the road, vast crags shouldered out of the foothills, huge granite faces seamed with fissures. Sharif's company slogged northwards through deep, shadowy gorges, the terrain growing ever more difficult; the floors of the ravines slanted steeply, and were covered with bits of loose fallen stone.

Late one morning, as Sharif reached the top of a steep grade between two leaning grey walls, he suddenly looked back at Erim and asked:

"Why don't you pray to him, then?"

"Pray?" Erim puffed, puzzled.

"To Essaj."

They were well ahead of the other men; Erim stood silently for a few moments, looking back down into the shadowy passage.

"Why don't you do it?" Sharif pressed.

"I'm not sure," Erim said. "It still strikes me as blasphemous, I suppose."

"You don't believe in him, then," Sharif said, sounding relieved.

"If only you were right," Erim replied.

"Surely if you believed in him, you'd be more enthusiastic."

"No. I've turned the corner. I'm committed. It makes me intensely uncomfortable, but . . ."

"You're not making sense."

"Remember what I said, back in the trial?" Erim asked. "How I detest Essaj's doctrines? That hasn't changed at all. If anything, I find them even more horrifying. This new faith is going to make terrible trouble for me. For the whole Order."

"Why should it? Who believes besides you?"

"*Sibi* Akram, I think."

"He's never even laid eyes on Essaj."

"I'm not sure that's necessary."

"You know, Erim," Sharif said, "I can't say I like this kind of talk from you . . ."

"Believe me, I understand. But you must promise me one thing. Don't let this business come between us."

"If it was just you and me . . ." Sharif shook his head. "But it's not. If I have to chose between you and the Order, I'm sorry . . ."

"An honest answer," Erim said. He sighed heavily. "Well, it hasn't come to that yet."

"And God willing, it won't," Sharif said. He jerked a thumb towards the men toiling up the slope below. "Look at that. Every one of 'em younger than us, and we're in much better condition!"

"What would you expect?" Erim asked.

<figure>
⊹
</figure>

Chapter 14

Sharif's map told of a cliff honeycombed with caverns at its base; Akram had instructed him to halt the advance column there. The main force arrived as twilight was deepening, and the Sharajnaghim made camp in the tunnels. Fires were allowed, provided they were far back from the cave-mouths; Sharif had his first cooked meal in nearly a week, although he was much too tired to enjoy it. He dropped off immediately after eating, wrapped in his blanket.

To his tremendous annoyance, a loud din woke him sometime later, shouts and the clash of steel. The sounds seemed to be coming from one of the passages that connected with the other tunnels.

Did the Anarites find us? he wondered groggily, reaching for his quarterstaff. Then came Khaddam's unmistakable roar:

"Hold! Hold, or by the Almighty, I'll have you all shot!"

The uproar died down.

"Send for *Sibi* Raschid!" Khaddam cried.

A man came running out of the connecting passage.

"What happened?" Sharif asked.

"Some of Samadhi and Massoud's men," the fellow answered.

Sharif spat with disgust, settling back on the stony floor. With the exposure of Samadhi, and the appointment of new Masters at Intelligence and Doctrine, the friction between the two camps had assumed a strange new form—a competition to demonstrate ever greater extremes of obedience to the Order. As much as Sharif admired obedience, he thought there was something feverish and unnatural about this new development. Samadhi's men seemed obsessed with the need to wash away the stain of allegiance to their former Master; Massoud's, still seething with mistrust and nursing scores of private grudges, apparently felt the need to outdo Samadhi's. As a result, the fighting had ceased—until the outburst just now.

"Khaddam *should* have them all shot," Erim said nearby.

"Yes," Sharif said, closing his heavy eyelids. "But tomorrow."

Morning came as blue twilight in the valley bottom; the troops assembled outside the caves to watch the culprits flogged. Sayid and Arghun, who had replaced Samadhi and Massoud, wielded the whips. But the punishment for each offender was limited to five strokes; Khaddam had no wish to deprive himself of able fighting-men.

Soon after the discipline was administered, Sharif's party set off once more. Twin saw-toothed ramparts ran directly across their route.

"Think they'll be able to get the animals this far?" Erim wondered as they reached the crest of the first ridge, surveying the second, shading his eyes with an open palm.

Sharif looked back down at the main body. Hidden in places behind outcroppings, the column appeared to have split into several segments; the troops were tiny with distance.

"They seem to be managing," Sharif announced.

"Someone should carve a road through here," Erim said.

"Well," Sharif said, "when this is all Sharajnaghi territory, perhaps we will."

They waited for the remainder of their detachment to catch up, then started downhill. Crossing the valley, Sharif's company spent the better part of the afternoon conquering the next incline. As they neared the top, Erim asked:

"Do you hear anything?"

The air hung thin and chill; Sharif paused, listening.

"Hammers?" he asked.

"Or pickaxes," Erim said.

"Miners?"

"Maybe the Anarites aren't waiting."

"Eh?" Sharif asked.

"For us to build that road," Erim answered.

The other men labored up to them. Sharif detailed one to return to the main column:

"Tell *Sibi* Khaddam that there might be an Anarite work-gang ahead of us."

Instructing the rest to remain where they were, he crept cautiously up the incline with Erim, slipping from boulder to boulder. At last he peered cautiously over the top.

Two Anarites in chain mail and peaked helms stood on a small patch of level stone. One had his back to Sharif, and was talking animatedly to his comrade. Nodding absently, clearly disinterested, the other was looking past him. He seemed not to notice Sharif.

"And then I sliced it off!" the first Anarite said, laughing. "How she squealed—"

The second's eyes flew open wide; his comrade turned.

Sharif smiled.

"Two of them," he told Erim out of the corner of his mouth, turning slightly. "About twenty feet from me."

Erim's blades whispered from their scabbards.

The Anarites started forward, reaching for their scimitars. Sharif waved, letting them close half the distance before telling Erim:

"Now!"

Leaping up, Erim hurled the blades. A silver-inlaid hilt sprouted beneath one man's chin.

His companion started to duck, catching the other blade in the cheek, the broad blade cutting part way through his nose. Dropping his weapon, he tried to pull the knife out with both hands, doubling forward.

Erim vaulted onto the shelf, ran up to him, and drove his shortsword deep into the hollow of the man's shoulder. Removing it and his knives, he wiped the blades on his victims.

Sharif dashed past him, making for the far edge of the shelf, intending to scan the valley beyond. But even as he approached the rim, two more Anarites climbed up in front of him.

Sharif continued his headlong rush, swinging his staff, crushing a helmet; leaping back to avoid the Sharajnaghi's next blow, the other man toppled over the edge on his own.

Sharif stepped up to the stony brim. Beneath, the Anarite lay sprawled on a ledge, gasping.

Wind knocked out, Sharif decided, and jumped down, guessing the man was helpless for the moment. A trail led away to the right; looking over the side of the ledge, he saw that the ground dropped sharply, and that the path, apparently chiselled out in spots, zigzagged back and forth across the steep grey-blue face. A battalion of laborers was at work on the lower reaches of the trail, widening it with picks and sledgehammers; there was a camp some distance from the base of the cliff, with at least a dozen tents. Armored figures moved among the workers. Sharif's first impulse was to try and count them; but without warning, the fallen Anarite got up and sprinted away along the path, shouting.

Stretching his long legs in mighty strides, Sharif raced after him, bringing his staff down on the peak of his helmet. The Anarite slowed, stumbling. Unable to check his momentum on the grade, Sharif tried to dodge, but bumped the tottering figure ever so slightly to the left. He turned to see his victim dropping over the cliff.

The Sharajnaghi crouched, watching him plummet. Colliding with an outthrust pier of rock, the corpse began to spin wildly, crashing at the feet of an overseer some hundred feet below Sharif. The man looked up. Sharif leaned back quickly.

Erim came down beside him.

"Khaddam will have my head for this," Sharif said.

"I saw it all," Erim answered. "It wasn't your fault."

"We can't let any of them escape," Sharif said. He peered over the edge once more. A small group of Anarites had collected by the corpse. Swords drawn, they started upwards. "If they'll just keep coming up here . . . Go back and get the others, quick."

Erim hastened away.

Sharif stood, hefting his staff. He moved some distance along the path, then halted, leaning the weapon against the cliff-wall. Assuming a Dragon Stance, he waited.

The overseers rounded the bend below him, sighting him and breaking into a run. He remained motionless, perfectly content to let them drag their mailed bodies up the incline.

Their pace soon slowed; he let them slog ten more yards or so, then pummelled them with cataract-bolts.

Shielding their faces with their hands, armor absorbing much of the force, the Anarites continued upwards. At last one fell, then another; Sharif seized his staff and hurled himself upon the rest. Swords shattered beneath his strokes; noses flattened, pouring out blood. Bodies rocked against the wall to the right, lurched out into the void on the left. A few heartbeats, and only one Anarite remained on his feet.

Holding the staff like a spear, Sharif feinted at the man's stomach, then drove the butt into his lips, feeling the teeth give behind them. Several inches of the stave plunged into the Anarite's mouth; levering the weapon upwards with a swift jerk, Sharif snapped his neck, kicking him off the end as he sagged.

Sharif looked back up the path. His reinforcements were nowhere in sight.

He glanced back over the edge. Another, larger contingent of Anarites was toiling up towards him. Far below them, guards were gathering by the tents, craning their heads back and pointing.

Sharif eyed the gorge beyond the tents. If the fools had sent anyone for help, he could see no sign of it.

The second group of overseers rounded the bend. But as they did so, a man cried out, and their pace slackened. Slowly they proceeded up the incline, conserving their strength. Three had crossbows.

"Put your staff down!" one of the arbalesters commanded.

Sharif complied, whispering a formula. As he came to the last word, he reassumed his Dragon Stance, just in time to trigger the spell.

Dark grey, almost indistinguishable from the stony floor of the path, a Shroud-That-Crawls materialized in front of the crossbowmen, rearing up before they could shoot, a writhing wall.

Sharif thought of conjuring a second demon, but the Influences were against him; seizing his staff once more, he sped forward.

The Shroud settled over the foremost Anarites, bowing them beneath its weight. Sharif rushed up over the struggling, blanketed forms, men charging at him from the far side; howling, he caught two across the face with his first stroke. As they slumped, he burst in among the ones behind, crushing a throat, destroying a knee, passing clear through the knot of foemen, halting his rush after a few steps, wheeling, bashing an Anarite from the path, jabbing another in the groin.

Ahead, the Shroud reared up once more, smoke belching from beneath it. Sharif heard something that might have been a clatter of bones. The creature lunged farther down the slant, enveloping several of his victims as they tried to rise.

The Anarite who had been struck in the groin got back up, rushing at Sharif from the side. Sharif stepped out of his way, then cracked him against the back of the helm with such force that the Anarite sailed far out into space, beginning a lazy somersault as he dropped from view.

Banishing the Shroud, Sharif looked to see if any more Anarites were coming. To his delight, the remaining overseers on the ledge, now heavily outnumbered by the slaves, were falling beneath hammer and pickaxe blows. But the Anarites who had been standing by the tents were now rushing to help their comrades.

Sharif heard footsteps above him—there were his men at last, racing down the slant with Erim at their head.

"About time!" Sharif cried, and fell in beside his friend. Together they led the troop in a wild descent.

The overseers were all dead by the time the Sharajnaghim reached the slaves; shouting encouragement in several languages, the thralls flattened themselves against the cliff, allowing their benefactors to sweep past.

The Anarite column snaked into view below. Rounding the corner, the black-robes halted, assuming stances.

But they had let the Sharajnaghim come too close. Sharif took a blast in the chest, shrugged it off and plowed into the Anarite formation, beating with his staff. Chaos engulfed him; entangled by thrashing limbs, he fell. Someone toppled onto him and scrambled off. Spittle spewed up into his face; an Anarite was struggling beneath him. The man's mouth seemed preternaturally huge—he had teeth like a horse, and they clacked shut an inch from Sharif's nose.

One of the Sharajnaghi's hands was still on his staff, the other on the hilt of a dagger in the Anarite's belt. Sliding the knife out, Sharif wrestled it twice through the man's chain mail, then hurled himself to his feet, roaring.

Before he could get both palms back on his staff, an Anarite knocked the weapon from his grip. Assuming a stance, Sharif pushed his fist almost into the Anarite's face, discharging a bolt into his eye. Blood slapped Sharif's knuckles, splattering up his forearm. One whole side of his face obliterated in scarlet, the Anarite went over like a falling tree.

Snatching his staff back up, Sharif dashed the life from three more. Off on the fringe of sight, Erim was slashing with shortsword and knife; some distance ahead, two greyclads were fighting frenziedly.

The press began to break up. The remaining Anarites were fleeing.

"Cut them down!" Sharif bellowed hoarsely to his men. "We can't let any escape!"

The Sharajnaghim bolted in pursuit, around the bend, down the last hundred feet of ledge. They rapidly outstripped their armored prey, cutting them down from behind. A few Anarites reached the bottom and ran in among the tents; crossbows finished them before they got much farther.

"I'll give them this," Erim said, panting beside Sharif. "They had more nerve than most Anarites. I wouldn't have thought they'd try to hold the path like that."

"They probably thought I was alone," Sharif said. "Once that last group started up the cliff, they wouldn't have seen the rest of us until it was too late. Not with the way those ledges over-hang—"

He broke off, startled by a series of wild whoops. Having smashed their chains, the slaves were even then pouring down off the ramp, hugging every Sharajnaghi within reach.

"Well, we've certainly made *them* very happy," Erim said.

"I hope Khaddam's as easily pleased," Sharif answered, just as a sweat-soaked Tarchan with filthy straw-colored hair hurled himself into his arms, kissing him loudly on the cheek. Gasping, staggering, Sharif glanced at Erim, embarrassed beyond words.

"Sharif, stop!" Erim cried. "What would Zehowah say?"

Chapter 15

In Khaddam's absence, Mufkadi Umar, the new Sorcery Master and foremost member of the Knot, had been left in command at Qanar-Sharaj. Soon after the raiders departed, Sigrun encountered him in the Women's Quarters. She liked Mufkadi a great deal; he had an excellent sense of humor, and he always listened closely to what she had to say, without the least trace of condescension. Moreover, he was extremely good-looking, with the blackest eyes she had ever seen, and a delightful, if somewhat lascivious, smile that only raised one corner of his mouth. Taller even than Khaddam, and very powerfully built, he was the object of much discussion among the women.

"Might I have a word with you, *Sibi*?" Sigrun asked.

"*Sibi*," Mufkadi laughed, signalling his guards to halt.

"Well, you *are* a Master now."

"It's taking me a while to get used to it."

"Are you here to see Bhanavar?"

"Yes, I am." He seemed somewhat impatient. "What can I do for you?"

"I'd like to go into Thangura with some of the other women, to buy cloth," Sigrun answered. "I know you've placed the men on alert, but . . ."

"You're wondering if I could spare you an escort."

"Yes."

"The city's probably safer than Qanar-Sharaj—no sendings. But you'll have your guards. When do you wish to go?"

"Tomorrow."

"Very well. But you must be back before sundown."

"Of course," Sigrun said. "How do you like being a Master?"

"Well," Mufkadi began, "it's very nice being obeyed by practically everyone. Even so, it's much too much work, at least for the time being. As a matter of fact, I haven't seen Bhanavar in four days . . ."

Sigrun stepped aside, motioning him forward.

"If you insist," Mufkadi said.

"*Sibi*," she answered, bowing.

Sigrun's party left early in the morning. There were fifteen women in all, including Zehowah and Khalima; Mufkadi had assigned an equal number of guards. To Sigrun's surprise, Nawhar came along as well.

"To what do we owe the honor?" she asked the captain of the escort, who rode along beside her.

"He wants to consult a book in the library of the Grand Temple," the Adept replied. "I thought it would be better if he joined us."

She could hear Nawhar behind her, speaking to one of the guards. The conversation had something to do with "traitors." She listened very hard, turning slightly in the saddle, but most of the words eluded her, eventually fading; evidently Nawhar and the other fellow were falling back in line.

But presently she caught another conversation—Khalima and Zehowah were telling Murad's concubine Ahesha about Essaj. Ahesha did not sound convinced, but she seemed to find the matter very interesting. Ever since Sigrun took the sisters under her wing, a number of the other women had warmed to them as well. Sigrun was not surprised. As far as she was concerned, the pair were the most interesting development in the Women's Quarters in quite some time; their enthusiasm was very refreshing, if admittedly a bit childish.

At length they rode up on her right.

"Did you make any progress with Ahesha?" she asked.

"No," said Zehowah.

"Yes," said Khalima. "She's thinking about it, I can tell. Murad's talked to her about it himself. And he voted for Essaj at the hearing."

"Not exactly," Sigrun answered. "He voted not to indict him—for now."

"If you're not against Essaj, you're for him," Zehowah replied. "That's what he always says."

"Well then," Sigrun said, "I suppose that means I'm for him too."

"Of course you are," Khalima said. "You're coming right along."

Sigrun could not suppress a laugh. "Thank you."

"Think nothing of it," Khalima answered, then knit her brows. "What's so funny?"

Entering Thangura just before noon, they proceeded along the broad thoroughfare that led to the temple. The clothseller's bazaar lay just south of the shrine.

As always, the sight of the temple left Sigrun in awe. Surrounded by four soaring minarets, it loomed like a mountain at the end of the avenue, snow-white but for its vast central dome, which blazed with gold leaf. If indeed the Kadjafi God was real, she could easily imagine that this was his earthly abode.

A large crowd had collected before the steps; halfway up, a tall figure in a brown robe was addressing the throng.

"That's him!" Zehowah said. "That's Essaj!"

"The fellow on the stairs?"

"We should go and listen," Khalima said.

Sigrun considered this, turning to the captain of the escort. "What do you think?" she asked.

"I'm curious about the man myself," he replied.

They halted at the fringe of the crowd. Several men near the front had begun to berate Essaj, but before Sigrun could discover the issue, Nawhar appeared alongside the captain, and demanded indignantly:

"Why have we stopped? What's the meaning of this?"

The captain put a finger to his lips.

"You have no business exposing the men to this poison!" Nawhar shouted, so loudly that many in the crowd turned their heads.

"Quiet, please," the captain replied.

Nawhar hissed in frustration.

Sigrun barely suppressed a smile.

"It is the Father who glorifies me," Essaj was saying. "The very one that you claim is your God, even though you don't know Him. But *I* know him, and I keep His word. Your father Ibrahim rejoiced that he might see my day. He saw it and was glad."

Ibrahim? Sigrun thought. *What is he talking about?* The first of the Kadjafi Patriarchs, Ibrahim had been dead for two thousand years . . .

"You're not yet forty!" a man cried. "How can you have seen Ibrahim?"

Essaj shrugged. "I'm telling you the truth. Before Ibrahim was born, I AM."

Nawhar muttered something under his breath, and the captain laughed in disbelief. A brief stunned silence descended over the crowd; furious cries followed. Sigrun saw men unsheathing daggers, prying up cobblestones with them. Essaj remained where he was, looking out over the throng, shaking his head.

"There's going to be a riot," the captain told Sigrun. "We'd better leave—"

"Make way!" a voice bellowed. "Make way!"

Armored in burnished scale mail, a troop of temple guards were approaching, a tall greybeard in a white turban riding along behind them.

"Make way!" the foremost guard cried once more. "Make way for Gamal Al-Din, High Priest of Thangura!"

Sigrun's party moved aside, and the crowd opened; dismounting, the High Priest took the steps two at a time. Sigrun expected some sort of furious exchange between him and Essaj; instead, drawing himself up to his full height on the stair beside the would-be messiah, the old man looked him over, then turned to face the crowd.

"What's all this, then?" he demanded. "Are those *stones* I see in your hands? By the Almighty, I hope not!"

"He blasphemed, *Sibi!*" someone answered.

"Blasphemed?"

"He called himself by God's True Name!"

"Well, then," Gamal answered, "let us suppose he did. Has there been a trial?"

"We heard him, Master!" another man bellowed.

"Quite beside the point," the High Priest answered. "No trial, no execution. That's the Law. You've heard of the Law, haven't you? If there's a case to be made against this man, the Sharajnaghim will deal with it. In the meantime, I've been on the road, I'm very hungry, and I'm ordering you to disperse!"

"What have we come to?" a voice wailed. "Our own High Priest defending heretics on the steps of the temple itself!"

Sigrun was astonished at such defiance; but hadn't Khaddam once mentioned certain radical elements that held the High Priesthood in utter contempt?

"Kill the blasphemer!" another voice screamed. A stone sailed through the air, bouncing from Essaj's shoulder. Barely flinching, he reached up slowly, gripping the place where he had been struck, working the joint.

"Guards!" Gamal cried.

The soldiers assembled in front of him and Essaj, staring sullenly at the crowd from behind a fence of spearpoints.

"I'll send for reinforcements if you insist!" Gamal shouted. "Now go!"

The crowd began to break up. Cobbles dropped to the street.

But directly before Sigrun, a bald man stood his ground, swearing, still hefting his stone.

"Put it down!" a guard barked from the steps.

The bald man snarled and hurled it.

The stone went several feet to Essaj's right, knocking the turban from Gamal's head. The High Priest howled with surprise and pain.

The troublemaker bent to snatch up another. As he leaped up again, cocking his arm back, two of the guards hurled their spears.

To Sigrun's mind, the weapons sailed very slowly, one behind the other. For some reason that was quite unfathomable to her, the ruffian made no effort to dodge. One of the spears opened the side of his throat; a fine mist of blood sprayed from the wound, reddening one whole side of the spear-shaft as it shot past.

Sigrun was fascinated. It was only when the first spear struck her horse that she realized she was in danger. Legs buckling, the beast collapsed as though the street had given way beneath it.

Missing the wounded man entirely, the second spear caught Sigrun just below the right breast. Suddenly unable to breathe, she gaped down at the shaft, still seated on her horse.

The animal began to heel over slowly. Sigrun threw herself off, falling onto her back. As she settled on the cobblestones, gripping the spear with both hands, she felt a sharp stroke of pain deep inside her body; the shaft jerked several inches upwards. Having come out her back, the point had been pushed inside again.

Khalima and Zehowah rushed up with the captain.

"God!" the captain shouted. "Oh God, no!"

Sigrun stared at him, coughing. Warm thick drops landed on her face. Grimacing, she tried to pull the blade the rest of the way out. The captain knelt, swatting her hands away.

"No," he said. "Leave it in."

"Help me," she said. The words bubbled with blood; could anyone even understand her?

Faces milled round, peering down at her. Someone took her hand; Sigrun saw that it was Zehowah. Zehowah's palm was very warm, almost hot; Sigrun felt increasingly cold, and a blurry greyness was creeping in at the edges of her vision. How preposterous this was! She would never see Khaddam again, not because he had gone off to war, but because *she* had gone into Thangura to buy cloth.

The city's probably safer than Qanar-Sharaj, Mufkadi had said.

The High Priest appeared. White robes shining through the spreading greyness, he looked like an angel. But unlike an angel, he only shook his head in helplessness.

"I'm so sorry," he said. "This is terrible, terrible." Then, to someone she couldn't see: "Quick, man, fetch my doctor!"

The grey was darkening now. Before long, she seemed to be looking along a tunnel.

"Please," Sigrun said. "Help . . ."

"No!" came the captain's voice. "We should leave it in till the doctor's here!"

Was he talking about the spear again? Who was trying to pull it out this time?

She felt it slide from her chest in a smooth, swift motion; her body rose up slightly from the cobbles and settled again. All in one rush, the tunnel pinched shut. She could see nothing for a few seconds.

Suddenly light blossomed. The world reappeared. At first she thought she was getting slowly to her feet, surrounded by a thick press of people. Then it dawned on her that she was floating, and that all of them, her friends, the men of the escort, the temple guards, were simply looking past her.

Through her.

Except, perhaps, for the High Priest.

And Essaj, who was now at his side. Without a doubt, Essaj saw her floating away. The bloody spear dripped in his hand.

Below her, a woman was stretched out on the pavement. Her eyes were open, but sightless. The cracks between the cobblestones surrounding her ran with blood; she seemed to be lying on a scarlet net.

Dead, Sigrun thought. *I'm dead.*

"Not yet," said Essaj.

She looked at him; he was reaching out to her.

"Come back," he said, taking her by the arm. She was no longer sure she *had* an arm; after all, wasn't her body lying on the ground? Nonetheless, he was tugging on her now, forcing her back down. She experienced a moment of profound horror as her chill flesh closed over her once more, drowning her in blackness. Then, dimly, she felt a touch by her wound, and the coldness was gone.

She opened her eyes. Essaj was leaning over her.

"Better?" he asked.

She nodded. Almost unconsciously, she tried to probe the wound with her finger; but even though the hole in the cloth remained, the opening in her flesh was gone. Had she been wounded at all? She searched herself with both hands, sitting up suddenly. Most of the onlookers drew back, gasping.

"You're all right," Essaj told her, motioning her to her feet. Very much to her own amazement, she stood.

"Thank you," she said, quite dazedly, even though her mind seemed unnaturally clear.

"I was glad to do it," Essaj said. "Khalima, Zehowah! Is this a friend of yours?"

"Yes," said Khalima. "Her name is Sigrun."

Coming forward, the High Priest peered at Sigrun's face. "How do you feel, woman?" he asked.

"Very well," she answered.

"And the wound?"

"It's not there anymore."

Gamal glanced at Essaj, then back to her. "I've a doctor coming. Would you permit him to examine you?"

"I'd feel much better if he did," Sigrun admitted.

"It's not necessary, really," Zehowah told her. "You're fine." But Sigrun was not quite ready to accept that.

"And *you*," said Gamal, rounding upon Essaj. "Just who do you think you are, starting riots from the steps of my temple?"

"*Your* temple?" Essaj asked.

"Don't quibble with me," Gamal said.

"I was given permission to preach. Your subordinate, Saadek—"

Gamal slapped himself on the forehead. "Saadek," he growled, then pointed at Sigrun. "What exactly did you do to her?"

"Healed her," Essaj replied. "Do you intend to interrogate me?"

"Perhaps," said the High Priest.

"Then hadn't we better go inside?"

Chapter 16

The Sharajnaghim and the women waited outside on the steps, some distance from Essaj's disciples. The doctor arrived shortly, and went into the temple with Sigrun.

To Nawhar's intense displeasure, though not surprise, the healing had made a tremendous impression on his comrades, not to mention the sows; and Khalima and Zehowah had leaped immediately into the breach, doing everything they possibly could to exploit the situation, telling of other wonders they had witnessed. Nawhar counterattacked with all the force and skill at his disposal, but no one seemed to be listening to him. Even the captain had apparently lost his wits. Nawhar reminded him that Essaj had, in using the three-letter name of God, incontrovertibly identified himself with the Deity; the captain just shrugged. Even when Zehowah and Khalima summoned the disciples to aid them in their proselytizing, the blockhead made no protest. Nawhar almost screamed at him. Only with the greatest effort did he hold himself in check.

Going back down the steps, he sat on the rim of a small fountain, shaking his head. The corruption of the Order would proceed much more quickly now. Once the party returned to Qanar-Sharaj, Sigrun's "miraculous" recovery would be the sole topic of conversation. And Sigrun herself would do everything in her power to sway Khaddam.

Women, Nawhar thought. *All of them, all the same, with their tiny minds, doing his work for him . . .*

Given the doctrine of incarnate divinity, it was not difficult to see why they were Essaj's natural allies. If God was flesh, was not flesh God? And what were women capable of, beyond excreting new generations of bodies?

Nawhar stared venomously at the fools milling about on the steps above. One figure stood apart, off to the left—Jalloud. He came slowly down the steps, pausing and looking over his shoulder more than once. By the time he reached the bottom, Nawhar was waiting for him.

"Why aren't you up there with your friends?" the Sharajnaghi asked.

Jalloud stepped round him silently.

Nawhar followed.

"What's the matter?" he asked. "Why won't you speak to me?"

"Once was enough," Jalloud answered.

"So," Nawhar replied. "There was merit in nothing I said? None of my arguments carried any weight at all?"

"None," Jalloud said, striding from the square.

"I don't think I believe you," Nawhar went on. "I watched you carefully after we spoke. I noticed a distinct cooling between you and Essaj—"

Jalloud halted. Nawhar stepped in front of him.

"You've seen through him, haven't you?" Nawhar pressed. "Aren't you going to thank me?"

"I don't know what you're talking about," Jalloud said.

"You still believe in Essaj?"

"And what if I don't?" Jalloud demanded. "Why should I show *you* any gratitude? You, of all people? Do you have the slightest idea of what it means to believe in someone?"

"Someone?" Nawhar asked. "Do you mean God?"

Jalloud stared at him narrowly.

"Or someone that you *thought* was God?"

"I hate you," Jalloud said quietly.

"I don't hate you," Nawhar said, marvelling at his own feigned sincerity.

"Then stop trying to hurt me."

"Hurt you? How have I done that? I'm trying to *cure* you. To set you at ease with your conscience."

"You're trying to put me at odds with my whole life. My very soul."

"And if your soul is at odds with the whole universe?" Nawhar asked. "With reality? With God Himself? Think, Jalloud. At best, at *best,* Essaj is a madman. At worst, he's wicked beyond belief. How much longer are you going to count yourself among his followers? And if you're still a disciple, what are you doing here with me, when you could be spreading the word about him?"

Nawhar laughed inwardly. *Spreading the word.* All he could think of was a farmer, fertilizing his fields with manure.

With prime matter . . .

"Does it have something to do with Anwar?" the Sharajnaghi asked. "Essaj chose him as his right hand, didn't he? I seem to recall overhearing one of your friends saying something to that effect . . ."

"What do you care?" Jalloud demanded.

There was no need here for any pretense. Nawhar answered with a righteous ferocity that came straight from his heart:

"I care that this heretic that you *still* call your master is corrupting the people. I care that he's infecting my Order with his lies. Already the Council stands impotent, unwilling to indict him. You saw what he did just now. When my comrades return to Qanar-Sharaj, the seeds he planted will bear evil fruit. I can hardly force myself to consider it—the *Comahi Irakhoum,* the ultimate guarantor of religious truth, transformed into an instrument for the promulgation of heresy! And no one is listening to me. No one but you. I've watched my friends drop away, seen the Masters of my Order begin to waver. But *you've* heeded my words. You, one of *his* disciples. I'm not about to abandon you. You're my foothold inside Essaj's company, the wedge I can use to destroy him."

"Destroy him?" Jalloud asked. "How? Your own Council won't indict him."

"We must *both* work against him," Nawhar answered. "Within the Order and without."

"But could we *prevail?*" Jalloud spat, wiping his mouth. "I've seen much more than you have, Sharajnaghi. He can banish storms from the sky . . ."

"He didn't cow that mob," Nawhar said.

"He didn't *choose* to," Jalloud answered. "For some reason of his own, he decided to suffer them. You asked me if I'd seen through him; believe me, it's impossible. There's something inside him. Every once in a while, you glimpse it in his eyes. And it has plans for you, plans so difficult and knotted you couldn't begin to understand them . . ."

Nawhar nodded. "I know. I've seen it too."

"The devils in Hell obey him . . ."

"I've seen that as well," Nawhar replied. "But who do the devils serve? And what does that tell us about Essaj?"

Jalloud's look grew puzzled. "And yet . . ."

"And yet?"

"I've never felt any evil in the man."

"Then maybe he *is* a madman," Nawhar answered. "Maybe he's quite innocent, and the demon possessing him cloaks itself in his innocence. What difference does it make? He's spreading heresy wherever he goes. And you must betra—*fight* him."

"Betray him?" Jalloud said distantly. He stared at Nawhar for a long time. Finally he laughed, shaking his head like a man who had just been released from a spell. "I cannot *believe* I've been standing here listening to you. After all the pain you've caused me . . ."

"You're listening because you know I'm right," Nawhar broke in. "Because I can see into your heart. What objections did you raise? *Practical* objections. Nothing about the morality of it."

"That's not true," Jalloud protested, with some justice.

But Nawhar was unconcerned. Smelling blood, he took up where he had left off:

"The treason had ceased to trouble you. I sensed the burden lifting from your shoulders. Liberation! No more guilt, just tactics. And fear—but we all have to live with some measure of that. Think, Jalloud! You can have that freedom back again! Turn on him! Help me destroy him. You have nothing to lose but your chains."

Jalloud lifted his hand as if to strike him. Nawhar only smiled.

"Please," the Sharajnaghi said. "I'm quite safe with you. And we both know it."

Jalloud marched past him. Nawhar elected not to follow; there was no need. The man was already a traitor, even if he did not know it yet.

*   *   *

Sigrun waited outside until the doctor arrived, then accompanied him through the temple to the residence, where Gamal was already questioning Essaj, assisted by several priests.

"Ah, Feisal," Gamal said, beckoning the physician. He was holding a small bowl of dates.

"Your instructions?" Feisal asked.

Gamal had taken a bite of date; chewing, he held a hand up for a few moments, then replied: "That woman was struck by a spear. In the breast, right about here—" Pointing the half-eaten fruit, he indicated the spot on himself, then directed Feisal's attention to Essaj. "This fellow healed her, to all appearances. I want you to examine her and give me a full report."

"Where should I take her?" the doctor asked.

"My wife's quarters," the High Priest answered. "She'll show you to a room." He popped the rest of the date into his mouth.

"Very well, My Lord," Feisal replied, rejoining Sigrun and conducting her deeper into the residence. "Spear in the chest, eh?" he asked as they walked along.

"Yes, doctor."

"I don't believe it for an instant."

"Didn't you listen to the soldiers outside?"

"Louts."

"One of *them* struck me with it."

"A likely story."

She plucked at her shift. "Where do you think all this blood came from?"

His eyes darted to the stain. "Who knows? I don't know why Gamal's even bothering with this. Obviously, the time to examine you was when the spear was still *in*."

"He was convinced—"

"Yes, yes," the doctor said impatiently. "What's your name?"

"Sigrun."

"Kragehul," he said knowingly—and sourly. He sniffed, as though she smelled; Sigrun was deeply offended. She was perhaps the most fastidious person she knew.

"Where's your husband?" he asked.

She decided not to mention that she was unmarried. "Off on business."

"What's his name?"

"Khaddam Al-Ramnal."

Feisal stopped dead. "The Sharajnaghi?"

"The Grand Master," Sigrun said.

"Do you think that will make me more likely to believe your story?"

"Is there anything that would?"

"Frankly, no."

While Feisal was examining Sigrun, Gamal's wife Soraya waited just outside the room; Sigrun heard her pacing back and forth. When the doctor opened the curtain, pronouncing Sigrun perfectly fit, Soraya's plump face opened in one of the brightest smiles Sigrun had ever seen. She declared herself incomparably relieved; apparently she had believed that Sigrun had still been in some danger, and had been horribly put out by the fact that the temple guards had inflicted the wound. She gave Sigrun a garment to replace her stained clothing, but when the fit proved far too tentlike—Soraya's figure had gone well beyond opulent—she summoned the wife of a lesser priest and instructed her to surrender a gown of her own.

"There," Soraya said, when Sigrun had donned it. "Doesn't settle all accounts, exactly, but . . ."

Feisal and Sigrun returned to the audience-chamber, where the interrogation was still in full swing. Told to wait outside, they deposited themselves on a marble bench. It seemed at least an hour before Essaj and Gamal emerged, followed by the latter's assistants.

"Do you think it's an accident that one of the Names of God is 'Gods'?" Essaj was saying. "Remember, He appeared to Ibrahim as *three* men."

"But two were angels," Gamal replied. "When they enter the Cities of the Plain, they're clearly identified as such."

"But God also says that *He* is going. Not that *He* is sending them."

"You're making too much of that," the High Priest answered, then noticed Feisal and Sigrun. He motioned them into the audience-chamber.

"What did you find?" he asked the doctor.

Feisal described Sigrun's condition.

"Enough," Gamal said. "No wound at all, that's what you're telling me."

"Yes."

"It was a trick," said one of the lesser priests. "It *had* to be a trick."

Sigrun stamped her foot. Between Feisal and this cretin, she had had quite enough. She did not know what to think about Essaj's claims; but she knew what he had done for her.

"I was at death's door, My Lord," she told Gamal. "*Through* it, maybe. And you saw what happened. You saw me—my soul—floating out of my body. . . ."

"Perhaps," Gamal conceded.

"Master," his assistant cried, "even if it's true, what difference does it make? Essaj denies that God is One. I heard him, just now, and that's not even the worst of—"

Gamal silenced him with a curt gesture. "The Sharajnaghim will judge him."

To which another lieutenant replied: "Then why question him yourself, Master?"

"I wished to make up my own mind. I have my flock to think about."

"And what conclusion have you reached, My Lord?"

"He healed this woman," Gamal replied. "Although by what power, I don't know. Moreover, we must balance his works against his apparent heresies. If he's not from God, his doctrines will wither, and his works will come to nothing. If the Sharajnaghim find him guilty, and he's executed, and rots in the earth, we will have our answer. Otherwise, we'll simply have to live with the irritation of his presence." He turned to Essaj, plainly exasperated. "For the life of me, I don't know what to make of you."

"If you're not against me, you're for me," Essaj answered.

"Don't you imagine that for an instant," Gamal answered.

Essaj's eyes flashed. For a moment he seemed to tower over the High Priest.

"I will imagine what I please," he said. "Count yourself blessed." He bowed slightly, added, "Peace be with you," and made for the door.

"What a character," said Gamal under his breath, then shooed Sigrun after him.

✙

Chapter 17

The first Masters to reach the Anarite çamp were Arghun Khan and Sayid Al-Mashat; they marched directly up to Sharif. Erim stood near, hoping to testify on behalf of his friend.

"Sharif, you idiot!" Arghun exploded. Even though the outburst was not directed at him, Erim found the man's expression particularly hateful; whether it was the sheer intensity of the look, or the twisted foreign features, he was not sure. But if he had been in Sharif's place, he would have felt a strong temptation to strike Arghun.

"Engaging such a large body of them!" Sayid growled, like a great bear. "What possessed you?"

"I had no choice," Sharif answered. "I looked over a rock, and one was staring straight at me. Erim killed him and his friend, but two more blundered onto the scene . . . one thing led to another. Finally the only thing to do was slaughter them all."

"What if some had escaped?" Sayid demanded, his red beard bristling.

"Meaning no disrespect, *Sibi*, but . . . none did."

"Are you sure?" Arghun demanded.

"Yes. They didn't seem to realize how desperate their situation was. And none of them started to flee until it was too late."

Sayid turned to Erim. "And what's your opinion?"

"I believe Sharif acted properly, *Sibi*," Erim replied.

"And what else is he going to say?" Arghun asked Sayid. "They're best friends!"

For now, Erim thought.

Arghun continued: "We should demote the both . . ."

But at that moment, Khaddam and Akram rounded one of the Anarite tents. Smiling, they made directly for Sharif; the Grand Master clapped Sharif on the back.

"I've been told you held the path single-handed," he said.

Sharif nodded.

"Stumbled right into a nest of 'em, eh?" Akram asked him. "Well, you certainly made the best of a bad situation."

"Damn good job," Khaddam said.

"And what if he'd alerted the enemy?" Arghun asked.

"Oh, will you be quiet?" Khaddam answered fiercely. Then his expression softened. "Please."

Arghun subsided.

From the slaves they learned that the Anarites had begun the road some weeks before; several gangs were at work in various locations, all of them along the course that Akram had chosen.

"The Anarites want a shorter route to the Great Slave Road," Akram said. "They picked the easiest path."

"We want to avoid those other work-gangs," Khaddam said. "Is there another way?"

"We *could* swing to the west," Akram answered. "We'd lose half a day, but . . ."

"Can't be helped."

"What about the dead Anarites?" asked Sayid. "If they're discovered . . ."

"We could leave a force here," Arghun said. "They could ambush anyone who comes too close."

Khaddam looked to Akram.

"Can't spare them," Akram said.

"What about a landslide?" Raschid Zekowi asked. "To bury the camp? Surely we could contrive one."

"We can't spare the power," Khaddam said. "We couldn't hope to recover before we launch our attack. I think we'll simply have to take our chances. Even if the bodies *are* found, we'll probably reach Khaur-Al-Jaffar before the news does."

"What do we do about the slaves?" Raschid asked.

"They'll have to come with us, of course," Akram replied.

"And if some of them are spies?" Sayid asked. "They might try to slip away, warn the Anarites."

"You're in charge of Intelligence," Khaddam said. "Have them watched. And questioned, tonight." He looked at the sky. "I'd say we still have two hours before nightfall. Gather up the men. We've wasted enough time here."

The following day, the advance column sighted the distant cone of a volcano in the gap between two peaks. A dark, spired mass rose above its rim.

"That's Khaur-Al-Jaffar, isn't it?" Erim asked.

"It must be," Sharif answered.

How tiny it looks, Erim thought.

"Pity we have to go any closer," he said.

"Lost your enthusiasm, have you?"

"Yes."

"Just don't let the others hear you," Sharif replied.

As Akram had predicted, the change of course set the Sharaj-naghim back by half a day; just before sundown, they arrived in a valley near the foot of the volcano. The plan had called for an afternoon's rest before the assault, but Khaddam decided to press ahead anyway, reasoning that the risk of being discovered was simply too great so close to the fortress.

The ten that had been chosen to penetrate the stronghold assembled at his tent. All were experts with crossbows or throwing-knives, save for Sharif; most had been members of his advance column. Their heads had been shaved after the fashion of the Anarites, leaving only a topknot; each man bore a waterproofed pack containing a hooded Anarite robe, and five *benshaqars*.

Raschid Zekowi and an assistant administered Shoua's night-vision drug, jabbing the raiders in the shoulder with coated needles. Large quantities of the drug had been prepared; eventually it would be given to the other troops, but in a much smaller—and safer—dose. If all went well, they would need it for a far shorter time than Sharif's men.

Khaddam led the raiders in prayer; then, as they were about to depart, Akram took Sharif aside.

"Which tower controls the portcullis?" he asked, for the third time.

"The eastern tower," Sharif answered.

"And as you come out of the keep . . ."

"The eastern tower will be on my left."

"What's the signal?" Akram asked.

"Three sweeps of a torch."

"God go with you," Akram said.

As the troop slipped away into the gathering dusk, he turned to Khaddam.

"Don't worry," the Grand Master said. "We're going to win. I can feel it."

"I'm delighted to hear it," Akram replied. "But will you and I live to see tomorrow?"

Khaddam laughed. "Such trivial concerns you have."

"Will we live?" Akram pressed. "What does your intuition tell you about that?"

"I'd better not vouch for *your* future. Just think how annoyed you'd be if I told you you were going to survive, and—" He drew his finger across his throat.

"You're right."

"Those damn mortal wounds," Khaddam went on. "They always annoy *me*."

Raschid turned to them with a puzzled expression. He was well known for his complete humorlessness. "Pardon me," he said. "What are you talking about?"

"Don't trouble yourself," Khaddam said.

Akram nudged him with an elbow. "Remember the time we were *both* killed?"

Erim had never been subjected to the night-vision drug before, and at first he was not aware of its effect—the dusk merely seemed to last a very long time, fading gradually into something very much like very bright moonlight. There were no colors, just a bluish shimmer off the rocks, and the grey glow of flesh, cloth and leather; the sky was very pale, the stars like diamonds.

The group proceeded to the base of the volcano. Actually there were two cones; the outermost had a gradual slope, hard frozen lava, fairly smooth to the touch. Here and there jagged towers rose from the incline, ancient crags that had been imprisoned when the volcano had first formed. After what he had been through in the last few days, Erim found the first part of the climb no great difficulty.

Worse lay ahead. A moatlike ring of water had collected between the first crater and the second; it was bitterly cold, practically robbing Erim of breath—simply entering it was like being struck in the chest. At first he could barely swim, even though exertion warmed him after a while. He was glad to know that the inner lake, with its submerged vent, would not be so chill; reaching the far side, he gasped a prayer of gratitude.

But scaling the inner cone proved every bit as much of an ordeal. Giving off a sulphurous reek, the grade was steep, and composed of some sort of gritty clinker, strewn with chunks of pumice. Many spots were loosely packed and treacherous; the pumice crumbled underhand, the fragments very sharp. By the time the group gained the top, Erim's hands were raw and bleeding.

The crater-rim had been levelled to form a broad road. Erim could see several small campfires located at intervals along the path. Khaur-Al-Jaffar lay directly across from the Sharajnaghim, carved out of the mightiest pinnacle that had been swallowed up by the volcano, a crag which formed part of the crater's inner wall. The fortress was a vast black outline against the sky, lights showing in scores of tiny windows; to Erim's altered sight, the casements blazed with a fierce brilliance.

Beneath the stronghold a huge opening shone grey. *Sewer-mouth*, Erim thought. He had been told that blood glowed brightly, even when dry; tens of thousands of sacrificial victims had been pushed down that slide into the lake—hence the illumination. Undoubtedly the slant was crusted inches thick with gore. But that fact, loathsome as it was, would ultimately work for him and his companions; the crust would give purchase to cleated sandals and climbing-claws.

If we ever reach the sewer, he told himself.

Gigantic shapes swam slowly before the aperture. Circling with a grace that utterly belied their vastness, they submerged and sur-faced as though gliding through a cloudy sky, fogging the water with their light. There were crocodiles with paddlelike feet and tails, shark-shapes with dragonlike heads and triple dorsal fins; a colossal long-necked turtle climbed out of the water onto a ledge, staring about balefully with eyes like points of fire. Some of the creatures were so strange that Erim had to struggle to make sense of what he was seeing—several looked for all the world like long diaphanous ribbons, moving with a bizarre corkscrew motion, while others seemed to be long trains of pinions, like a dozen huge stingrays or bats linked together.

"All right, you've seen the bastards," Sharif said. "Time to visit those campfires."

After dispatching men to kill the sentries at the southernmost, he led the remainder towards the nearest, which lay directly across the crater from the fortress. Three Anarites in blankets were sitting by the small blaze, while a fourth was leaning on a spear, looking out over the slope. None seemed aware of the approaching threat.

Sharif whispered instructions to his crossbowmen, assigning targets. The Sharajnaghim drew very close to the Anarites before the man on his feet cocked his head as though he had heard something.

Sharif raised his hand. His men halted.

"Password?" the Anarite called, reaching for a horn on his baldric.

"Now," Sharif told his men in a low voice.

Speeding shafts blurred into long grey beams. Erim saw a flash as one struck the upright Anarite between the eyes; blood flew like sparks from the deep-buried missile. Two of his comrades were punched straight back like overturned idols, but a fourth bent forward at the last moment, reaching for a bottle, the bolt meant for him plucking his hood back from his head.

"Erim," Sharif said.

Erim drew a knife and sprinted towards the Anarite. Sitting up, swearing, the man clapped a hand to his pate as though the quarrel had cut him, then stared wildly about at the corpses. Erim put a knife in him, just above the collarbone.

Sharif and the others came forward. Erim retrieved his blade.

The crossbowman who had missed, a fellow named Fadlallah, apologized to Sharif.

"I'm without excuse, sir," he insisted.

"Nonsense," Sharif answered. "He ducked."

Going to the fire, he took a brand burning at one end and tossed it down the slope; that was the signal for the men carrying the sheep-blood. If all had gone well, they were already past the moat-lake.

"You and the others go on ahead," Sharif said to Erim, nodding towards the last fire. "I'd best remain here."

"You think we can manage by ourselves?"

"Get moving," Sharif replied.

⊹

Chapter 18

Some time later, the cask-bearers reached the crater-rim, one hundred of them, each with a two-gallon keg strapped to his back; the blood had been been drained at Qanar-Sharaj, and treated to prevent clotting. Once Sharif's party reassembled, he ordered the barrels broached and lowered into the crater at a spot where the wall hung sheer. Before long, a glowing pennonlike stain was spreading along the edge of the lake, carried on the current towards the sewer-mouth.

On the opposite side of the crater, trotting along the road with his men, Sharif looked now and then at the stain; it lengthened quickly, and he was delighted by its progress. But Erim was not so pleased.

"The current's much faster than we were told," he whispered.

"So?" Sharif asked.

"We'll have a harder time swimming against it," Erim said. "And it'll sweep the blood back to us that much sooner."

They moved as close to Khaur-Al-Jaffar as they dared; some two hundred yards from the fortress, Sharif signalled a halt, trying to make out the troop's ultimate objective, the gatehouse that warded the southern approach. Its form was lost amid the shadow of the mountainous structure looming behind it; all he could see were the windows, diamond slits cut through the darkness.

Beside the road, the cliff-wall had remained sheer, grooved with vertical gutters eaten in the packed ash by rainwater. Donning their

137

climbing-claws, the Sharajnaghim descended along one of these chimneys as quickly as they were able.

Sharif began to hear great splashes; looking out through the front of the gutter, he saw luminous shapes slipping past, off on the far side of the lake, following the blood-trail. The lure was working.

Nearing the bottom, he told his companions to wedge themselves in place, then lowered himself into the lukewarm water. He swam a few yards from the chimney, out into the current. As Erim had predicted, it was quite strong. Swiftly carried away from the gutter, he swam back to the cliff-wall, hauling himself along with his climbing-claws.

Eyeing the sewer-mouth, he saw that the guardians were gone— except for one of the gigantic turtles. It lay totally motionless on its ledge, neck extended on the stone. He wondered if it might be dead.

Slowly its head came up, then dipped, snout disappearing beneath the surface of the water. An instant later, the monster slid into the lake with a thunderous splash; so suddenly had it moved that Sharif thought for a moment that the ledge must have upended beneath it. Swiftly it paddled after the other beasts.

Sharif hauled himself back to the chimney, whispering to Erim: "They're gone. Come on."

He heard Erim pass the order. Moments later Erim slipped down beside him.

"Feels good," he said, treading water, glowing hands sweeping beneath the surface like submerged firebrands.

"You were right about the current," Sharif told him. "We'll have to cling to the cliff."

"That might be easier than what we planned," Erim said.

They moved out of the chimney to make room for Fadlallah; another man followed shortly, one named Samir.

This isn't going too badly, Sharif thought—

Just as the wave from the turtle's plunge came rolling up.

Feeling the lake heave around him, Sharif reacted instinctively, pushing off from the wall with his legs, diving straight into the swell. Water rushed in his ears. The wave enveloped him, pushing him against the stone, his pack taking most of the brunt. Kicking back to the top, he surfaced in the foaming backwash, the bubbles about him shining brilliantly in the starlight. Erim and Fadlallah rose on either side of him. The current carried the three westwards some distance before they managed to snag the wall once more.

Sharif looked back towards the chimney. A body floated towards him, face down in a blot of milky radiance, the back of its head one huge incandescent wound.

Samir, Sharif thought, grabbing him and turning him over. The man was dead, beyond a doubt. Sharif guessed the wave had caught him on the surface, smashing his head against the cliff.

Sharif let him go, the current dragging the corpse from his hand. He and Erim pulled themselves back to the crevice once more. Labibh Terzi was clinging desperately to the side of it with one hand, climbing-claw sunk into the soft stone.

"The wave," he said. "It spurted up the chimney, wrenched me loose—my left arm's numb."

"Broken?" Sharif asked.

"I don't know."

"Everyone all right up there?" Sharif whispered to the men above.

"We're fine," one answered. "Where did that wave come from?"

"One of the creatures leaped into the water. We should be all right from now on, though." *I hope,* Sharif thought. "Come on."

"What about me?" Labibh asked.

"We're not going to leave you," Sharif said. "You can cling to me."

As the other men descended, Sharif removed the claw from Labibh's hand and let him take hold of his pack, then hauled himself back out of the chimney, moving towards the sewer-mouth. Burdened as he was, and fighting the current, he found the going slow and difficult, the others bunching up close behind.

By then, the pennon of sheep-blood, much diluted, had reached them; the water was a swirling grey mist, the cliff-face dimly painted by its light.

At length Erim volunteered to take Labibh. Sharif looked back towards the place where the casks had been lowered into the water. The monsters had collected there, swimming back and forth, their movements stirring the surface of the lake into thousands of coruscating wavelets.

Sharif continued towards the sewer. His head was beginning to hurt; he guessed it was the drug. *Sibi* Raschid had warned them about that—they had been given such a massive dose. Sharif wondered when it would wear off.

Up ahead, the glow from the sewer-mouth was swiftly intensifying; he could see white streams crawling down the ramp into the water, brightening the cloud of sheep-blood. It could only mean one thing: sacrificial victims sliding slowly down the slant, preceded by their own runnelling gore.

Before long a tangled knot, somewhat darker than the blood, came rolling sluggishly into view, like a clot of rainwashed mud. It vanished in the water, then surfaced again, much flattened, a raft of cadavers, drifting on the current.

"Good God," Sharif heard Erim gasp.

Soon a second mass appeared, larger by several times, hitching for a moment on the threshold, just long enough for the upper portion to spill forward, sending a huge crescent of bodies out into the lake.

The fog of sheep-blood about Sharif turned swiftly to grey fire. The first raft of corpses drifted near, rotating slowly. It passed by the Sharajnaghim, but came close enough for Sharif to get a good look at the bodies.

All were naked, and horribly splayed. They floated limply, flesh conforming to the heavings of the wavelets with perfect jointlessness. Great wounds split their arms and legs, gaped in their backs.

Boned like fish, Sharif thought. What monstrous rites would require such mutilations?

The second mass swirled near, its fringes brushing the side of the cliff. Sharif closed his eyes, shuddering as a body touched him. It wrapped partially around him, and he felt a tremendous pressure; looking down at his shoulder, he saw that three corpses had broken free from the raft, and backed up against him like floating, sodden blankets. The weight almost pulled him from the wall, but he managed to flatten himself against the stone, and the current immediately dislodged the bodies, which whirled away to the side.

As the Sharajnaghim pressed closer to their goal, more of the hideous mounds slid down into the water. Several formed rafts so large that the troop had to submerge to avoid being swept away; Sharif helped Erim with Labibh, who seemed to be getting steadily weaker. Each time they surfaced, the injured man begged their pardon for the trouble he was causing them.

Finally the sewer's grisly discharges ceased, at least for the time being. The group made better progress. Fadlallah took Labibh from Erim.

Abruptly the rock wall changed, packed ash giving way to black stone; they had reached the mighty pier that had been swallowed up by the crater.

Pausing, Sharif looked up along the cliff-face. From its base, he could not see the fortress but knew it lay directly above, partially made of hewn blocks, partially carved from the pier itself, the stone beneath it honeycombed with tunnels.

He returned his attention to the water-beasts. Several thousand yards away, they were directly across from him.

But even as he watched, some began to move southeastwards along the rim of the lake. He did not need to be told the reason; the blood from the sewer-mouth had reached them on the current, perhaps even some of the bodies.

No matter, he thought. *We've more than enough time to reach the opening.*

But he had not reckoned on the black stone. It was smooth and impenetrable; the climbing-claws could find no purchase on it. That left the Sharajnaghim with only one choice—to try and breast the current.

It proved terrifically hard. They made some headway, but very slowly. An Adept called Wakim joined Fadlallah in bearing up Labibh; before long, Sharif heard a commotion behind him, and looked back to see Wakim thrashing in the water, both hands clapped to his temples, blood spurting from his nostrils. It looked as though he were exhaling flame.

The drug, Sharif guessed. *It's bursting his veins . . .*

Wakim started to scream; reaching around the man's head, Labibh gagged him with his wrist. The victim jerked back, but his voice had deserted him. With a hiss he dropped from sight, straight down as though he had been made of lead.

God, Sharif thought. *Eight men left, and one of them crippled . . .* He wondered if anyone above had heard that shriek.

Time and again he twisted to look at the monsters. As far as he could tell, they were *all* coming now; he could hear immense splashings, and sounds like vast shears opening and closing—all too vividly, he found himself picturing ravenous jaws rending boned flesh.

"We're not going to make it," someone panted.

"We'll make it," Erim answered. "The corpses will keep them busy."

But for how long? Sharif thought. He reckoned the distance to the sewer-mouth at perhaps two hundred feet—but it might as well have been a mile.

His headache grew steadily worse. He became aware of a hot, rusty smell. Exertion clearly aggravated the drug's effect—were his veins about to burst too?

"Don't scream!" he heard someone whisper. "Whatever you do, don't scream!"

Looking over his shoulder, Sharif saw a second man floundering in the water, his whole lower face dripping with light. Others closed in, bearing him up. His struggles ceased.

But he didn't die. Muttering, head twitching, he bobbed in the water.

"What should we do?" asked the men holding him.

Sharif swore under his breath. "Bring him," he answered.

"But, sir—"

"We can't let him drown," Sharif answered.

The current had carried them back fifty feet at least. Making up the distance was murderous work. Sharif began to feel sharp pains in his skull, very different from the throbbing he had endured so far; the rusty smell intensified, burning his nostrils, and he thought:

Any second now, and your skull's going to split.

Even so, he struggled to force more speed into his increasingly leaden limbs: the chop-and-splash of monstrous jaws had drawn ever closer.

There's hardly any blood in the water here, he told himself, battling his fear. *Maybe they won't come any closer than that last raft of corpses . . .*

But hardly had the thought passed through his mind when the water in front of the sewer-mouth suddenly flamed silver; radiant torrents spilled into the lake, followed swiftly by the vastest knot of bodies yet.

He glanced back at the creatures. Two long chelonian necks lifted high above the wavelets; the turtles were clearly staring at the sewer-mouth, limp shapes swaying from their closed bladelike beaks. Leaving the other creatures behind, they came plowing through the water like moving islands.

And if that sight were not fearsome enough, several of the crocodiles and dragonsharks came speeding in their wake.

Sharif turned once more. The corpses were almost upon him. He dived beneath them, swimming underwater. Lungs nearly bursting, he surfaced in the midst of the human flotsam, head pushing up between flaccid bodies, cold flesh trailing down his face; gulping air, he struggled loose and submerged again.

When he rose at last beyond the raft, he saw that he was only thirty feet or so from the sewer-mouth. His vision wavered; pain and dizziness assailed him.

Still his limbs churned through the water. Temples about to crack, he locked his fingers over the side of the entrance, then halted, seizing air in great wracking gulps.

Someone seized his tunic.

"Sharif," came Erim's voice. "Thank God."

Sharif hardly had the strength to look at him.

Fadlallah thrust past them, without Labibh.

"They're coming," he breathed. "We must get up on the ramp!"

Sharif raked himself up the thickly crusted slant, driving with his cleated sandals. The incline was covered with an oozing film, but solid underneath, slightly porous, like weathered brick. They went a few yards up the slope before exhaustion stilled them once more. Claws embedded in the clotted gore, they hung belly-down on the incline.

Sharif heard other men scrambling up behind them; hanging on with one hand, he thrust himself up onto his side, squinting at them. There were only two, one named Abdollah, the other Nakir.

A wave washed up over the threshold, almost reaching Sharif's feet; Abdullah managed to hold on, but Nakir, farther back, started to slide.

Draconian jaws blossomed out of the water, huge teeth clotted with strings and fragments of meat; Sharif was not sure, but he thought he saw Labibh's sheared-off head wedged between two serrate fangs.

Nakir slid to the fence of teeth rising from the dragonshark's lower jaw, the fangs themselves halting his descent. He started to claw his way upwards once more.

A vast speeding shape snaked around the lefthand corner of the sewer-mouth, knocking the dragonshark's head aside. Before Sharif could flinch, the turtle snapped Nakir up, then retracted its serpentine neck.

Sharif clambered upwards as quickly as he could. Claws hooked his trouser-leg, and for an instant he was sure he was finished. Then he heard cursing, and realized that Abdollah, flailing his way up the slope, had apparently snagged his leg by accident.

There came a titanic slap of impact, and a blast of air fierce enough to toss Sharif's sodden hair; the climbing-claw jerked against his trousers, and he felt Abdollah's weight lessen sudden- ly—and drastically. Accompanied by a sharp, shrieking whistle, a heavy rasp shook the passage, the sound of a monstrous body sliding down the incline.

Sharif glanced back at his leg. Abdollah's hand was still hooked on the trouser-leg, but nothing remained of the man below the shoulders. Beyond, a crocodile was slipping slowly back into the water on its stomach, nostrils emitting the whistle, vapor jetting from the openings. Sharif was struck by just how tiny they looked. Hitching his leg upwards, he plucked Abdollah's hand loose.

But to his horror, Abdollah's expression changed; first dismay, then accusation flooded the staring eyes as the mangled remnant glided downwards on the blood-slick surface.

"Forgive me," Sharif sobbed, averting his gaze. Despite the danger, it was a few moments before he could continue his ascent.

He heard vast movements below, splashing and roars; had the creatures fallen to fighting each other? In any event, there was no more pursuit.

He was exhausted to the marrow, but mercifully, the pain in his head had lessened. It seemed the light from the crusted blood had dimmed somewhat—was the drug wearing off?

Erim and Fadlallah were some distance above him; he saw them vanish into an opening in the righthand wall, and crawled in behind them. The passage was a tributary conduit, water trickling along its bottom.

Sharif settled on his side, massaging his aching skull.

"Is anyone else left?" Erim asked.

"No," Sharif answered, the image of Abdollah's receding face still imprinted on his mind.

☩

Chapter 19

The sentries mounted on the western battlements of Khaur-Al-Jaffar could see nothing of the lake below; the fires of the watch-men were all they could discern along the crater-rim. By the sound of it, the water-beasts seemed unusually active, but there was nothing alarming about that. Even when the splashings and roarings grew fainter, as though the creatures had crossed to the far side of the lake, the sentries paid scant heed; some of the beasts had hollowed out nests there, and battles frequently erupted as they transported great cropfuls of carrion to their young.

True, one of the sentries thought that he heard a man scream; but his companions dismissed the idea. If he had heard anything at all, which they doubted, it had been one of the beasts expelling air through its nostrils.

"It wasn't like that at all," the man insisted.

Laughing, shaking their heads, they simply walked away from him.

One of the Sharajnaghim who had borne the blood-casks nudged a large chunk of burning debris from the western watchfire, then kicked it powerfully down the slope.

Below, the main body had paused at the moat between the craters. Seeing the signal, Khaddam ordered his men across. All had been given doses of Shoua's drug, just enough for them to find their way on the slopes.

Khaddam was astonished by the lake's coldness. Akram's teeth chattered loudly; it was like listening to birds pecking grain off a sill.

"Beyond endurance," Akram grumbled under his breath. "If I'd known—"

"What would you have done?" Khaddam asked.

"Laid on some fat."

"Doesn't help," Khaddam answered.

"I'm freezing!" someone gasped behind them. "I'm going to sink!"

"Don't be an idiot!" Akram answered, raising his voice just shy of a shout. "It's nothing!"

Lying in the conduit, his strength returning, Erim grew aware of a far-off rhythmic crackling.

"Do you hear that?" Sharif asked.

"Yes," Erim said.

"What do you think it is?"

Erim would not hazard a guess. But Fadlallah said:

"Bones?"

"What makes you think that?" Erim replied.

"Remember the bodies?" Fadlallah asked. "The Anarites must do something with the skeletons. Maybe they're grinding them up."

"What for?" Sharif asked.

"Don't they use powdered bone in their rituals?"

"Not by the ton—"

Sharif broke off; Erim heard something moving outside. A mound of bodies slid past the mouth of the conduit.

Erim blinked, rubbing his eyes; even though they still pierced the murk, he could no longer see quite so clearly. That slight headache was also fading.

"We'd better get up into the fortress before the drug wears off completely," Sharif said, as though reading Erim's mind. "Could we use this conduit?"

"We don't know where it comes out," Erim answered. "We'd better follow the route Akram gave us."

Sharif in the lead, they climbed back out onto the ramp. The air was thick and rancid; they passed large protuberances glued to the slant, aggregates of corpses that had stuck and withered, drying like clumps of beached seaweed.

Far ahead, Erim could see the top of the incline; a black archway yawned above the dimly glowing ramp. The crunching came from the opening, along with loud thuds and scrapings. A low barrier—bodies, apparently—ran across the threshold.

Something massive heaved into view above the grisly wall, hulking from side to side. Erim had a brief impression of vast shoulders, thick limbs, plates and knobs; he could not clearly distinguish a head or face.

The shape moved back out of sight, but not before shoving a small hill of cadavers through the wall. The glutinous pile tumbled slowly down the slant, like chopped bait overturned from a cup.

The Sharajnaghim crawled to one side, the corpses passing with a mucky squelching sound.

"What is that thing up there?" Fadlallah whispered. "I couldn't get a good look at it."

"We'll find out soon enough," Sharif said.

They resumed the ascent. Several times Erim saw the creature move past the opening, but no more corpses were thrust down the incline. Presently Sharif told his companions:

"No use risking all three of us. Wait here."

Erim wanted to follow, but Sharif's decision made perfect sense. Heart in his throat, Erim watched him drag himself up to the gap that had been thrust in the wall of corpses.

After a time, Sharif beckoned. They crawled up with him, peering over the edge.

Beyond lay a colossal circular chamber, like the bottom of a well; it corresponded to nothing in the route Erim had memorized. Had Akram's information been faulty? The plans of Khaur-Al-Jaffar's interior *were* twenty years old . . .

The floor was heaped with human remains, bones and corpses, divided into separate piles, the walls charcoal-grey in their glow. Most of the bodies appeared to be intact, except for wounds across the throat; but there were no whole skeletons. Skulls, ribcages and limb-bones were jumbled all together.

In the midst loomed a monstrosity like an enormous armored ape, impossibly broad, leaning forward on bulging arms. Its head barely rose above the line of its knobbed shoulders; the eyeless face fell sheer beneath a spiked brow, mouth a vertical slit between two hammerlike mandibles.

Reaching with an enormous four-fingered hand, the creature seized an entire pile of bones. The jaws opened, disclosing a second set of mandibles, which yawned to reveal yet a third.

The thing heeled back. For the first time Erim saw that it had no legs, but was balancing itself on a thick insectlike abdomen.

The Titan's fist opened. Bones rained into the clashing mandibles; chips flew from the punishing jaws. Fadlallah had been right, at least in part—the skeletons *were* being ground to powder.

The thing leaned forward once more, walking on its knuckles, the vast bag of its body dragging behind. Greedily it went from bone-pile to bone-pile, devouring them all.

Then it turned to the corpses.

Long bladelike claws sprang from its fingertips. Holding a body in one palm, it slashed it with five swift cuts, then flicked the skeletons piecemeal out of the flesh with its claw-tips. Each body was boned in seconds; tossed aside, they slapped the floor like wet garments. Fascinated by the monster's dexterity, Erim was amazed at how little the spectacle sickened him.

"Second line of defense," Sharif whispered. "The Anarites send it their sacrifices, and it guards the ramp . . ."

"But how do we get past it?"

A bottomless chasm of a voice answered: "YOU DON'T."

Erim gaped at the Bone-Eater. Its blind face was trained directly upon them.

"Back down?" Fadlallah asked Sharif.

All we can do, Erim thought. The colossus couldn't possibly squeeze itself through the archway.

It might reach a long way in, though . . .

"Back down," Sharif said, letting himself slip.

But only if it threw itself onto the floor . . .

Pushing off with its knuckles, the creature bounded forward.

"Erim!" Sharif cried.

Erim ignored him, climbing up into the chamber. As the monster crashed nearer, he slipped out of his pack and flung it; once it landed, he primed the *benshaqars* inside and retreated back onto the blood-greased slope, his feet going instantly out from under him. Landing hard on his stomach, he began to slide . . .

The Bone-Eater seized him before he went two yards.

Chest well clear of the pack, it was resting on one arm. Squeezing the breath from Erim's lungs, it pulled him out of the sewer, then dropped to the floor, its free hand lunging after his companions.

Erim heard a blast, almost completely muffled by the monster's body. The Bone-Eater jerked; the hand holding Erim sprang open.

Getting to his feet, the Sharajnaghi backed swiftly away, watching as the thing pushed itself off the floor and tilted backwards, a five-foot-wide hole blown in the middle of its chest, the wound pouring forth a phosphorescent cascade. Tottering, it turned towards Erim.

"YOUUUU. . . ." thundered the gargantuan voice. Then the creature folded backwards over its tail, arms outstretched on either side of it.

Erim raced back to the archway. "It's dead," he called.

Sharif and Fadlallah clambered to the top.

"How did you kill it?" Sharif asked.

Erim explained.

"Destroying your pack in the process," Sharif said. "So much for your Anarite garb."

"I'll waylay someone when we get out of here," Erim answered.

"If there *is* a way out of here," Fadlallah said.

The walls of the chamber were at least two hundred feet high, completely smooth and sheer; dim flickering light played over a domed ceiling.

"We may have to go back to that conduit after all," Sharif said.

"No," Erim said. "Look."

Three figures had appeared at the lip of the well.

"Ghashar!" one cried. "Ghashar!"

"They're calling to the monster," Sharif whispered.

"Must've heard those shouts," Erim said.

One of the figures vanished from the edge. A ghostly rope-ladder descended along the side of the wall. Erim could hardly distinguish it—the drug's effect was barely a fraction of what it had been. Two of the Anarites started down the ladder, carrying torches.

"Do you still have your knives?" Sharif asked Erim.

"Some of them."

"Good," Sharif said, taking off his climbing-claws and his pack. "Fadlallah, it's time for us to switch sides."

At the bottom, the Anarites started across the floor; even with the torches, they still could see nothing of the Bone-Eater.

"Ghashar?" they called.

"He's dead," a voice replied.

Cowls raised, two men came towards them, pulling a third in Sharajnaghi garb.

"This bastard killed him," said the tall fellow on the left.

"How?" one of the Anarites demanded.

"Knives," said the captive.

"Knives? Against *Ghashar*?"

"It was easy," the prisoner boasted. "Let me show you."

His captors let him go. The last thing the torchbearers ever saw was the Sharajnaghi's hands darting into his sleeves.

Erim took the robes from the corpse most nearly his size. Then he and his companions stamped out the torches and went to the rope-ladder.

From the far side of the chamber, there came a deep moan, as of a great ship straining against its cables. Erim squinted through the thickening darkness. A faint shimmering mass, the Bone-Eater stirred; back to the Sharajnaghim, it rose like a moonlit thunderhead.

"NOT . . . DEAD . . . YET," it rumbled, and spun, abdomen dragging over the stone.

Sharif in the lead, Fadlallah last, the Sharajnaghim hastened up the ladder. The well reverberated with the boom of the Bone-Eater bounding on its knuckles.

"COME BACK!" Ghashar bellowed.

A cross-piece snapped beneath Erim as he set his weight on it. He howled in surprise, his foot shooting onto the round beneath, which gave as well.

"COME BACK TO THE FEAST!" Ghashar cried.

Taking hold of the vertical strands, Erim hauled himself upwards.

By the sound of it, the Bone-Eater's pace was slowing. Its breath bubbled and wheezed. Erim prayed desperately for the thing to succumb to its wound; it vented a volcanic, tearing cough, and he heard fluid splatter. Ghashar drew to a halt.

God is Great, Erim thought.

Almost immediately, the booming began once more.

Erim looked down. The Bone-Eater arrived at the foot of the ladder. Its intended victims were too far up to pluck off, but Ghashar could simply pull the whole ladder down . . .

Fadlallah drew a dagger, and just as the creature caught the ladder, sliced the strands below his handhold, the severed section dropping away. Ghashar roared in frustration. Gripping the knife between his teeth, Fadlallah resumed his climb.

Erim thought surely they were safe after that; but he had not counted on the monster's intelligence.

"DIE, DAMN YOU!" Ghashar bellowed, just before a whistling shower of bones struck the side of the well.

Fadlallah shrieked. Erim saw him pitch backwards from the ladder, tumbling end over end. The Bone-Eater spread its manidibles wide, awaiting the pure pleasure of crushing Fadlallah's life out between its multiple jaws.

Prime your benshaqars, Erim thought. *That's what I'd do. . . .*

Fadlallah dropped into the hideous maw. The innermost jaws snapped on his legs; the outermost clacked closed, obscuring him from view. Erim never heard the middle set shut; there was only the thump of the *benshaqars* detonating.

Splendid, Fadlallah, Erim thought, tears welling in his eyes. *God go with you.*

And Ghashar the Mighty slumped down along the wall.

Chapter 20

Kneeling on the rim of the inner crater, Khaddam and Akram peered through the night towards Khaur-Al-Jaffar. Now that their first dose of the drug had worn off, the fortress was invisible except for its redlit casements.

"They should be deep inside by now," Akram said.

"And going the right way, God willing," Khaddam answered. "I hope those diagrams of yours are still accurate."

"They were the best I could do," Akram said.

There was a long silence.

"What are you thinking about?" Khaddam asked.

"The fact that we've come to the endgame at last."

"Things could go wrong," Khaddam said. "Perhaps you'd find that something of a relief."

"In some ways," Akram admitted.

"Still worrying about the Same Old Thing, eh? What we'll do when the Anarites are gone?"

"And also, if truth be told, whether we're doing the right thing now."

"You *still* think they might not be responsible?" Khaddam asked.

"Oh, I'm fairly certain. But not enough to feel completely comfortable, if you see what I mean."

Khaddam laughed. "You sound so irresolute. It's really rather deceptive of you, you know. You never show the slightest indecision once the slaughter starts, yet you feel compelled to torment yourself beforehand."

"*Torment*'s too strong a word," Akram replied.

"Perhaps. But whatever it is that you do to yourself, you should stop it. You're a warrior. Shedding blood is what you do best. You should *see* yourself when someone shows you a new way to slaughter your foes. Your eyes *shine*."

"They don't," Akram protested.

"Ask anyone," Khaddam replied.

Akram grunted. "I suppose they might at that," he said. "But there's nothing I hate more than seeing my boys killed. I'd give it all up gladly if we never had cause to fight again."

"In short, you're aching for the end of the world," Khaddam answered. "Well, then, be of good cheer. If those dreams are any indication, it's right around the corner."

Sharif climbed over the edge of Ghashar's well, finding himself in a broad circular chamber with a domed ceiling; torches guttered along the walls.

There was no rail around the pit. The rope-ladder hung from a reel attached to the ceiling. Fresh and dried blood covered the floor. Sharif perceived only the faintest glow from it now; he reasoned it had leaked from the sacrificial victims as they were brought to the pit.

Five men came through a doorway towards him. He remembered the three standing at the top of the well; one had departed before the others climbed down—had he gone to fetch reinforcements?

Erim climbed up next to Sharif. Sharif immediately took him by the shoulder.

"Pretend you're wounded," Sharif whispered, supporting him. "Fall down, crawl behind them."

Gasping with mock pain, Erim affected a severe limp as Sharif led him towards the Anarites.

"Who are you two?" the foremost demanded.

"We heard Ghashar bellowing," Sharif said. "I think he's dead . . ."

Erim chose that moment to fall to his hands and knees.

"But what were you doing down here?" the leader asked.

Erim let out a sob, working his way forward.

"Can't you see he's wounded?" Sharif asked.

The leader's hand drifted to his swordhilt. "What were you

doing down here?" he growled once more.

"Are you just going to let him die?" Sharif answered.

"Majid, Tahir," the leader said, over his shoulder.

"Sir?" two of his men replied.

He indicated Erim. "Get him on his feet."

They went to the Sharajnaghi.

"Stand up," one snarled.

Erim only moaned and laid down. They kicked him, but he would not stir.

"Pick him up!" the leader cried.

They bent to comply. Sharif slipped a climbing-claw over his hand.

The leader drew his scimitar. "What've you got there?" he demanded.

Majid and Tahir shrieked. Rearing up between them, Erim elbowed them aside, red knives in either hand.

Stepping forward, Sharif tore out the leader's throat with the climbing-claw, simultaneously seizing the black-robe's scimitar.

As the body sank, Sharif found himself staring into the goggling eyes of another Anarite; without hesitating, he lashed out with the sword. The Anarite's head flopped backwards over his shoulders, hanging by a thread.

The last was on his knees, one of Erim's blades in the side of his head, the other in his neck. Erim had to let him fall and set his foot on the carcass before he could pull them out.

Hurriedly the Sharajnaghim dragged the corpses to the pit and pushed them in. Then Sharif unslung the case which held the halves of his quarterstaff and screwed the pieces together. Originally it had been an Anarite weapon—Sharif had taken it from a dead black-robe ten years before. The Anarites were known for their skill with such arms—the stave's first owner had very nearly killed Sharif.

"Do you have any idea of where we are?" Sharif asked Erim as they set off through the door.

"Yes," Erim said. "Remember the plans Akram showed us? The incline grew much steeper towards the top of the sewer. I think that stretch was carved out into Ghashar's well. If I'm right, we're directly below the main slave-pens, about three hundred feet under the ground floor. And right on course."

"Only two of us left," Sharif said. "Think we'll still be able to do any good?"

"We've still got your *benshaqars*," Erim replied. "Even if we don't raise the portcullis, we'll surely clean out one of those towers."

They approached two long rectangular bays that opened opposite each other. Fluid tapped against the floor.

Looking inside one of the bays, craning his head back, Sharif saw a great platform descending along the shaft, and caught one of the falling drops on his hand. Moving back out into the torchlight in the corridor, he saw that the liquid was blood.

"This must be where they lower the victims from the altar-room," he said.

Going to a stairwell, they climbed several flights, finally emerging in a gallery that overlooked a vast excavation, several hundred yards long, crowded with naked slaves, male and female, young and old. Most were Tarchan, by their look; the stench of unwashed bodies was abominably thick and sour.

Equipped with crossbows, armored overseers watched from the gallery, but allowed Erim and Sharif to pass without so much as a word. Going through a tunnel, the Sharajnaghim came out in another such gallery; but here the pit was only half full. On the level above, they discovered two enclosures that were completely devoid of prisoners.

"We're close to the main altar-room," Erim said. "These pits must've been emptied."

Presently they came to the ground floor. Up ahead, a long line of slaves was creeping along the wall; there seemed to be at least one guard for every three captives. Going nearer, Sharif saw that the prisoners were chained together at the neck, and that their wrists and ankles were manacled. The line vanished inside a towering doorway, from which came a steady chorus of howls and screams; Sharif began to pick out several voices chanting in Old Malochian.

Two great carts rumbled through the doorway, drawn by bleeding thralls; overseers lashed out with many-thonged whips, the leather strands tipped with metal balls.

The carts were piled high with corpses.

When the Sharajnaghim came to the arch, Sharif was unable to

keep himself from halting and looking inside. Three black altars
stood at the end of the cavernous hall. An idol loomed behind
each; Sharif had participated in the destruction of several Anarite
shrines, but had never seen such images. One was a serrate wheel,
another the mutilated statue of a naked woman; the last seemed to
be a child covered with insects.

The line of slaves went almost to the dais; there the foremost
were uncoupled from the rest, dragged to the slabs, and slaughtered. Three priests wielded the knives; headdresses flanked by
small ram's horns marked them as Masters. The man in the
middle, a tall spidery figure, drew Sharif's attention.

"That's Achmed Hakkar," Sharif whispered to Erim. "The
Grand Master."

They continued on their way.

Sharif added: "I saw him once, at the Khan's Court. His eyes
are hideous. He looks like he could kill with a glance."

They soon passed from the keep into the inner courtyard. There
were no troops to be seen, even on the formidable wall that
separated it from the outer courtyard. The gate was wide open,
and the Sharajnaghim went through without challenge.

The outer courtyard was likewise empty, but sentries stood on
the battlements, armor shining in the light of several fires. Eyeing
the casements, Sharif could see men moving inside the gatehouse
towers. He paused, telling Erim:

"Get your toys."

Reaching beneath Sharif's cloak to his pack, Erim took out the
benshaqars.

"You handle 'em," Sharif said. "I'll watch your back."

"Fair enough," Erim answered, slipping all five into his robe,
tucking them down near his belt. "Ready?"

"Ready."

A flight of steps led up onto the battlement beside the tower;
the Sharajnaghim crossed to the stair.

As they ascended, a group of Anarites came trotting down
towards them, laughing, the firelight at their backs. Sharif could
not see their faces.

One launched into a joke, then fell silent, halting. Sharif could
feel the man's eyes upon him. Breath catching in his throat,
he wondered what this portended, but forged upwards anyway,
following Erim past the black-robes.

* * *

After the revelation that his company of twenty had been drubbed by three Sharajnaghim at the inn, Torthas Al-Tarcha had been flogged and demoted by Mahayoun; upon returning to Khaur-Al-Jaffar, he had been assigned to guard duty.

His troop had just been relieved when he spotted that oddly familiar face on the steps. At first he couldn't quite place it—perhaps it was the fact he never would have expected to see it here, in Khaur-Al-Jaffar. But seconds after the man went by with his companion, Torthas was jolted by recognition. Reliving all the pain and humiliation in one red instant, he remembered the Sharajnaghi's mocking voice so clearly that the bastard seemed to be shouting in his ear:

My name, dog, is Sharif Ben Shaqar.

Torthas whirled.

Erim and Sharif placed themselves on either side of the tower's doorway.

"Now," Sharif said.

Erim primed a *benshaqar* and tossed it through. There was a startled cry from inside, and a clank as of the bomb striking the floor—but no explosion.

"What happened?" Sharif asked.

"Shhh!" Erim answered, muttering a second priming-spell.

"Sharajnaghim!" a black-robe bellowed from the steps. "Shoot them!"

Three of his companions cocked crossbows. Sharif heard a hiss of fabric as Erim hurled a second *benshaqar* into the tower.

Clank.

Footsteps clattered inside, racing towards the doorway.

"What's wrong?" Sharif cried. A quarrel grazed his temple, spanging off the wall behind him.

Another whistled by; Erim grunted in pain.

A third stuck in Sharif's staff—if not for the weapon, it would have caught him in the midriff.

The footbeats were almost to the threshold. Sharif looked round to see Erim, a bolt buried in the big muscle of his shoulder, toss the third *benshaqar* through the doorway with his good arm.

Work, you pig! Sharif thought.

A vicious peal ripped the night. Blood and mail-links sprayed from the arch.

Beyond the door, Erim was crumpling, clutching at the missile in his flesh.

More movement inside the tower; men cursed and coughed. Sharif glanced in. Through the smoke, he saw troops getting to their feet.

He looked back at the steps. The black-robes there were rushing to the top. If he tried to hold them off, the ones from the tower would take him from behind.

"Sharif," Erim called, fumbling inside his robes, rolling the remaining *benshaqars* across to him. Snatching one, Sharif missed the next, which fell into the courtyard. Priming the first, he straightened and plunged through the arch, holding his staff in his left hand.

A blood-spattered Anarite took a thrust on the chin, toppled. Two more stumbled close, another some distance behind them. Sharif hurled the *benshaqar* at the straggler.

The Anarite's head and shoulders disappeared in a crimson flurry. Fragments of his byrny and headgear tore through his companions in puffs of vaporized blood, a jagged crownlike hole opening in the front of one man's helmet; flying gore whipped Sharif's face like grains in a sandstorm, and a tremendous concussion tossed him backwards off his feet. He could feel that he had been pierced in several places.

"Sharif!" a voice called joyfully from outside the tower. "Sharif Ben Shaqar!"

Sharif turned over onto his stomach. An Anarite came rushing towards him. It was hard to tell with that smashed nose, but he thought he recognized the fellow; wasn't this the black-robe chieftain he had humbled at the inn?

Sharif lurched to his feet, lifting his staff.

But the Anarite had a staff of his own; Sharif took three crashing blow, and found himself careening across the chamber, dropping once more to the floor.

Hardly had he landed when a keen point jabbed him in the thigh, another in the side. Through slitted eyes, he saw two Anarites with swords preparing to stab him again when the man with the blond topknot cried:

"He's dead. I felt his skull split."

Did you? Sharif thought. *I believe it.*

Even though his eyes were not fully closed, his vision blurred and darkened. Something struck him, foot or quarterstaff, he could not tell.

"And *my* name, dog," came the leader's voice, "is Torthas Al-Tarcha."

Chapter 21

When Khaddam ordered Shoua's drug given to the Sharajnaghi
main body for the second time, it was discovered that the men
detailed to carry the substance had picked up the wrong packs; as
it transpired, another pair had brought the drugs up the mountain,
but it was some time before this became apparent. Raschid and his
assistants were still administering the drug when two explosions
thudded in the distance. Horns began to bray inside Khaur-Al-
Jaffar, but there was no signal from Sharif.

"He must've failed," Khaddam said after a time. "We'll have
to try and blast our way through the portcullis."

"They'll be ready for us," Akram said.

"Not for a while," Khaddam answered. "Not completely, at
least. If we can cross the courtyard swiftly enough, we might be
able to take the inner gate."

"I'm not sure . . ."

"We haven't come all this way to give up now. As soon as
Raschid's done, we move."

Erim was vaguely aware of the Anarites hauling him down from
the battlements. Aside from the pain in his shoulder, his clearest
perception was of the way his boot-tips shocked from step to
step.

He lapsed in and out of consciousness. First he was being
dragged along a gloomy hallway full of hurrying troops; then
he was going up an endless staircase. Finally, inexplicably, he

found himself sitting in a black stone seat. Somewhere horns were blaring. A chill breeze blew from an unseen aperture behind him; his mind cleared somewhat.

Black-robes milled about him. A hand locked in his hair, yanked his head back. Looking very like the Anarite leader Sharif had demolished during the journey to Bishah, a man with a blond topknot peered into Erim's eyes.

"Doesn't even know you're there," another man said.

"Wake up," the first one growled, grabbing the bolt in Erim's shoulder, prying it sideways in the bone. Erim howled, thrashing against the back of the seat.

"Do we have your attention?" the Anarite asked.

His whole body quivering, Erim nodded. Sweat spilled from his brow.

"Someone wants a word with you," said the blond man, stepping aside.

Achmed Hakkar came forward. Netted with wrinkles, his face was a bitter mask, cheeks shrunken, nose a long sharp blade; his thin drooping moustache and plaited beard were a filthy ivory color. He trained his eyes full on Erim; contrasting startlingly with their red-rimmed lids, they were a flat bluish-white, like those of a dead fish or cat. The pupils appeared completely obscured. Erim wondered how Hakkar could see. But the blankness of those orbs simply made the Grand Master's gaze all the more dreadful. Indeed, just as Sharif had said, the man looked like he could kill with a glance.

With him were the other two Masters who had been in the altar-room. One was broad-shouldered and barrel-paunched, the other small and thin, wearing a black veil; where his nose should have protruded beneath the cloth, the fabric sagged slightly, revealing the outline of a ragged cavity.

"There was another one, Torthas?" asked Achmed Hakkar, in a voice clenched with fury.

"I killed him," the blond man answered.

"What were those blasts?" asked the man with the veil.

"They were hurling these things into the tower, *Sibi* Aswarak," Torthas replied, holding up a *benshaqar*. "I found this down in the courtyard."

The one Sharif missed, Erim thought.

"And you brought it *here*?" shouted the heavyset Master.

Torthas blinked. "*Sibi* Mahayoun . . . I . . . I thought . . ."

"Take it out!" cried Achmed Hakkar.

"*Sibi*," Torthas answered, cringing, "I think they only explode when they strike something. And they have to be primed. I heard this fellow—"

"Enough," the Grand Master snarled.

Torthas laid the bomb on a table.

"Shouldn't we go down to the south gate?" Mahayoun asked.

"There's no immediate danger," Aswarak answered. "How can they attack in pitch blackness? *If* they're out there?"

"*If?*" Mahayoun demanded. "What's in that tower? The wheel that controls the portcullis."

"They're out there," Ahmed Hakkar said, still staring at Erim. "But I want to know why."

"I've told you," Mahayoun replied. "They think we've been murdering their Masters!"

"Nonsense," said Achmed Hakkar. "There must be more to it than that. Isn't there, Sharajnaghi?"

Erim said nothing.

The Grand Master demanded: "You hypocrites used to make such a show of never attacking first. Do we have a whole new *Comahi Irakhoum* to deal with? No more pretense?"

Erim was deeply puzzled. What was the man talking about? How could he not know why they were being attacked? It had to be some sort of ploy . . .

With a speed that would have been astonishing in a man of twenty, Hakkar jammed the heel of his palm against the butt of the quarrel in Erim's flesh. Erim jerked, sliding a full foot up the back of his seat. Hakkar hissed and thrust his face forward.

"We *abided* by the treaty!" he shrieked, spittle spewing over Erim, his breath stinking like plague. "We did *nothing* to molest you! My council argued constantly for war; I alone staved them off. And how did you repay me? With treachery! With this attack!"

Blinking, squeezing tears and sweat from his eyes, Erim marvelled at the man's expression despite his pain. Hakkar's cloudy eyes twitched in their hollow sockets; great veins swelled and throbbed on his forehead, like blue worms beneath his ice-pale skin. He seemed to hold Erim personally responsible.

And if his outrage was merely feigned, Erim was mad.

"Why?" Hakkar shrieked. "Why have you done this?"

Erim flinched, struggling to think:

But if he's not trying to fool you . . .

"What does it matter now?" Mahayoun cried. "What about their numbers? Their disposition?"

If the Anarites weren't behind the killings at Qanar-Sharaj . . .

Hakkar ignored Mahayoun, seizing the quarrel.

Then who—?

Hakkar twisted the bolt. For the next several seconds, all Erim knew was a white glare of pain.

Hakkar let go of the shaft. The glare faded slowly.

"Why?" the Grand Master shrieked.

Panting, Erim wondered what to do. He was loath to give the Anarites any information; but if they *had* dispatched the sendings, he would only be telling them what they already knew. If, on the other hand, the sendings were *not* their work, then *both* Orders were facing the same hidden enemy . . .

A messenger raced into the room. "They've been sighted," he cried.

"Where?" asked Mahayoun.

"Out on the crater, *Sibi,*" the messenger answered. "Master Haroun sent out a patrol . . ."

"How many?" Aswarak demanded.

"Several hundred. Off to the west."

Ha! Erim thought. *They've underestimated our numbers, thank the Almighty. . . .*

"Several hundred?" Aswarak asked. "That's nowhere near enough to take this fortress."

You're right, fool.

"Were they advancing?" Achmed Hakkar asked. The news seemed to have sobered him a bit.

"No."

"They'll have to wait until first light," Aswarak insisted.

"Certainly," Hakkar sneered. "And I suppose they didn't climb the mountain in the dark."

Aswarak had no answer for that.

"Did they see our patrol?" Mahayoun asked the messenger.

The latter nodded. "Only one man escaped."

Hakkar pondered the news for a few moments. "Obviously, our scouts didn't sight the main body. The force they saw was much too small. Any attack on the south gate will just be a feint." He looked at the messenger. "Go to Haroun. Tell him he must change his dispositions. The main assault will come from the north or east."

The messenger disappeared.

Hakkar's terrible eyes trained upon Erim once more.

"Now," he said, reaching for the quarrel again. "Tell me."

Akram's men in the vanguard, the Sharajnaghim raced along the crater-rim. Bolts came whistling from the gatehouse and the rampart to the right. But as yet the attackers were too far from the fires on the battlements for the crossbowmen to find clear targets.

Deadlier by far were the demons that collected above the road. Batwinged hags swooped in gales of ragged laughter, tearing at men with nails like knives; skeletal horses thundered through the air, hammering at heads with fiery hooves. Glittering with hot jewels that dazzled and seared, phantom outlines plummeted like constellations sundered from the heavens.

Akram called a halt, ordering his men to use their explosive quarrels. Flying bodies shattered; to eyes conditioned by the drug, the blasts were like sunbursts, great flares of white sparks. Wounded demons dropped amid the Sharajnaghi vanguard, raging among the troops until more quarrels put an end to them. By the time the last creature was killed, fully half of Akram's arbalesters lay dead or wounded. And most of the explosive bolts had been expended.

Nevertheless, Akram rallied his men and pressed on towards the gate. As they neared the walls, the fires revealed them plainly; the Anarite crossbowmen extracted a heavier and heavier toll.

The Sharajnaghim loosed bolts at the portcullis, but the thick metal was impervious to the blasts. Akram summoned the men with the *benshaqars*. The bombs were more effective against the towering steel grate, opening several twisted vents; but the holes were not big enough to admit more than a few men at a time. The Anarites held the gaps easily.

Akram raised his horn and blew the retreat.

*   *   *

After an eternity of pain, Erim began to hear detonations. Aswarak and Mahayoun rushed past him.

"They're attacking!" Mahayoun cried. From the sound of his voice, Erim guessed he was outside, probably on a balcony. Momentarily the pair returned.

"We must join Haroun!" Aswarak insisted.

"No!" Hakkar replied. "This is the feint. And since we don't know where the real attack will come . . ."

"But what if it isn't a feint?" Aswarak answered.

Instantly Erim made up his mind to speak, if only to distract Hakkar; the longer the Grand Master persisted in his delusions, the better.

"You want me to talk?" Erim asked.

"Silence!" Aswarak cried, veil fluttering up. Erim caught a glimpse of ulcered flesh and grinning molars.

"Go ahead," Hakkar told Erim.

"But—" Aswarak began.

Hakkar motioned him to be quiet.

"You know as well as I do why we've come," Erim said. "Half our Council was killed by your sendings."

"I told you!" Mahayoun roared at Hakkar. "I told you that's what they believe!"

Hakkar's face pinched; he was clearly mystified.

"But why would they—" His voice faltered.

"Your men were sighted during the last attack," Erim said. "Precisely at the spot where the sending was conjured."

Hakkar eyed him in silence. "When was this?"

Erim told him.

"Mahayoun," Hakkar said. "Weren't you returning from Dhamar—"

"That was later," Mahayoun replied. "I had business with the Khan . . ." He turned slowly, looking at Torthas. "But I was so sick of this fool that I sent him and his clowns on ahead. He must've given you that letter—the one that explained how I'd demoted him. . . ."

"Was it your sending, Torthas?" Hakkar whispered, not even glancing at him.

Torthas went to his knees, head bowed behind clasped hands. "Please, *Sibi!*" he wailed.

Hakkar unsheathed a knife. An instant later, half of Torthas's right ear landed on the floor. The slash was dealt with consummate speed and skill; dagger-man that he was, Erim could only nod in professional admiration.

Hakkar screeched like a panther: "Get up!"

Whining, gripping the side of his head, Torthas obeyed, nose streaming snot. Hakkar sliced him across the chin.

"I'll tell, I'll tell!" Torthas screamed.

Hakkar wiped the blade on Torthas's cheeks with two lightning sweeps. "Oh, you will," he promised.

"We were after Sharif Ben Shaqar," Torthas said. "The man I killed in the tower just now . . ."

"What?" Hakkar exploded.

"Sharif Ben Shaqar. The one who defeated me at the inn. I wanted revenge. So did the rest of my men. So when we came north from Dhamar, we stopped near Qanar-Sharaj. The Influences were with us—we managed to conjure a very powerful demon. *But we were only after Sharif.* We weren't trying to kill the Masters . . ."

"Sharif and I were at a Council when the sending attacked," Erim said.

"The Masters must've gotten in the way," Torthas said.

"But what about the other killings?" Hakkar asked.

Indeed, Erim thought. The attack by the Thornwitch had forced him to abandon his theory about the Knot of Serpents; had his suspicion been justified after all?

Was the killer a Sharajnaghi?

Out in the hallway, the shouting grew suddenly louder; the messenger reappeared, quite breathless. It was a few moments before he could speak.

"Grand Master," he said, "*Sibi* Haroun feels it unwise to take men from the south gate . . ."

"Tell him my order still stands," Hakkar answered. "He must continue to reinforce the east and north."

"But we're under attack, *Sibi*!" the messenger cried.

"It's a feint. Now go."

Aswarak indicated Torthas. "What about him?"

"Return to your post," Hakkar told the blond man.

Torthas bowed. "Master," he said, and dashed off with his men.

"We'll deal with him after the battle," Hakkar informed the other Masters. "When there's enough time."

"But why fight?" Erim demanded. "If you weren't behind the killings, why not ask for a parley . . ."

"A parley?" Hakkar laughed. "When we've been given the chance to crush your Order?"

"But—"

"Afterwards, we'll deal with you too. You and Torthas together."

"Why not kill him now?" Aswarak asked.

"Without learning how he penetrated our defenses?" Hakkar replied. He shook his head, summoning two guards. "Bind this man."

Chapter 22

Feigning death, Sharif had remained perfectly still. The Anarites left him sprawled on the floor.

"We'll take *this* one to *Sibi* Achmed," came Torthas's voice; Sharif guessed he was referring to Erim.

By that time, other Anarites had arrived, drawn by the blasts. One asked:

"Were there any more?"

"One," Torthas answered. "He's in there, dead. Didn't have too much trouble with him. Blew himself up."

There was a groan and a scuffling sound—had they just pulled Erim to his feet?

"All right, then," Torthas said. "We're off. Good luck up here."

The newcomers entered the tower. Boots stamped back and forth. Sometimes the Anarites leaped over Sharif; sometimes they trod directly onto him, often stumbling in the process. It was all he could do to keep himself from flinching.

"Get those corpses out of here!" someone bellowed. "Toss 'em into the courtyard!"

Sharif heard grunts of effort, things dragging. But momentarily a second officer came bellowing into the room:

"Throw those bodies in the corner and come with me!"

Two men pulled Sharif up onto his heels; sharp jabs of pain lanced through his body. With a heave they deposited him atop the pile. Partially propped against the wall, he watched the Anarites through slitted eyes, wondering if he could move. His head felt hot and swollen, as though the whole inside must be one massive bloodclot. Wounds throbbed all over his limbs and torso; he was covered with blood, but how much of it was his, he had no way of knowing.

"The Sharajnaghim!" men shouted presently, within and without the tower. "Here they come!"

Arbalesters loosed quarrels through the casements; once it seemed no one was looking his way, Sharif tried to flex his limbs. The pain was intense; his mind darkened.

When he regained consciousness, the fighting seemed to be over.

Suddenly he realized that he was moaning.

"This one's alive!" a man called.

Oh, God, Sharif thought.

"I don't recognize him," another Anarite said. "Is he a Sharajnaghi?"

"There was only one of the bastards," the first declared.

"No, two," the second replied.

"That's right," said a third man, who wore a buff eyepatch. "They carried one off to Master Achmed. But *that's* the other right there, with his top half gone. Blew himself up. Torthas said so."

He thrust a bottle between Sharif's lips. "Here you go. Won't heal you, but it'll help with the pain until the surgeons get here."

Guessing it would also dull his wits, Sharif had no desire to drink; but with the Anarites staring at him, he swallowed anyway. The liquid had a sweet, surprisingly pleasant flavor.

"Whoa," said Eyepatch, pulling the bottle away.

"What is that stuff?" the first man asked.

"My brother's formula. *Sibi* Aswarak's been testing it—"

"What are you doing?" an officer cried. "Get over here!"

The three rushed off.

Sharif sat up against the wall, discovering that the fluid had a vicious aftertaste. His mouth flooded with saliva.

Like strong wine on an empty stomach, the elixir went directly to his blood; he could feel it spreading through his body. His skin began to tingle. Contrary to his expectations, the pain did not fade, but grew strangely *agreeable*.

Shouts from the courtyard; the officers swore.

"Reinforce the *other* gates?" one thundered. "I wonder what *Sibi* Haroun thinks about that?"

But whoever Haroun was, and whatever he thought of the orders, evidently he complied; after an exchange with a messenger, one of the officers took half the men from the chamber, and Sharif heard large numbers clattering down the steps outside.

The Sharajnaghi stood slowly, working his arms.

"Feel better already, don't you?" called the man who had given him the liquid.

Sharif nodded, looking slowly about the chamber. Ten Anarites remained, most of them standing by the slit-casements. A few were still cradling crossbows, but the rest had leaned theirs against the wall. As far as the Sharajnaghi could tell, none of the weapons were primed.

Directly across from the arch through which Sharif had entered, there was a second door; beyond was the bridge leading to the tower on the western side of the gate. Stout lengths of wood were attached to the walls beside the openings, held upright by hooks; swinging them down and barring the doors would be a very simple matter. Sharif thought it an ingenious arrangement—if the fortress were penetrated, the chamber could be sealed at a moment's notice.

He eyed the device that controlled the portcullis. Obviously, it had originally been a simple capstan; but the spokes had been removed, leaving a line of empty sockets around the outside of the wheel. Atop the wheel a brass cylinder had been attached, its crown heavily embossed with sorcerous formulae. A demon was imprisoned inside, Sharif knew; its power rotated the wheel. And unless Akram's information was outdated, Sharif knew the entity's true name—

Tsumir.

Sharif considered the black-robes once more. He could count on surprise; but since the Anarites were armored, he could not be sure of stunning them with magic-bolts.

He looked for his staff; it had been kicked across the chamber. A fallen scimitar lay closer to hand.

He picked it up and went to the eastern door. Pushing it shut, he dropped the bar into place and turned.

Eyepatch was coming towards him.

"Why did you do that?" the Anarite asked.

"Are you speaking to me?" Sharif replied, just as the man stepped within striking range. The Sharajnaghi opened him beneath the chin with such speed that the Anarite did not even seem to realize that he had been cut. Eyepatch's lips formed the words *yes, you*, but he made no sound. An expression of puzzlement passed over his blanching face; he was still standing as Sharif rushed by.

Racing towards the men at the casements, the Sharajnaghi slashed one across the back of the neck, caught another in the face as the fellow looked round; a third black-robe's arm parted at the elbow, and a fourth man took the return stroke through the side of the helmet.

The rest boiled Sharif's way. The foremost had drawn their swords; those behind were fumbling with crossbows.

Scimitar clenched in his right fist, Sharif assumed a Dragon Stance, driving four cataract-bolts into the swordsman farthest on the left. The Anarite stumbled and fell. Sharif bounded over him, smashing into an arbalester behind, laying him low with a forearm to the mouth and a thrust through the belly.

Another crossbowman pivoted, off on the fringe of sight. Loosed a split-instant too soon, a bolt caught Sharif on the point of his cheek, continuing past his face, drawing a line of blood in the air.

Dashing for the western archway, the Sharajnaghi saw a crowd of Anarites speeding towards it along the bridge. Reaching the door, he hurled it shut.

As if out of thin air, a quarrel appeared in the wood above his hand. Others thumped into the door's far side.

Footsteps hammered up behind him. Knocking the hook from the bar, he whirled as the beam dropped into place.

A black-robe sliced at him, scimitar burying itself in the door to Sharif's right, notching his ear. Mouth gaping, eyes blazing in a swarthy face, another Anarite lashed out from the left.

Sharif ducked the blow, shoving his blade under the hem of the second man's short mailshirt as the Anarite's edge sank into his comrade's jaw, biting it through at the hinge.

Sharif straightened, the black-robe he had stabbed dropping at his feet. Jaw hanging, the other tottered away like a man slipping in mud.

The remaining swordsman lurched near, still stumbling from the effects of Sharif's bolts; behind him, the two arbalesters were repriming their weapons. Parrying a clumsy stroke, Sharif caved in the swordsman's shoulder and butchered the crossbowmen before they could fit their quarrels.

Someone brushed him. Sharif clapped both hands to his hilt and spun, mail and flesh parting beneath his edge. Blood splattering from a rent in his side, the Anarite with the ruined jaw took a few aimless steps and lay down as though going to sleep.

Sharif looked at the other wounded. They seemed to be unconscious.

The Anarites outside discharged volleys of strikes. The doors shook under the impacts, but he doubted the black-robes could blast them down—the barriers were very thick, and reinforced with iron bands.

Sharif loosed several more cataract-strikes, then assumed a binding-stance, training his concentration full upon the cylinder surmounting the portcullis-capstan. In a low voice he called three times the name of the being within.

"I hear and obey," answered Tsumir, voice a shrill buzz behind the brass.

"Raise the portcullis," Sharif commanded.

Green energy snaked from the cylinder, racing over the surface of the capstan. Slowly, the wheel began to turn; somewhere gears rumbled and chains clinked.

"The gate!" wailed voices from outside. "The gate's rising!"

Plucking a torch from a socket, Sharif went to a casement. Beyond, he could see nothing but blackness; was anyone watching? Praying, he waved the torch three times.

"Please," he muttered. "Let them see."

"Look," said Khaddam. "Sharif's signal."

"God is great," Akram answered.

Khaddam squinted; the drug was fading. "The gate's only halfway up."

"The *benshaqars* twisted the metal," Akram answered. "The portcullis won't slide all the way into its slot."

"But halfway's enough."

"Yes," said Akram.

He rallied his men for another charge.

* * *

Shouts drifted up into the keep, along with distance-muted screams and the crack of magic-bolts.

"Something's happening at the south gate!" Achmed Hakkar cried from the balcony.

Aswarak and Mahayoun rushed past Erim.

"They're trying to smash the doors," said Mahayoun. "Some-one's holding the tower!"

"But who—?" Aswarak began.

Hakkar broke in: "Perhaps Torthas didn't kill that other Sharajnaghi after all."

Sharif's alive? Erim thought, shocked with joy at the possibility.

"Look!" Mahayoun shouted. "The portcullis—"

"I don't believe it!" Hakkar screamed.

"Just a feint, eh?" Aswarak demanded. "The Sharajnaghim were waiting for this all along!"

"At least we know where they're coming," Hakkar answered, sweeping back into the chamber. Pointing to Erim, he told the guards: "If the Sharajnaghim break through, kill him."

"*Sibi*," said the guards.

One was holding the *benshaqar* that Torthas had brought from the gate.

Hakkar, Aswarak, and Mahayoun hastened away. The guard with the bomb showed it to his companion.

"What is this thing, anyway?" he asked.

While the Anarites outside were still trying to blast their way in, Sharif reentered his binding-stance, seizing the crown of Tsumir's cylinder in an invisible grip. It was relatively easy to unfasten—the demon was restrained by the spells on the cap, not the cap itself.

The top sprang off, and a seam appeared in the front of the cylinder. Long black lines, almost parallel, thrust outward on either side of the fissure; it was an instant before Sharif realized they were prying spidery fingers, several feet long, with ten knuckles at least. The wings of the cylinder opened wide, then snapped back together like the sides of a scroll as the brazen tube fell backwards over the capstan.

Revealed was a thin, tar-black pillar; except for the crossed hands extending on either side, the demon still retained the cylinder's shape. An elongated, mummylike head jerked up from a depression in the entity's chest, grinning at Sharif. The hands flew towards him, many-elbowed arms unfolding with a series of sharp popping sounds.

"Tsumir!" Sharif bellowed.

Clutching spiky fingers halted just before his face.

"By your true name I command you, Tsumir!" Sharif cried.

"I hear and obey," the demon answered.

Outside, the force-bolts had stopped; the Anarites were conjuring. Parchment-flat, working its way side to side with a dry slithering noise, a reed-demon insinuated itself under the western door, peaked head and long serrate arms climbing the wood like shadows.

"Kill it, Tsumir!" Sharif shouted.

Tsumir leaped into the air like an exploding bundle of sticks, all joints and fleshless limbs; lighting near the reed-demon, it drew a sharp fingertip across the demon's neck, flicking away the head.

Bending his will upon the bar across the door, Sharif tossed it upwards, then swung the door wide. A crowd of Anarites stood on the far side, flinching with surprise, mouths slack.

"Take them, Tsumir!" he shouted.

The demon leaped, falling over them like a black net.

Sharif swung the door shut and dropped the bolt once more.

Slitherings behind him; two reed-demons were sprouting from cracks in the floor, another from the ceiling.

Snatching a torch, he ran to the one hanging head down. A sawtoothed arm nicked his brow; his scimitar bit left and right. The arms dropped to the floor, curled like shavings. He thrust the torch against the edge of the serrate head. Tiny filaments sparkled and blazed. Flames climbed along the suspended body.

By then the others had almost pulled themselves free of the floor. Sharif hurled the torch. The head punched into the demon on the left, sticking before it penetrated too far. The being writhed, screaming, trying to pull the brand out.

The second burst from its fissure an instant before Sharif brought his sword down on the peak of its head. There was a sound like ripping linen, and the demon wobbled, one side of its body curling forward, the other backwards. He struck it across the waist, and the demon vanished in three pieces.

Sharif eyed the eastern door. Did the men beyond know what he had done to their comrades on the bridge? Conjuring a huge badgerlike beast, he unbarred the door and opened it.

The Anarites flooded in as soon as it swung wide.

Snarling, the badger flung itself at them. One black-robe dived under it, but the rest were borne backwards.

Sharif slashed at the Anarite on the floor. The blow tangled in the man's cloak, could not bite through the mail beneath; the Anarite rolled aside.

Sharif bounded to the door. Just before he slammed it and dropped the bar, he had an astounding glimpse of the badger racing back and forth *over* the Anarites outside, leaping from shoulders and backs, snapping, jaws running with blood.

Sharif turned. The black-robe had risen; with both hands he held a mighty staff. There was a gash on his chin, and a huge red stain covered one side of his head; one ear had been partially sliced away. He blinked at Sharif.

"You!" breathed Torthas Al-Tarcha.

"You should have made sure of me," Sharif answered, snapping into stance, aiming two strikes directly at the Anarite's bleeding chin.

Torthas raised his staff, splitting the bolts. Light splashed away on either side of his head.

With a shriek he charged, thrusting with the stave.

The butt connected with Sharif's forehead at the very instant that he loosed two more bolts.

The Sharajnaghi smashed backwards into the door, skull full of lightning. Eyepatch's cordial transformed the pain, but the pure shock set Sharif's stomach heaving. His legs folded, and he landed hard in a sitting position, shaking his head.

Torthas was laid out on his back, but he was stirring. The Anarite sat up slowly, grimacing, rubbing his eyes, blood reddening the mucous oozing from his nose. He reached for his staff, leaning on it as he pulled himself back to his feet.

Sharif fought to a crouch, discovering that the scimitar was no longer in his hand.

Torthas pitched towards him, howling.

*   *   *

Akram's vanguard raced once more for the gatehouse. Anarites
with spears and shields awaited them; but far fewer demons swept
from the sky, and the crossbows on the battlements were idle.
Akram could see some sort of chaotic activity on either side of
the eastern gatehouse tower; since the gate remained up, he could
only assume that Sharif's troop still held the upper chamber.

Akram's men had only a score or so *benshaqars* left, but they
were more than enough to shatter the shieldwall. The Sharajnaghim
rushed into the gap, driving forward, splitting the Anarites before
they had a chance to retreat.

Surging in behind the vanguard, Khaddam's men widened the
lane; Akram's dashed madly to the inner gatehouse, which lay
undefended. Unslinging their crossbows, they mounted the wall,
showering quarrels on a mob of black-robes even then emerging
from the keep, routing them back through the arch.

Swiftly finishing the Anarites in the outer courtyard, Khaddam's
company poured through the inner gate, speeding to the entrance
of the keep, which the Anarites had abandoned in their panic.

The worst's over, Akram thought, looking down from the
gatehouse bridge.

✛
Chapter 23

Sharif straightened, trying to assume a stance. Torthas swept a leg out from under him, but just as he lifted his staff to strike again, another reed-demon materialized in the chamber; mistaking him for Sharif, it slashed the Anarite across the back.

Torthas rounded on the demon. If the thing's blow had cut through his mail, he betrayed no hint of it. A sweep of his staff sent the demon whirling, torn almost in half.

Sharif scrambled to pick up his scimitar. Torthas raced to intercept, lashing out. Sharif dodged away, stumbling towards the wall on the right—and *his* staff.

Torthas cracked him across the back. Hurtling forward, Sharif crashed into the wall, arced along it to the floor, landing atop his stave.

Seizing it, he rolled aside, heard Torthas's weapon connect with the wall. Bounding up in the center of the room, Sharif turned to face the Anarite.

There followed the most ferocious exchange of blows that Sharif had ever experienced; a poor sorcerer Torthas might have been, but he was a true master with a staff. Strokes rained on Sharif's weapon, glanced off his skull, clipped his chin. Parrying furiously, circling slowly to the right, Sharif realized he was overmatched.

There came a series of detonations from outside, distracting Torthas just long enough for Sharif to leap backwards and hurl his stave at the Anarite's face. Torthas swept it aside; Sharif drove two cataract-bolts into his chest. Torthas snarled, foam flying from his lips, teeth snapping rabidly as he came on again.

Sharif gave him two more. Torthas kept his feet, but Sharif blasted him steadily backwards, towards the western door. When he struck the barrier, Sharif could easily have used it for an anvil, pinning him against it, crushing his life out.

Instead, the Sharajnaghi paused.

There was an image graven on the wood behind Torthas, although Sharif had not noticed it before. The figure was considerably taller than the Anarite; eyes closed serenely, the Thornwitch's beautiful feminine face was in full view.

How could he have conjured her? Sharif thought.

But the black-robe had not summoned the demon. That became plain as she slipped a dark leg about his waist and began raking his chest with her talons. Obviously the Anarites outside had sent her; and just like the last reed-demon, she had mistaken Torthas for Sharif.

Her eyes and mouth opened, bristling with black points. Wrenching her head forward from the wood, she rained spiny kisses on the side of Torthas's face and neck. Her claws ripped through mail, then flesh and ribs. Blood washed in waves down his belly and thighs. Torthas rocked and thrashed against her; the toes of her lifted foot began to curl, as though in fierce passion.

Torthas slumped. She emitted a gasp, slowly lowering her leg. He sank in a glistening pile. The Thornwitch freed herself from the door, face trained on Sharif.

"Sharif Ben Shaqar?" she asked in a whistling voice, stepping gracefully over the corpse.

"Remember the worms?" the Sharajnaghi replied.

As if she remembered all too clearly, she dissolved before his eyes; but Sharif knew she had not withdrawn of her own volition. Conjured beings fought under compulsion; they could not discorporate unless they achieved their objective, or their physical forms were damaged beyond use.

A tremendous din of battle was pouring through the casements. Sharif went to one of the slits that faced the courtyard. A wedge of Sharajnaghim was smashing its way towards the inner gatehouse. Whoever had conjured the Thornwitch, Sharif evidently was no longer their most pressing concern.

Thank you, Lord, he thought, sinking to his knees in exhaustion. The pains were changing, returning to their previous hideousness. His skull grew heavy; his chin sagged onto his chest, and that little movement seemed enough to unbalance him, pulling him forward onto his hands.

It was time for another sip from Eyepatch's bottle. As he dragged himself towards the man's corpse, he felt a brief twinge of sorrow at having killed him.

As Khaddam's troop pressed farther into the keep, Akram led his men into the galleries beneath, slaughtering the guards, freeing the captives in the pits. The male slaves took weapons from the dead Anarites; their liberators gave them all the arms they could spare. Then, marshalled by Tarchan-speaking Sharajnaghim, the slaves followed Akram's company up into the keep.

In the corridor outside the altar-room, black-robes rushing from the north gate had collided with Khaddam's forces, the sides locking together in an awesome contest of magic and steel; rounding a bend behind the Anarites, Akram saw a riot of bolts glancing and flashing through the air above the melee. Demons hovered and plummeted like eagles; towering over the human combatants, others strode through the press, dealing out murderous clawstrokes.

The clamor permitted Akram's column to close half the distance before any of the black-robes looked round; Akram saw their eyes bulge from fifty yards away.

Several ranks turned to face the Sharajnaghim. Beams flamed from upraised fists. But the range was still too great for them to do much damage. Akram's troops shrugged off the strikes.

Demons coalesced near the ceiling. The Sharajnaghim had no choice but to halt and assume stances, forceletting.

An intense scarlet blaze appeared, hanging in midair between the lines. Out of it an oval face materialized, twin tongues dangling. *Morkulg,* Akram thought.

The demon's eyes bulged and glared white, as though swelling with energy. Akram had one shield up; he raised a second, overlapping them.

Energy stabbed from the glowing orbs. Akram's defenses protected him, but the men on either side, each with a single buckler, were ripped asunder.

The demon roared—in frustration, Akram guessed.

He's after me.

Then he saw that the Anarite demons had begun to swarm about Morkulg, talons raking. The mask launched two more beams, but they struck the floor far short of Akram. Whirling, Morkulg revealed his second face to the Sharajnaghim, blazing fire down into the Anarites.

But why did the Anarites attack him? Akram asked himself. Hadn't the black-robes conjured him in the first place?

By then, enough Sharajnaghim had finished forceletting to conjure their own demons, swiftly doubling the swarm assailing Morkulg. Great strings and fragments of flesh rained to the floor.

Tongues whipping, eyes seething white fire, the Mask fought back frenziedly, spinning. It availed him nothing. Surrounded on all sides by pinioned attackers, falling to shreds, he began to sink, eyes closing, his tongues torn away. At last he vanished.

Instantly the Sharajnaghim turned their demons against the Anarites'.

Akram stared at the carnage in the air, but could not focus his attention on it, mind fixed by a terrifying question.

If the Anarites hadn't conjured Morkulg, who *had*?

Pinned between Khaddam and Akram, the Anarite main body, commanded by Achmed Hakkar himself, was slowly forced into the altar-room. Coming up behind Akram's column, other Anarites made fearful headway against the freed slaves that made up his rearguard; but they were too few to break through to the altar-chamber.

Raschid Zekowi, Arghun, and Sayid joined Khaddam; Akram fought his way through to them soon after. Pooling their strength, the five summoned the most terrible beings a Sharajnaghi could command, enjoining them to appear behind the vast barred doors, which the demons quickly swung open; the troops directed scores of lesser entities into the chamber as well.

The Anarites attempted to reply in kind, but were no match for the Sharajnaghi conjurers. Abandoning sorcery for steel and desperation, they made a fierce effort to force their way from the trap. In this some succeeded, as most of the freed slaves had been killed holding off the reinforcements, and the Sharajnaghim were still outnumbered, although no longer so severely; one large group of black-robes managed to smash through Akram's badly depleted forces. But the rest were either killed or driven back into the altar-room. Haroun and several other Anarite Masters were struck down on the threshold; the Sharajnaghim poured in over their bodies.

Black-robes began to surrender, hurling themselves to their knees and begging mercy. The Sharajnaghi vanguard drove towards the rear of the chamber with little difficulty. Dripping shortsword in one hand, Malochian longsword in the other, Khaddam led the thrust, absorbing bolts, a shirt of stout chain mail beneath his robes.

Ahead, a crowd of Anarites had gathered in a corner, three of them Masters, all in binding-stances. Demons appeared and disappeared, alternately straining at projections from a bas-relief and trying to blast the wall down.

Secret passage, Khaddam thought. *There's a moving panel, and it's hitched on something . . .*

Suddenly one of the beings managed to pull a section of wall forward, just far enough for one man to slip through at a time. The Anarite Masters rushed forward; a subordinate that tried to slip in ahead of them was decapitated by Achmed Hakkar, who vanished an instant later. Aswarak went next, then Mahayoun, who barely forced his bulk through the fissure.

The Sharajnaghim plunged among the demons and black-robes that had been left behind. Swords whirling, Khaddam ripped straight through, cleaving a cobra-headed figure from snout to mid-chest before reaching the entrance.

Lunging inside, he had the impression that his men were right behind them; but as he raced along in total blackness, it became clearer and clearer that he had simply been hearing echoes from the altar-chamber . . .

His feet banged from stone to metal; hinges squealed. The floor began to drop from under him, but caught for a moment, allowing him to race up the slope. Just as he reached the far side, he heard the hinges shrieking once more, and the bang of the metal panel striking the wall of the shaft. Things roiled and gnashed in the pit.

Up the hall, someone whispered a spell; Khaddam heard a sharp tapping of claws, as though a huge quadruped were racing towards him. Throwing himself to one side, he slashed in the direction of the sound. The edge clipped through something, a limb perhaps; there was a yowl, and the unseen beast struck the floor, sliding past him into the pit.

He continued forward. There came a hollow splash, and the sounds of a ferocious struggle.

"Bolts!" a voice cried.

Khaddam flattened himself against a wall.

Blue light filled the passage. Mahayoun, Aswarak, and Achmed Hakkar were standing a few feet away; a sheaf of strikes swept by the Sharajnaghi.

There was an instant of darkness. Khaddam ducked and hurled his shortsword underhand.

More beams flew, this time over his head. He saw Mahayoun staggering back with the blade in his shoulder.

Another heartbeat of gloom. Illuminating his hand, Khaddam sprang up and assumed a stance. Achmed Hakkar struck him with two bolts, but Khaddam caught Aswarak full in the face with a spiral strike, blowing away the veil and a large expanse of diseased grey cheek. Maggots squirmed from beneath the heaving skin, trailing over denuded teeth. Screaming in a high voice, Aswarak stumbled back with Mahayoun, covering the wound with his hands.

Achmed Hakkar had raised a shield; Khaddam aimed a blow at him with the longsword. The Anarite jerked back, the blade passing harmlessly through the top of his buckler. Khaddam stepped closer, sword poised for another stroke.

Loosing a tremendous howl, the black-robe banished his shield and flung his hands towards Khaddam, a torrent of rats pouring from either sleeve.

Khaddam barely had time to cover his eyes with a forearm. An instant later, from knees to scalp, all he could feel was claws and gnawing teeth. He rushed blindly forward, wading in rats, sweeping the longsword.

It connected with something massive. He let out a howl; immediately a furry head invaded his mouth, and he felt sharp jabs on the top and bottom of his tonguetip. Biting down on the rodent, he swept the sword back again, struck his target once more—and suddenly the rats were gone.

Achmed Hakkar wobbled in front of him, sliced once across the chest, and again in the side of the head, the slash passing all the way through one milky eye and partway into the next. Vivid red rivulets snaked down his pallid face.

Khaddam thrust him aside; it was like knocking over a rootless rotted sapling.

Trembling, jowls wobbling, Mahayoun was on his knees, trying to pull the shortsword from his shoulder.

Aswarak was conjuring; an apparition like a huge severed hand materialized between him and Khaddam, armed with cruel bird-of-prey talons.

But Khaddam recognized the demon, and knew its name; reassuming his stance, he seized control of the being. Fingers spread in a broad fan, the hand spun towards Aswarak.

Aswarak hurled up both shields. The talons rebounded, but Aswarak was jolted out of his stance, bucklers dissipating. The hand lunged forward, pressing him to the floor, grinding him against the stone with the heel of its palm. His feet knocked savagely from wall to wall. When at last the hand lifted, Khaddam saw that the Anarite's whole upper body was splayed and flattened, the head reduced to a gelatinous pulp.

Wrenching the shortsword from his shoulder at last, Mahayoun floundered to his feet. The hand whirled, talons sighing through him horizontally. His head jumped from his neck; his arms flew into segments. Blood sheeted from three parallel incisions in his torso, the wounds yawning as his corpse arched backwards.

Hearing voices behind him, Khaddam banished the hand and turned. A crowd of his men raced towards him, pausing at the brink of the pit.

"Grand Master!" they cried. "Is there a way across?"

Khaddam looked round, quickly spotting a small lever. "I'll have that plate back up in a moment," he said.

Shortly they were crowding round him, gaping at the corpses.

"Three Masters," one breathed. "My God, *Sibi,* you killed *three Masters* single-handed."

"Not since Zorachus—" another began.

"This is very different," Khaddam answered. "The Masters he killed were much stronger than these fools."

"Even so, *Sibi*—"

Khaddam laughed. "I suppose it *is* impressive, at that."

"Why do you think they turned to fight, Grand Master? Why didn't they keep going?"

"It's plain enough," Khaddam answered. "There's no way out."

A short distance past Mahayoun's corpse, the passage ended in a blank wall.

"There must be another moving panel," Khaddam said. "It's my guess that they couldn't open it. They had a devil of a time with that one in the altar-chamber, and that plate in the floor almost didn't drop. The mechanisms hadn't been tended—at least not recently. Someone was lax in his duties . . ."

It was growing hard for him to talk; his tongue was swelling from the rat-bite. Luckily, though, there was no chance of infection; any contagion transmitted by conjured beings vanished with them. A brief healing-trance would deal with the wounds themselves.

"Come on, then," he said. "Back to the altar-room."

Judging by what Erim could hear, the fighting had passed from the courtyards into the keep. The din faded, but after a space, swelled once more; increasingly panic-stricken, his guards positioned themselves at the door, looking outside every few seconds or so.

"They've broken through," one said.

"We can't be sure, Hanif," the other replied.

"Then what's that racket in the stairwells?" Hanif asked. "We should kill him now. There still might be some way to escape."

"I don't know . . ."

"Listen. I'll stay right here. You go and do it. Then we'll leave."

" 'You go and do it,' " Hanif's companion said. "You go and stick your neck out. You take the blame if he's killed too soon. . . ."

"Well then, Saddam," Hanif said. "Let's put it this way. If you ever expect me to sleep with you again, you'll kill the bastard and do it now."

Saddam glared at him, then turned towards Erim, still holding the *benshaqar* that Torthas had brought. He had, at intervals, been tossing it up and catching it; now he began to do it again.

"Go on," Hanif urged.

Erim considered priming the bomb. He doubted it would detonate—it was not striking Saddam's hand with any real force. Still, he had nothing to lose, and tried it anyway.

Just as he had expected, there was no explosion.

"Get rid of that damn thing and kill him," Hanif said.

Saddam tossed the bomb over his shoulder and started forward, reaching for a knife. Erim hunched to one side, pulling his legs up, grimacing in anticipation of the blast.

The device went off with a murderous crack. Saddam sailed into the air, a red flap of scalp swinging forward over his eyes; his heels came up, and he landed face-first, his back laced with smoking wounds.

Looking past him, Erim saw nothing that could be recognized as Hanif.

The Sharajnaghi had felt a fragment graze him along the edge of one calf; he moved the leg and wiggled his toes, deciding he had taken no serious hurt.

Men came clattering along the hall. He slumped, closing his eyes. The footsteps paused by the threshold.

"What happened in here?" someone demanded.

"Who knows?" another answered. "Let's go."

The footbeats hurried off.

After the death of Achmed Hakkar, Khaddam's men spread out from the altar-room, shouting the news, telling the remaining Anarites to surrender. Refusing, some escaped through the northern gate; others fought to the death. Even so, the Sharajnaghim gathered up five hundred prisoners, who were herded down into one of the slave-pits.

After entrusting one group of captives to the guards, Arghun Khan and Akram were making their way along a corridor with their men when they saw a column of Anarites sprint across a junction up ahead; in moments the Sharajnaghim were in full cry.

But it proved to be an ambush—more Anarites lay in wait, and as soon as the pursuers rounded the corner, the hidden black-robes pounced.

The Sharajnaghim almost slashed their way free, but the Anarites managed to contain the thrust; cut off in the forefront, Arghun and Akram fled down a narrow stairway, illuminating their hands.

Anarites followed, but the Masters rapidly outdistanced them. At the bottom the pair halted and conjured. Their powers were virtually drained; even so, the demon they summoned was enough to drive the black-robes screaming back up the steps.

Banishing it, the Sharajnaghim sprinted along the passage, coming shortly to a yawning gulf where the floor had collapsed. Out of the abyss came a dim rush of running water.

"This will do nicely," Arghun said.

Akram looked at him. "What?"

Arghun thrust his sword sidewards.

His intended victim leaned back, the edge cutting him across the chest.

Akram brought a fist down on Arghun's hand. The blade bounced to the floor and into the gulf. Akram pivoted.

Seizing his sword hand, Arghun unsheathed a dagger and jabbed him in the stomach.

Akram shrieked, kneeing him in the groin. Arghun loosed his hand and retreated. Akram followed, gripping his wound, blood streaming through his fingers.

Straightening, Arghun kicked the sword from his grip and closed with him once more, dagger lifted on high. Aiming for the hollow of Akram's shoulder, he plunged the blade straight downwards.

But the old man swayed at the last moment; the point glanced off his collarbone, driving down between pectoral muscle and ribcage.

"Why?" he gasped.

Tearing the blade out, Arghun just laughed and stabbed him in the eye. Akram turned, tottering on the brink. Arghun drove the knife into his back, using it to tip him into the chasm.

"Why indeed?" he asked.

✛

Chapter 24

Soon after the deaths of Saddam and Hanif, a group of Sharajnaghim reached the chamber where Erim sat bound. Untying
him, they led him down to the vast barracks-hall that Raschid
Zekowi had chosen to serve as an infirmary.

"Is Sharif here?" Erim asked one of Raschid's assistants.

The doctor pointed. "Right over there—"

"Behind all those men?" Erim asked.

"This has to stop," the doctor said, stamping. "He's going
on about his heroics in the tower again." Erim following, he
marched over to the small crowd. "Back to your beds! Enter
those trances!"

They limped away.

Sharif was sitting on an uncomfortable-looking bed, back against
the wall, wearing nothing but a breechclout and red-spotted band-
ages, a dozen at least. His face was badly swollen, splotched with
purplish bruises.

"You're an even bigger mess than I am," Erim observed.

Sharif started forward off the bed, but Erim put his hands up,
wincing.

"Let's not embrace, what do you say?" he asked.

"Suit yourself," Sharif replied. "Quarrel in your shoulder,
I see."

"Yes."

"Hurts, I'd wager."

"It does."

"Myself, I can't feel a damn thing," Sharif said. "An Anarite mistook me for one of his, gave me a drug. Took two more sips before they brought me here. Amazing stuff . . . I couldn't enter a trance if I wanted to."

"Well, you'd better try," the doctor said, then told Erim: "Your friend's lucky he's still alive—"

"Now *there's* an understatement," Sharif broke in.

"*Sibi* Shoua tested that formula fifteen years ago. Half the subjects died after the second dose."

"Well," Sharif said, "I've had four now, and I'm still going strong." As if to prove his point, he began slamming his head against the wall.

"*Stop* that!" the doctor cried.

"I suppose you're right," Sharif answered. "But it feels so good."

"*That* felt *good?*" Erim asked.

"Whole point of the drug. It's a shame they took my bottle away. I'd fix you right up."

"Don't listen to him," said the doctor, taking Erim by the arm.

"Man's a fool," Sharif called after them. Erim heard his head strike the wall again.

The next day, after Erim woke from his trance, he and Sharif were told that Khaddam wished to see them.

"He's in the altar-room," the messenger said. "Do you know the way?"

"Not from here," Erim answered.

"I'm not sure," Sharif said.

"No matter," the fellow replied. "I'll show you."

On the way, in the course of conversation, he mentioned Akram's death. Erim and Sharif halted.

"You hadn't heard?" the runner asked.

Sharif swore under his breath. "Every Master that I truly loved, Iyad, Massoud, Shoua—now Akram."

"How did it happen?" Erim asked.

"He and Arghun Khan were ambushed last night," the messenger said. "They were forced down a staircase, and a group of Anarites blasted Akram over the edge of a chasm. But Arghun managed to drive them back."

"He was the sole witness?"

"The sole *Sharajnaghi* witness."

Of course, Erim thought.

"Were any of the Anarites captured later?" he asked. "Questioned about this?"

"I don't know. What difference does it make?"

All the difference in the world, Erim thought.

"None, I suppose," he said. He had told no one of his conversation with Achmed Hakkar, although he had considered going to Akram.

Sharif brushed tears from his face, then drew himself upright, his eyes tightening. "Well, at least Akram didn't die in vain. We're rid of the Black Orders once and for all."

But not the murderers, Erim thought. *Not Arghun, at least.*

Khaddam was overseeing preparations for the exorcism of the altar-room; as Erim and Sharif came up, he put an assistant in charge, then took the pair into a small adjoining chapel, where he questioned them about their adventures. He seemed particularly impressed when Sharif told him how he had used Tsumir to defend himself.

"It seemed a better choice than conjuring a demon of my own," Sharif said.

"Indeed," Khaddam answered. "I used a similar stratagem last night . . ."

"Against Aswarak, *Sibi*?" Sharif asked.

"How did you know that?"

"It was all over the infirmary, Grand Master," Sharif answered. "No one wanted to hear about me anymore . . ."

"I wouldn't worry about it if I were you," Khaddam said. "You've proved yourself several times over. As a matter of fact, I think it's high time we ordained you a Master."

Sharif bowed his head. "*Sibi!*"

"Subject to the approval of the Council, of course."

Sharif looked at Erim, beaming.

Erim grinned back and clasped his hand.

"Congratulations," he said, trying to sound enthusiastic, pained by his own dishonesty. As much as he loved Sharif, he did not believe he deserved elevation, no matter how heroic his exploits. A mighty warrior and sorcerer Sharif might have been, but his mind was simply second-rate, as Sharif himself cheerfully admitted.

Perhaps, after the passage of time, experience might substitute for native wisdom, but—

"Erim," said Khaddam.

"Yes, *Sibi?*"

"I understand you were found in the Council-chamber."

"Yes, *Sibi.*"

"Did they bring you before some of their Masters?"

"Yes," Erim answered. "Mahayoun was there, along with Aswarak—"

"And Achmed Hakkar?"

"Yes."

"Did they interrogate you?"

Erim ached to give him the truth, but dared not.

Lay low, he told himself. *If it reached Arghun, he'd turn his eye on you . . .*

"They started to," he answered. "There was a quarrel in my arm, and Hakkar tortured me. I expect I would have cracked—"

"Everyone does," Khaddam said. "There's no shame in it . . ."

"But then I heard the outcry from the south gate—when Sharif took the tower. Hakkar left with the other Masters."

"But why were they still in the Council-chamber?" Khaddam asked. "Our intentions must have been fairly obvious after they caught you. And even more so after I launched that first attack."

"They thought that was just a feint," Erim said. "Their patrol underestimated the size of our main body."

Khaddam nodded. "That explains many things."

He questioned them further. When at last his curiosity seemed satisfied, he said:

"I think I'd better see how the preliminaries are coming along."

They went back into the main chamber.

"Those idols," Sharif said. "I've never seen anything like them, *Sibi.*"

"Are they images of Tchernobog?" Erim asked. "Different aspects? Washallah Irakhoum postulated a certain multiplicity inside angelic—or demonic—beings . . ."

"One of his more suspect lines of reasoning," Khaddam said. "Ultimately he postulated several persons inside God Himself— a position which he hastily recanted."

"But the idols, *Sibi*—" Sharif said.

"I believe they represent the Annunakim," Khaddam replied.

Erim considered this. In pagan lore, the name was given to the judges of the underworld; but according to Sharajnaghi teaching, the Annunakim were three lesser demonic entities, fallen angels who supposedly, after rebelling against God, rebelled against the Black Lord as well.

"That explains why the Anarites were shedding so much blood," Erim said.

"Yes," Khaddam answered. "Their new gods were far less powerful than Tchernobog, so they needed to compensate. Given the burst of energy that's released from a body at the moment of death—the *wave*, to use Samadhi's term—the sacrifices would have strengthened the Anarites no matter who they were dedicated to. Even *nonexistent* entities.

"But in departing from Tchernobog's fold, the Anarites were badly weakened nonetheless. Which is why, if you ask me, I managed to defeat three of their Masters at once."

"But why would they have turned against Tchernobog?" Sharif asked.

"Simple human nature," Khaddam answered. "He's capricious and cruel. The father of Mancdaman Zorachus rebelled against him, and tried to transform the Khymirian Black Priesthood into a mere secular government. Needless to say, Tchernobog responded with fury. Just as he has here, I think."

"So we're the wrath of Tchernobog?" Erim asked. "Not God?"

"Tchernobog apes God, certainly," Khaddam replied. "And given that the Anarites offended both God *and* the Black Lord, it's reasonable to think that both had a hand in their destruction. Especially when one considers that the Annunakim don't even exist."

Erim was puzzled. "Don't even exist?"

"They're mere fictions, created by Tchernobog to test the loyalty of his subjects."

"But with all due respect, *Sibi*, it's generally assumed that the Annunakim are real, even if their existence hasn't been proved beyond a shadow of a doubt . . ."

"Is it?" Khaddam asked.

"Grand Master," called a voice.

They turned. Arghun Khan was coming towards them with several of his men.

"I found this in their Council-chamber," he said, signalling. An adept laid a leather sack on the floor.

"And?" Khaddam asked.

"There are five severed hands inside."

Khaddam exhaled heavily, slowly looking away from the bag. "And the rings?" he asked.

Arghun nodded.

You filth, Erim thought. *The Anarites had nothing to do with the murders, yet somehow the sack found its way here. . . .*

"Is Ahwaz's hand there?" Khaddam asked.

"There's one with the Grand Master's ring—" Arghun broke off suddenly. "Why are you staring at me, Erim?"

"I . . . I . . ." Erim fumbled.

"Yes?"

"I was wondering how you must have felt."

"Felt?"

"Making such a horrible discovery."

Plainly Arghun was not satisfied with that answer. But before he could press Erim, Khaddam said:

"Bring the bag to my quarters."

Arghun nodded to one of his underlings. The Adept departed with it, passing Sayid Al-Mashat, who had just entered the altar-room.

"*Sibi* Khaddam," Sayid said as he came up, "what about the prisoners?"

"They're bound and gagged, are they not?" Khaddam asked.

"Quite helpless," Sayid said. "But surely we're not leaving our garrison here just to play nursemaid."

Sharajnaghi practice was to release captured sorcerers, but only after "gelding"—the destruction of their capacity to express their powers. Tongues were slit to prevent the pronunciation of spells, and certain nerves were severed in their limbs. It was a cruel expedient, but at least it made it possible to spare the prisoners' lives; Erim fully expected Khaddam to order the operations. What other choice was there?

"Kill them," Khaddam said.

"Master?" Erim asked in disbelief.

Khaddam regarded him mildly, as though he had expected

some such reaction. "I have the right. Properly interpreted, the prohibition against killing prisoners of war never had the force of law. Even Akram was forced to concede the point, when I wrote my treatise—" Suddenly he began to laugh. "What am I doing? I don't have to explain myself to you."

He turned to Arghun and Sayid, who laughed as well.

"But, *Sibi*," Erim protested. "Sharajnaghim have *never* slaughtered their prisoners. We're not executioners. Who will stoop to carry out this order?"

"Stoop?" asked Khaddam. "Does a Sharajnaghi demean himself when he obeys his Grand Master?"

"The men won't do it, *Sibi*!" Erim answered.

"Do you really think we're all so dainty as you?" Sharif snapped.

Erim looked at him in horror.

"You poor little flower!" Sharif said. "Does the thought make you wilt?"

"How dare you?" Erim demanded. "I've put my life on the line for the Order, time and again."

Sharif's tone softened: "I wasn't questioning your courage."

"You weren't?"

"But would you actually disobey *Sibi* Khaddam for the sake of a few murdering black-robes?"

"He needn't worry," Khaddam said. "I understand his objection. And I honor it, believe me. I wouldn't order Erim to violate his conscience. Not when there are others who will do my bidding gladly, men who have been humiliated past endurance by the Anarites. Who have been *competing* to display the most absolute obedience . . ." He shifted his gaze to Sayid. "Select your teams from among Samadhi's followers. And Massoud's."

"*Sibi*," Sayid said, and made for the door.

"Erim, you're dismissed," said Khaddam.

Erim bowed and turned. As he walked off, he heard Khaddam say:

"Now then, Sharif. A few more words about your elevation . . ."

Erim continued forward, trembling, hot nausea crawling in his stomach.

Chapter 25

Sigrun was gardening when the Adept came.

"My Lady," he said. "*Sibi* Khaddam has instructed me—"

She virtually flew to her feet, flinging aside her trowel. "He's back?"

"No, but the column's only a few miles away."

"Is he all right?"

The grey-robe smiled. "He's fine."

Sigrun hugged him fiercely. He gasped and loosed a callow-sounding giggle. Realizing what she was doing, she stepped back quickly.

"Sorry," she said, feeling the blood rushing to her cheeks.

The Adept did not seem too put out. "Think nothing of it, My Lady." He giggled again.

Zehowah and Khalima dashed near.

"What about Erim?" Khalima asked anxiously.

"And Sharif?" demanded her sister.

"Alive and well," the Adept said.

Zehowah drew him instantly to her bosom, kissing him passionately on the cheek and clasping him significantly longer than Sigrun had; Khalima had told Sigrun that her sister had been *very* troubled during Sharif's absence.

"Excuse me," Zehowah said, stepping back.

The messenger stared at her with a vacant expression. "Of course," he said numbly.

"The Anarites were defeated?" Sigrun asked.

"Utterly," the Adept said.

"Praise God," Khalima said.

"What was Khaddam's message?" Sigrun asked.

"He wishes you to welcome him in his quarters," the Adept replied.

"What?" Sigrun asked. "I've never been allowed to visit him there, let alone . . . welcome him."

"He's decided to change the regulation," the grey-robe answered. "Many things are about to change, now that he controls the Council . . ."

"I thought it was evenly divided."

The messenger's gaze fell. "That was before the raid, My Lady. *Sibi* Akram was killed."

"Oh," Khalima gasped. "How terrible. He was such a sweet old fellow . . ."

The Adept evidently did not think this an apt description, but said nothing.

"He was very nice to *me*," Khalima said earnestly.

"And me," said Sigrun. "I always felt that he genuinely liked women."

"He did," Khalima replied. "I heard him say so."

There was a silence.

Sigrun told the messenger: "If there's nothing more . . ."

He took his leave.

"Poor Akram," Sigrun said.

"He's with God, surely," Khalima replied.

"I wish I had such faith."

"After what Essaj did for you—" Zehowah began.

"I haven't made up my mind," Sigrun answered.

"That's very ungrateful of you," Zehowah said.

"So it's a matter of gratitude, eh?"

"You could look at it like that," Khalima said.

"Well, then," Sigrun laughed, "perhaps I'm on my way. Let's go in."

Khalima expected Erim to make love to her as soon as he reached her apartment; in truth, she suspected she was every bit as eager as her sister.

But Erim had something else on his mind. He embraced her desperately, then sat her down on the bed and began to pace.

"I have to tell you something," he said. "I suppose I shouldn't speak to anyone at all, but my skull's about to burst, and I need advice."

Khalima grew alarmed; all thought of lovemaking vanished from her mind.

"You can trust me," she said.

Erim's anxiety seemed to hover over him like a shadow. "You can't tell anyone. Not even Zehowah."

"I promise."

"Swear by God. By God and Essaj."

"Erim, you're my husband. I wouldn't—"

"Swear."

"I swear by God and Essaj. Now what is this all about—"

His voice fell to a whisper: "The Anarites weren't behind the murders."

She whispered back: "What about the attack on the Council? They were *seen*."

He sat beside her, taking her hand, his palm clammy with sweat. "Do you remember the black-robes that tried to rape you?" he asked.

"Could I possibly forget?"

He told her of Achmed Hakkar's denials, and Torthas's confession.

"But why would you believe Achmed Hakkar?" she asked.

"What could he have possibly gained by lying? If he was behind the killings, and he thought I knew it, why try to confuse *me*— a solitary prisoner—if the rest of *Comahi Irakhoum* also knew, and was knocking at his door? He was furious at us for breaking the treaty. Furious at *me*."

"Then who *do* you suspect?"

"For one," Erim answered, "Arghun Khan. I don't think he's been acting alone, but I'm fairly sure *he* killed Akram. And he found the hands—"

"Hands?"

"From the murdered Masters. Arghun claimed he discovered them in the Anarite Council-chamber. But if the Anarites didn't kill the Masters, the hands were put there to incriminate them."

"Was anyone with Arghun when he found the hands?" Khalima asked.

"Yes, but it doesn't matter. He could have used a demon to secrete them in the chamber."

"Why haven't you gone to Khaddam?"

"Because it might get back to Arghun, and I have no proof. Also, I'm not exactly in Khaddam's good graces."

"What happened?"

"I expressed certain . . . reservations about one of his decisions," Erim answered. "Rather too forcefully for my own good, I think. He ordered the Anarite prisoners killed."

Khalima was puzzled; did prisoners of war have a right to mercy? She wondered what Essaj would say. He *was* always talking about forgiveness, but if he extended forgiveness to everyone, he certainly gave no sign of it. He quite approved of the idea of Hell; moreover, she had seen him beat a man who was collecting alms while disguised as a priest.

"Isn't it up to the victors?" she asked.

"Sharajnaghim *don't* massacre their captives," he answered, startling her with his vehemence. "At least, there was a time when we didn't. An evil spirit has descended on this Order. You should have heard the men who did the killing. They *joked* about it afterwards. Some of them had sliced ears or fingers off the bodies . . ."

"Why, in God's name?"

"For trophies," Erim answered.

"What about Sharif? Did he stand up to Khaddam too?"

"Far from it. He wasn't ordered to take part, but he would've obeyed. He called me a little wilting flower. We had a great row on the way back, and haven't spoken since."

"Are we going to stay here?" Khalima asked.

"Am I going to remain in the Order, is that what you mean?"

"Yes."

He mulled the question. "Perhaps we *should* get clear of all this. I'm not going to be welcome very much longer, I think. Along with everything else, I believe in Essaj."

"But we're not alone here," Khalima answered.

"No," Erim laughed. "There's Zehowah."

"And Sigrun, perhaps."

"You managed to convert *her*?"

Khalima told him how Essaj had healed her. "The whole escort saw what happened. Now everyone who goes into Thangura tries to hear one of Essaj's sermons. Mufkadi's tried to put a stop to it, but he hasn't been too successful. Before long, we'll have allies everywhere in the Order."

"If only Akram hadn't been killed,'" Erim said.

"He'd want you to stay," Khalima answered. "Above all, to bring Arghun to justice." She paused. "You said you didn't think he was acting alone—"

"No single wizard could conjure a demon like Morkulg the Mask. Not in these latter days, at least."

"You suspect some of the other Serpents?" she asked.

"Some, the whole lot, it makes no difference."

"And Khaddam?"

"If he's part of it, I still can't imagine how. Or why controlling the Council should be so important to him. But the Order's his now. And it's all because of the murders."

"Perhaps you should speak to Kourah again," Khalima suggested. "He might have learned something while you were gone."

"I can't trust him."

"You're going to have to trust *someone* besides me."

"Am I?" he asked.

"You asked for my advice," Khalima replied.

"Yes, I did at that," Erim said. He smiled at her. "I did well to marry you."

"Yes," she answered.

Upon his return, Sharif had gone to his quarters to get fresh clothing, then to the baths. Erim was there, but they did not speak. Afterwards, Sharif went to Zehowah's apartment, his hair still wet.

The door opened at the first knock. Zehowah took him by the hand and led him wordlessly into the rear chamber. They stood for a moment beside the bed; she put her arms around his neck and drew his face down to hers, tongue thrusting. Suddenly her robe slipped from under his hands, and she was completely naked; how she had accomplished this, he was not sure—if her arms had left his neck, he had not been aware of it.

The way she removed *his* clothes seemed somewhat more comprehensible to him, though the grace of her movements was still quite magical enough. Finishing, she ran her long-nailed fingers down his hips, sitting on the edge of the bed, legs together, pointing on tiptoe; she was wearing the brass anklets that he loved. Trailing one of her tresses over her bosom, she gazed up at him and said:

"Welcome back."

"Ummm," he answered, thinking this was not quite eloquent enough.

She turned and went farther into the bed, flaunting her marvellous behind, looking back over her shoulder.

"Did you miss me?" he said.

She nodded and lowered herself onto her stomach, wriggled against the covers briefly, then turned over.

"How much?" he asked.

Fingering her nipples, she lifted her legs and slowly spread her pale-soled feet, anklets chiming.

"This much," she said.

After the second time, she asked:

"Is it true that you're going to be a Master?"

"If I pass the trials," he answered. "The second and third should be no problem. But I don't know what I'll do about the first. Especially if Erim doesn't help me."

"Why wouldn't he?"

"I'm not sure if we're friends anymore."

"Is it about Essaj?"

"No, believe it or not."

"What then?"

"Erim was being very unreasonable. We captured some Anarites when we took the fortress. Khaddam decided we really couldn't afford to keep them alive."

"Why not?"

"A wizard's no ordinary prisoner. He can strike at you from his cell, summon demons to help him escape . . . imagine trying to keep a hundred wizards in prison. Five hundred. Khaddam decided to kill them, and why not?

"But Erim was very upset. On the way back, he started badgering me, arguing that Khaddam had no business making such a decision. Now, as far as I'm concerned, the Grand Master's the best judge of such things. After all, who *is* Erim, anyway? A little Fifth-Level Adept. Someone who'll probably never make the

Sixth Level, let alone the Seventh. I got tired of listening to him whine about it. Especially after what I saw at Khaur-Al-Jaffar. The Anarites were sacrificing *thousands* of slaves. It was as if they'd completely lost their minds. If anyone ever deserved to be massacred, they did. They would have deserved it even if they *hadn't* been killing our Masters. And here's Erim, coming out with all this mealy-mouthed drivel about how we should settle for just gelding them. Well, the Hell with that."

"But are you really going to let this ruin your friendship?" Zehowah asked.

"I don't know. When I add it to everything else . . ."

"You *do* hold Essaj against him, don't you?"

"Maybe."

"Then why don't you hold him against me?"

Sharif almost answered: *Do you really think I don't?* Instead, he replied: "Because you're my wife."

"You're not going to have to choose, sooner or later? Between me and the Order?"

"Not if you don't try to convert me. We could simply not speak about Essaj . . ."

"I don't think I could keep silent, Sharif. Not if your Masters convicted him."

"Well, then," he said, "we'd better pray that he's found innocent. Because the Council *is* going to indict him. Now that Akram's out of the way, Khaddam will order an immediate trial."

"Has he said so?"

"Believe me, he will . . ."

Zehowah began to sob. "Please don't put me aside."

"Don't make me," he answered. Much to his surprise, he found that he was weeping too.

On her way to Khaddam's apartment, Sigrun met Ahesha, Murad's concubine.

"Where are you off to?" Ahesha asked.

Sigrun told her.

"That should raise a few eyebrows."

"He's changed the regulations," Sigrun said.

"It'll *still* raise a few eyebrows," Ahesha asked. "How powerful he's become! He's certainly benefitted from—" She broke off suddenly as though she realized she was about to say something impolitic.

"Benefitted?" Sigrun pressed. "From what?"

"Don't trouble yourself."

"Trouble myself? What were you going to say?"

"Simply that his position was much improved . . ."

"By what?"

Ahesha laughed. "The war."

"The killings, you mean?"

"You're taking this entirely the wrong way," Ahesha said. "Really, don't let me keep you any longer."

"Are you hinting he was behind the killings?" Sigrun demanded.

"What an imagination you have!" Ahesha answered, shaking her head. She started past.

"How *dare* you," Sigrun said.

"Enjoy your visit," Ahesha said, over her shoulder. "I'm sure his apartment's very nice."

Furious, Sigrun continued on her way. What on earth was the woman talking about? Admittedly, Khaddam had gained a tremendous amount of power. But he had suffered hideously himself . . .

It's all complete nonsense, Sigrun thought.

Indeed, it was even possible to draw a certain pleasure from Ahesha's malice, born as it was—clearly—of sheer envy. Ahesha's consort was virtually a nonentity, while Khaddam was indisputably the greatest man in the Order.

She was complimenting him, Sigrun told herself. *The only way the nasty little bitch could.*

Her temper began to cool.

She had a general idea of how to find Khaddam's apartment; it was in the west wing, on the second floor. With all the activity that followed Ahwaz's death, Khaddam had not yet appropriated the Grand Master's residence.

Sigrun received many hard stares along the way, especially from the older Adepts: one even went so far as to challenge her, informing her pompously that she was not allowed in this part of Qanar-Sharaj, even if she was—sniff—"The Grand Master's concubine." But her calm insistence that Khaddam had revoked the rule soon put the man in his place; encouraged by his failure of nerve, she even demanded—and received—directions from him.

Khaddam's apartment was very large, at least four times the size of hers, and full of books. It was all very orderly—that is, everything looked like it was in its place. But there was dust everywhere, often in great mouselike clots. The bedroom was huge but largely bare, not at all congenial.

And there was, of course, no kitchen.

The dust began to make Sigrun sneeze. Did Khaddam actually intend her to live with him here? She wondered how long it would be until they could move into Ahwaz's quarters, and whether there was anyplace to cook *there*. In the meantime, she decided, the dust *here* simply had to go.

Returning to the door, she summoned a passing brown-robe. The fellow seemed nonplussed to see a woman in Khaddam's lair, but was perfectly willing to fetch her a broom and other implements. She went promptly to work, raising large grey clouds, coughing steadily, eyes watering. Sweeping the dust into a flat scoop, she tossed it out the window in the bedroom.

More than once as she cleaned, her thoughts drifted back to Ahesha's veiled accusation; but refining and rehearsing her counterarguments made her work go more quickly. By mealtime, she had the antechamber, the study and the bedroom large-ly clean.

There was no sign of Khaddam, though that did not surprise her. After such a long absence, he undoubtedly had a good deal of business to attend to.

Still, she had grown quite hungry. She guessed Khaddam intend-ed to have a meal brought to them, but she needed something in the meantime. Out in the hall, the same brown-robe was going past again; she asked him to fetch her some bread and wine.

The latter was very good, but she made the mistake of drinking a half a cup before eating very much. The wine went directly to her head, and she dropped the pitcher in her lap, the contents splattering beneath Khaddam's huge desk. Pushing back the seat, she bent forward to see how much of a mess she had made.

To her disgust, she discovered that she had neglected the dust under the desk—there had evidently been a considerable rat's nest down there, though the wine had flattened it somewhat. Getting the scoop, she picked the stuff out by hand, making an interesting discovery in the process: a rectangular pale-blue jewel of moderate size.

And what were you doing there? she wondered.

Khaddam arrived soon afterwards. If he was hungry for anything but her, he gave no indication of it. For a moment she thought he was going to thrust her onto the carpet in the antechamber. But after his first, fierce kiss, he paused and looked about.

"You cleaned," he said, his hand still clasping one of her buttocks.

"It was about time *someone* did," Sigrun replied. "Why didn't you have some brown-robe take care of it?"

"Never occurred to me," Khaddam answered. "Does dust offend you?"

"Grievously," she replied. "Among other things, it makes me sneeze. I take it you expect me to stay here."

"Maybe. I'm going to recommend the abolition of the Women's Quarters."

"While keeping the women."

"Precisely. I'll show you Ahwaz's residence tomorrow. In truth, though, it's not that much bigger than this apartment, and I'm used to living here. What do you think?"

"Will you give me a free hand?"

"Except for my study. You can do what you please with the rest."

"I'll need a kitchen and a pantry. Big ones."

"You can use those two rooms in the back."

"Where will we eat?" Sigrun asked.

"We could knock a hole in the study wall, take a room from the apartment next door."

"I could manage," Sigrun said.

He looked down at the rug. "What do you think of the carpet?"

"It's nicely swept," she said.

He lifted her in his arms and laid her softly upon it. "Does that mean you won't sneeze?" he asked, tossing her skirt up over her stomach.

Afterwards, they adjourned to the bedroom. Lying beside her, raised on one arm, he scrutinized her breasts.

"What are you doing?" she asked.

"Looking for the scar."

"So," she said. "You heard about the healing."

"It was the first thing Mufkadi told me."

"Are you angry?"

"Because you let Essaj save your life?"

"Yes."

Khaddam laughed. "If he could save me, I'd do the same. But . . . you didn't draw any false conclusions from this brush with death, did you?"

"All I know is that he healed me."

"But is that all you *believe*?"

"He has powers," Sigrun said. "It doesn't prove anything."

He stroked her breast. "I'm glad you realize that."

Nonetheless, she was anxious to change the subject; eyeing his hand on her bosom, she remarked on a new ring.

"Badge of rank," he said. "It's the Grand Master's ring. You might remember seeing it on Ahwaz."

"Yes," she said. She had a particularly vivid memory of it from the banquet when Ahwaz had his first stroke; how it had glittered against his purpled flesh!

"Arghun found the hands at Khaur-Al-Jaffar," Khaddam went on.

"Ah," Sigrun said in disgust. "And you took that ring from Ahwaz's dead finger and put it on?"

"It's expected of me. I *am* his successor."

She shivered.

"I'm going to have it adjusted," Khaddam said. "Slipped on easily enough at first, but I think I'd lost some weight—all that marching and fighting. The return trip was less hurried, and I ate better . . ."

"Wasn't there a jewel?"

"A blue diamond."

She remembered the jewel she had happened upon, and was just about to ask him about it when he continued:

"Arghun said he saw it when he looked in the bag."

"What happened to it, then?" Sigrun asked.

"Someone might have stolen it," Khaddam said. "Or perhaps the prongs snagged on something, and the jewel spilled out. It might have happened when the hands were removed from the sack, and no one noticed."

As he spoke, she looked more closely at the ring. There were two intact prongs, as well as the remains of two broken ones; from the way they were arranged, she guessed the jewel must have been about the same size and shape as the one she had discovered. But why would the gem from Ahwaz's ring be lying on Khaddam's floor?

She began: "Strangely enough, I—"

The breath locked in her throat. A terrible possibility had occurred to her: what if Ahwaz's hand had been brought to the apartment?

"Sigrun?" Khaddam asked.

What if it was put in the bag here, before it was taken to Khaur-Al-Jaffar?

"Sigrun?" Khaddam said again.

Looking at him, all she could think of was Ahesha's words: *He's certainly benefitted.*

"I forgot what I was going to say," she answered, pulse racing. "Give me a moment . . ."

He looked mildly amused; there was nothing the least bit sinister in his eyes. Ahesha's voice began to fade from her mind; reason reasserted itself. Surely there was—there *must* be—another explanation for the jewel's presence.

Ahwaz came here, lost the jewel himself, she thought. *He wasn't entirely bedridden. He attended Iyad's funeral, and the Council afterwards . . .*

But Khaddam had said that he did so only with the gravest difficulty. Apart from that, Sigrun knew, the old man had ventured out only on trips to the baths . . .

The jewel's the right size, Sigrun.

The right shape.

The right color.

And besides . . .

Khaddam's certainly benefitted.

She found herself teetering on the edge of panic. One moment she had been safe, her beloved consort lying beside her, a living promise of comfort, of pleasure, of marriage and prestige. Now she felt as though she had awakened with a cobra at her side.

Oh, my love, my precious love. Not you—

"No use," she said at last. "I can't remember." She thought her voice sounded horribly strained, but he appeared not to notice.

"It mustn't have been too important," Khaddam said.

She had not alarmed the cobra—if cobra he was.

You must give him the benefit of the doubt . . .

"Could Ahwaz have lost the jewel himself?" she asked.

"I suppose. But the last time I saw the ring on his hand, the jewel was there."

The answer seemed straightforward enough, but she sensed an underlying slipperiness. He could easily have been referring to Ahwaz's *severed* hand, flaunting his own cleverness.

"Also, if Ahwaz *had* lost it," Khaddam went on, "Arghun couldn't have seen it at Khaur-Al-Jaffar."

"How do you know that he did?"

"Why would he lie about such a thing?"

She thought: *Maybe he feared your anger. Or only thought he'd seen the stone. Or misremembered. But the last time you saw the stone, it was here. And that's why you believed him . . .*

"You have me there," she said.

He looked at her narrowly. "Why all this curiosity?"

"Mysteries intrigue me. Besides, I don't really like Arghun, I think."

"He's not very likeable. But he does have his qualities."

She looked at the ring once more. Was she simply deceiving herself, or did the setting appear too small for the gem she had found? Was she jumping to conclusions, doing Khaddam a monstrous misservice? Despite her terror, she felt horribly guilty.

"Are you all right?" Khaddam asked, his expression sharpening still further.

He knows, she thought, guilt obliterated by a new rush of fear. *You roused his suspicions with your idiot questions, and he's realized the jewel dropped out here . . .*

"I had some wine before you came," she answered.

"So?"

He's reading every one of your stupid thoughts . . .

"I don't think it agreed with me," she answered. Suddenly a mysterious question leaped into her mind:

Why did Your Son heal me if I'm just going to die now?

Khaddam rubbed her flank, his face unreadable. Perhaps it was only her imagination, but his hand seemed icy, almost reptilian.

"Pity," he replied at last. "I assumed—"

"I think I'd better lie quiet for a while."

Spare me, she begged, not sure if she was praying to the Sharajnaghi God, or Essaj, or both. *If you're there, if you healed me, spare me now. . . .*

"Not a bad idea," Khaddam said. "I *could* sleep the night through." He ran his hand between her legs, cupping her briefly. "There's always tomorrow."

"Thank you," she said.

"Anything for my bride-to-be," Khaddam answered.

Once she was certain he was asleep, she went out to the antechamber, where her clothes were still lying on the carpet; she had put the diamond in a small purse attached to her belt. Taking it out, she returned silently to the bedroom.

"Sigrun?" Khaddam called.

"I'm here," she answered, still some distance from the bed.

He sat up. In the light from a small lamp, she could see his head turning, as though he was looking about; but his eyes were closed. She eased back into the bed, the jewel clenched tight in her hand.

"It's good," he said. "Don't be afraid of it."

"I won't," she replied, without the slightest idea of what he was talking about.

"No suffering, no guilt."

"Go to sleep," she answered.

He sank down again, yet within moments he was rubbing against her, stroking her, kissing her neck. To all appearances, he was still asleep; but horribly, his touch had never seemed more skillful. She found herself yielding to it, and as she responded, discovered a deep unwillingness to believe he was guilty. How could this man have committed such crimes? How could he have slaughtered his friends when she loved him so, when he was inside her now, giving her such delight?

And yet, there was no way to know *who* he was. Even now, she could not be sure that her Khaddam was real—or someone else, acting out one of his own dreams. Even after they both came, he never seemed to wake.

"I love you," he murmured, lowering himself beside her, right hand on his breast, the ring gleaming faintly on his finger.

She waited an eternity before asking:

"Khaddam?"

He made no response. He barely seemed to be breathing. His eyes were jerking back and forth under the lids, but that only meant that he was deeply asleep; he himself had told her what the movements indicated.

Rising on one elbow, she took the jewel between the tips of her fingernails and held it near the ring, comparing its size against the remains of the setting. She leaned farther, all but sliding the jewel beneath the remaining prongs.

The gem certainly looked as if it would slide beneath them and fit snugly in the socket. But for the sake of her love, and for her own sake, she had to know for sure . . . Even if Khaddam woke, she doubted he would grasp immediately what she was doing.

She eased the jewel onto the ring and nudged it under the prongs. With a little click, the jewel fell into place—

A perfect fit.

She closed her eyes in horror.

If I had poison, I'd drink it, she thought.

Yet if she truly wanted to die, why had her hands begun to tremble? Why was she so afraid that he might wake?

Opening her eyes, she drew in a deep breath, trying to control her quivering as she took hold of the jewel again. But withdrawing the diamond without tugging on the circlet was a much more difficult matter than simply slipping it into the socket; hesitant to use any real strength, she had made several tentative tries when Khaddam's hand suddenly pulled to one side, and the stone came free.

Her elbow flew back; she almost shrieked, then suppressed an equal urge to laugh.

"Absolute peace," said Khaddam.

His eyes were gleaming slits.

Gasping, she dropped the jewel beside him.

His body arched upwards as he reached beneath his back. She began to recoil, but his hand reappeared, sweeping towards her. Steel gleamed; then the edge was in her throat, like a breeze through her flesh.

"It's coming," Khaddam said. "And you won't stop it."

His eyes closed, and he rolled over.

Heart battering her ribs, she realized she was on her feet, beside the bed, hand to her throat.

But why wasn't she bleeding? She ran her fingers across her skin—there was no wound.

She had imagined it all.

All except the worst.

Searching the covers for the jewel, she retrieved it and put it back in her purse; then she lay down with the butcher once more, wondering frantically what she should do.

The night was very long.

✠

THE PLAYERS

Essaj Ben Yussef—A miracle-worker

THE SHARAJNAGHIM:

Literally "Bringers of Light," members of the *Comahi Irakhoum*, a brotherhood of white wizards dedicated to warfare against the so-called "Black Orders," and the upholding of religious orthodoxy

1. Sharajnaghi Masters:

Ahwaz—Grand Master of the Order

Khaddam—Master of Sorcery

Akram—Master of the Martial Arts

Iyad—Master of Logic and Doctrine

Massoud—Master of Science, then Iyad's successor at Doctrine

Samadhi—Chief of Intelligence

Shoua—Master of Medicine

Ghazal—Minister of State

2. The Investigators:

Erim—Fifth-Level Adept, expert in theology

Sharif—Sixth-Level Adept, Erim's best friend, said to be the mightiest sorcerer since Mancdaman Zorachus

Nawhar—Fifth-Level Adept, a specialist in the detection of false miracles

3. The Knot of Serpents—Followers of Khaddam:

Arghun Khan—Massoud's successor at Doctrine

Sayid Al-Mashat—Samadhi's successor at Intelligence

Raschid Zekowi—Shoua's successor at Medicine
Mufkadi Umar—Khaddam's successor at Sorcery
Ahmed Fawzi—Promoted to Master of Treasury and Trade
4. Others:
Kourah Kislali—a follower of Samadhi
Ezzedin Moukarbal—a follower of Massoud
Farouk—Massoud's assistant; killed attempting to murder Khaddam

THE WOMEN:
Sigrun—Khaddam's concubine
Khalima—Erim's wife
Zehowah—Khalima's sister, Sharif's wife
Yasmin—the mother of Essaj

THE MIRKUTS:
Ferocious barbarians out of the eastern steppe, conquerors of the Kadjafi lands
Batu—Khan of the Mirkuts, known as the "Scourge of Heaven"
Khassar—Batu's brother and minister of State and Intelligence

THE BLACK ANARITES:
An evil offshoot of the Anarite Order, slave traders and mortal enemies of the Sharajnaghim
Torthas Al-Tarcha—commander of a troop of Anarites bested by Sharif, Erim, and Nawhar
Mahayoun—Minister of State
Achmed Hakkar—Grand Master
Aswarak—Master of Sorcery
Haroun—Master of the Martial Arts

ESSAJ'S DISCIPLES:
Anwar—The first among Essaj's followers
Jalloud—Anwar's jealous rival

OTHERS:
Khaldun Al-Maari—a cedar-merchant, raised from the dead by Essaj; the father of Khalima and Zehowah

Hafez Shammar—an innkeeper

Gamal Al-Din—High Priest of the Grand Temple in Thangura

DEMONS AND MONSTERS:

Tchernobog—literally, "The Black God." Chief among the rebel angels; the emperor of Hell. Also known as Athtar the Fallen, The Black Lord, and Lord of Light

Horde—one of the Great Demons; a vassal of Tchernobog. Exorcised by Essaj; also known as Legion

Morkulg the Mask—one of the Great Demons, a vassal of Tchernobog

The Chopper—a manifestation of Morkulg

The Thornwitch—a lesser demon subject to the Anarites

Ghashar—a monster defending Khaur-Al-Jaffar; also known as the Bone-Eater